HIDDEN FIRE

THE FIREFIGHTERS OF STATION FIVE

JO DAVIS

D0011824

A SIGNET ECLIPSE BOOK

SIGNET ECLIPSE
Published by New American Library, a division of
Penguin Group (USA) Inc., 375 Hudson Street,
New York, New York 10014, USA
Penguin Group (Canada), 90 Eglinton Avenue East, Suite 700, Toronto,
Ontario M4P 2Y3, Canada (a division of Pearson Penguin Canada Inc.)
Penguin Books Ltd., 80 Strand, London WC2R 0RL, England
Penguin Ireland, 25 St. Stephen's Green, Dublin 2,
Ireland (a division of Penguin Books Ltd.)
Penguin Group (Australia), 250 Camberwell Road, Camberwell, Victoria 3124,
Australia (a division of Pearson Australia Group Pty. Ltd.)
Penguin Books India Pvt. Ltd., 11 Community Centre, Panchsheel Park,
New Delhi - 110 017, India
Penguin Group (NZ), 67 Apollo Drive, Rosedale, North Shore 0632,
New Zealand (a division of Pearson New Zealand Ltd.)
Penguin Books (South Africa) (Pty.) Ltd., 24 Sturdee Avenue,
Rosebank, Johannesburg 2196, South Africa

Penguin Books Ltd., Registered Offices:
80 Strand, London WC2R 0RL, England

First published by Signet Eclipse, an imprint of New American Library,
a division of Penguin Group (USA) Inc.

First Printing, December 2009
10 9 8 7 6 5 4 3 2 1

Praise for
Trial by Fire

"A five-alarm read . . . riveting, sensual."

—Beyond Her Book

"Jo Davis turns up the heat full blast with *Trial by Fire*. Romantic suspense that has it all: a sizzling firefighter hero, a heroine you'll love, and a story that crackles and pops with sensuality and action. All I can say is, keep the fire extinguisher handy or risk spontaneous combustion!"

—Linda Castillo, national bestselling author of
Sworn to Silence

"Jo Davis set the trap, baited the hook, and completely reeled me in with *Trial by Fire*. Heady sexual tension, heartwarming romance, and combustible love scenes just added fuel to the fire. . . . Joyfully recommended!"   —Joyfully Reviewed

"A brilliant start to one of the most exciting 'band of brothers' series since J. R. Ward's Black Dagger Brotherhood. It's sweet and sexy, tense and suspenseful, and—the best part—pushes the erotic envelope in a way that fuses emotional intimacy with hot, sweaty sensuality."   —myLifetime.com

"For a poignant and steamy romance with a great dose of suspense, be sure to pick up a copy of *Trial by Fire* . . . as soon as it hits the bookstores!"

—Wild on Books (5 Bookmarks)

"Hot, sizzling sex and edge-of-your-seat terror will have you glued to this fantastic romantic suspense story from the first page to the final word. Do not miss the heart-stopping, breath-stealing, incredibly well-written *Trial by Fire*."

—Romance Novel TV

To my grandmother, Ladine Howard,
who once fell in love with a handsome rogue who refused
to take no for an answer. You did your best to turn Papaw away
at the dance . . . and we all know how that story turned out.
But then, you always did love a happy ending.
Granny, Julian's story is for you.
I miss you.

ACKNOWLEDGMENTS

As always, my heartfelt thanks to:

My husband, Paul, for whisking me out of town for much-needed alone time after finishing a particularly tough book. And to our awesome teenagers, for their continued love and support.

Tracy Garrett and Suzanne Welsh, my critique partners, for your advice and friendship.

Debra Stevens, my lifelong friend, for forcing me out of my cave and handing out my reality checks when needed.

The Foxes, for keeping me sane. I love you guys.

Roberta Brown, my one-of-a-kind agent and friend.

My editor, Tracy Bernstein, and all of the fabulous folks at NAL. Your class is untouchable, bar none.

Captain Steve Deutsch for keeping my facts straight.

Author's note: Any mistakes I've made or liberties I've taken for story line purposes are completely my own.

1

Julian Salvatore sprayed a steady stream of water at Station Five's ambulance, rinsing off the soapsuds and gyrating around the vehicle to "Life in the Fast Lane" blaring from the radio just inside the bay.

Nothing like the Eagles to make a boring task bearable.

Using the nozzle as a microphone, he lip-synched a little Don Henley, punctuating the heavy downbeat with blasts to the bubbles. Watching them slide away. Thinking, yeah, he could relate. He enjoyed life a bit too fast.

Too bad he was on shift. He craved some action, and not the type to be found here, working with four guys he couldn't quite call pals. Not that he hadn't made an effort—no, screw that. Friendship shouldn't come with a set of conditions, and God knew his best was never good enough.

Forcing down the old disappointment, he conjured an image of feminine curves, toned thighs. Long, white blond hair draped over his chest, violet eyes holding him captive, while their slick bodies moved in time to the pounding music—

Which abruptly lowered several notches, poofing his fantasy to dust.

"Jeez, man. You selling tickets?"

Julian glanced toward the door to the bay. Zack Knight, A-shift's fire apparatus operator—aka engine driver—

straightened and turned away from the portable radio, cell phone to one ear. Knight leaned against the grille of the big quint, cooing into the phone like a frickin' turtledove.

". . . know I don't care, beautiful," Knight was saying, face glowing with happiness. "Whatever color you want me to stain it is fine."

Yep, totally whipped.

Rolling his eyes, Julian made an exaggerated gagging noise. Knight shot him the finger and a big grin, and Julian couldn't resist smiling back as he shut off the water. So, the geek had grown a big, steely pair after all. Love must do weird shit to a guy.

He wouldn't know. Nor did he care to.

"Salvatore!"

He started, stifling a curse. *Cristo*, the captain had a way of lying low, then leaping out of nowhere to lop off an unsuspecting victim's head like some sort of damned ninja assassin.

Julian turned, pasting on his most innocent expression— a stretch, even on his best day. "Hey, Cap. What's shakin'?"

Sean Tanner got in his personal space, vibrating with anger from head to toe. He rested his hands on his narrow hips, green eyes snapping. Hoo-yah, this was gonna be a scream.

"I'm going to say this once. The prepubescent shit is getting old. You're done."

Julian stared back. What the hell? "Am I supposed to know what you're talking about?"

"The tampon prank was funny the first time, although inappropriate. You're lucky Eve didn't make an issue of it before, but this? Stringing them across the ladies' restroom door is going too far."

Knight closed his cell phone, slid it into his pants pocket, and watched with interest. Julian laughed. He couldn't help it.

"Man, you need to lighten up. Eve's cool and you *know* she dishes out as much as she takes."

Tanner's face hardened. "I'm fed up, Salvatore. Knock that crap off before you wind up with a formal complaint in your file."

Julian's humor fled. "Why don't you look into the mirror, amigo, say that three times, and see if you land in Kansas. You're not the only one who's fed up."

Color flooded Tanner's cheeks as he sputtered, "What the fuck do you mean by that?"

"Want to make me spell it out? Fine. You're not doing such a great job yourself, but you don't hesitate to shout and bitch at everyone who doesn't meet your impossible standards." Julian sighed, shaking his head. "You know what? Forget it. I'm not doing this. The point is, I'm not the one who pulled the stunt. I don't have a clue who did, and frankly, sir, I don't give a rat's ass. If you'll excuse me, I have work to finish."

For the first time in his career, Julian gave his back to a superior. And it hurt a helluva lot more than he'd have thought.

Because in that moment, in a startling burst of clarity, he realized Tanner had lost his respect.

Everyone went through rough times, Tanner's rougher than most. But the captain wasn't the only one who'd faced total devastation and lived to tell.

Are you hurt, hijo?

No, mamá.

Oh, no. Not going there. Grabbing an old towel, he shoved the memory into its tamperproof compartment and began to dry the ambulance. He longed to get in Tanner's grille, set him straight. Tell the uptight bastard he didn't have the market cornered on pain and suffering. Tell him—

"Damn, you should've seen his expression," Knight remarked quietly, coming to stand beside him.

"He's gone?" Julian wasn't about to give Tanner the satisfaction of looking.

"After he gave about two seconds' thought to ripping your head off, yeah." Knight paused, blinking behind his wire-rimmed glasses. "You shocked him. I mean, I've gotten pretty good at not letting him get to me, but nobody stands up to him like that except Six-Pack."

"And Eve."

"True."

Lieutenant Howard "Six-Pack" Paxton was Tanner's best friend, Eve Marshall their sole female firefighter. Six-Pack was six and a half feet of towering muscle, Eve whipcord lean but tough. Neither of them took crap off anybody.

Julian started on the windshield, keeping his voice low. "Has the intervention been scheduled?"

"I was on my way out to talk to you about it when Cori phoned. Six-Pack needs to meet with all of us first so we're on the same page with how to proceed. Everyone else is free Friday afternoon. We were thinking around three, at Six-Pack and Kat's new house. Work for you?"

"I've got a date later, but sure. I'll be there."

Knight clapped him on the shoulder, then wandered off. Julian tried to imagine Tanner's reaction when he realized what they'd planned, and winced. No man wanted to listen to the people closest to him air his drinking problem in a public forum. He had a feeling this giant group hug was going to backfire something awful. For the record, he'd warned them.

Still, something had to be done before Sean killed himself.

Three loud high tones over the intercom system scattered

his thoughts. The pleasantly creepy computerized voice announced a kitchen fire at one of Sugarland's few high-end restaurants.

Pitching the towel into the bay, he sprinted for his gear, almost relieved for the distraction.

Almost. If he'd learned anything in all his years as a firefighter, it was that complacence on the job was usually followed by unmitigated disaster.

He might get a dark thrill out of tempting fate, but he wasn't stupid.

Julian grabbed a hose and jogged for the rear entry of the restaurant, Tommy Skyler at his back. Displaced diners milled around the front and side of the building, and Julian spared them a glance as he and Skyler approached the kitchen door.

Most of them appeared to have departed, but a few onlookers watched the proceedings with avid interest. As always, his roving eyes zeroed in on the women, some dressed business casual, but a couple in classy power suits. Including a tall, willowy blonde who seemed to be staring right at him.

Recognition zapped him as if he'd touched a live circuit, charging his libido. He stopped so abruptly, Skyler plowed into his back with a curse.

Grace McKenna.

Five feet eleven delectable inches of cream-your-boxer-briefs temptation. The violet-eyed beauty of his lusty fantasies, the Ice Princess who'd ignored every one of his advances. Well, except for that one toe-curling kiss all those months ago.

And Six-Pack's off-limits sister-in-law.

He couldn't have Grace.

Which, of course, only made him want her more.

"What're you doing, man? Go, go!" Skyler yelled.

Shaking it off and breaking eye contact, he ran. What *was* he doing? A split second of inattention on the job could get a firefighter killed. He wasn't ready to die today, and certainly not over a woman.

A woman who wouldn't suffer a moment of remorse if something bad *did* happen to him.

Focus. The kitchen was almost fully engulfed in flames, but he and Skyler managed to wrestle the blaze under control with relatively little difficulty. The stove provided the worst problem, since the extinguishing system in the vent hood over it had apparently failed. The unit, covered in grease and equipped with a vat for frying, had gone up like a torch, but was quickly subdued by Eve with chemical foam.

The heat was a nasty bitch, though, boiling his skin through the heavy protective clothing. He'd reek of smoke and sweat, and he hoped they had a long enough reprieve from the calls later to sneak a shower.

Through the kitchen entry into the restaurant's dining room, he saw Eve join Six-Pack to do a walk-through of the premises. Six-Pack gave him a thumbs-up for an all clear, so they had to concentrate only on the kitchen area and make sure no hot spots remained.

Leaving their buddies to handle that part, Julian and Skyler shut off the hose and exited the way they'd come in. Skyler took charge of helping Knight put away the hose, and as Julian removed his mask to let it dangle around his neck, he observed that the younger man had really started to mature in the past couple of months.

Julian shook his head with a rueful laugh. Yeah, he was such an expert on maturity.

Then he didn't have time to think about Skyler anymore because, *Dios mío*, Grace was striding toward him purposefully, lovely expression cool and composed as ever. If he didn't know better, he might have thought she was marching forward to serve him with a subpoena. After months of her ignoring his phone calls, he couldn't imagine what on earth she had to say to him.

But it couldn't be good.

And yippee, here he was caught off guard and out of his groove. With her crisp blouse under her tailored suit jacket and hair in an elegant twist at her nape, the woman looked like she'd just stepped out of the pages of *Vogue*. An equally sharp-dressed man trailed in her wake—her lunch date?—while Julian was a stinky, sooty old gym sock. Shit. Feeling self-conscious and hating it, he raked his fingers through his wet hair, pasting on a grin.

"*Querida*, you picked a fine time to accept my dinner invitation. As you can see, I'm a bit underdressed."

Grace stopped in front of him, huge eyes softening the merest fraction. "I had to stay and make certain you were all right," she said, her soft, melodic voice edged with a tiny hint of concern.

Just like that, his knees went weak. His heart thudded madly in his chest and for once in his life, he could think of nothing clever to say. The armor of his sarcastic wit deserted him, leaving him naked and squirming.

"I . . . I'm fine, Grace," he said, shrugging.

"And Howard?" She squinted toward the smoldering restaurant, worry for her sister's husband plain.

"We're good. Just another day in the jungle. How have you been?" *Why haven't you acknowledged my existence?*

Clutching her purse, she favored him with a polite smile that seized his lungs. "Busy. Half the population needs an attorney."

"And they're all innocent, I'm sure."

"Of course. Those are the only ones I defend." As though

suddenly reminded of her lunch date, she glanced to the man standing behind her and waved him forward. "Oh! Gentlemen, I apologize. Derek, this is an acquaintance of mine, Julian Salvatore. He works with my sister's husband. Julian, this is Derek Vines."

The name slammed into him, a double shot to the head and gut. His gaze swung toward the man's good-looking face. Fifteen years older, but the same face that haunted his nightmares, his every waking moment. One he'd never thought to see again in this lifetime, or the next.

He couldn't breathe. Was being held underwater. Vision graying at the edges.

Drowning.

"Julian? Are you all right?"

He blinked at Grace, fighting to breathe, the fog clearing some. He'd never fainted and he wasn't about to now, in front of her.

In front of the man who'd nearly destroyed him.

This must be cosmic punishment for his most terrible mistake and the promiscuous life he'd led since. Hadn't he suffered enough, simply struggling each day to rise above the past?

"Julian?" She turned to Vines. "Get one of the others—"

"No!" He gave her what he prayed was a reassuring smile, when what he needed to do was find a restroom and be sick. "No, I'm fine. It's just . . . all of this clothing and gear is hotter than hell. Vines, nice to meet you," he said.

Because that's how a normal person greeted another. A normal guy would shake the man's hand, too, but he couldn't bring himself to do it. Not even under torture.

Before Vines could open his mouth, Julian took Grace's arm. "I need to speak with you in private."

Vines wore a puzzled frown, not a spark of recognition in his eyes. Thank God. Julian steered Grace toward the back of the ambulance, aware of the captain's disapproving scowl and the other guys' curious stares. He ignored them all, getting right to the point.

"What the fuck are you doing with a slimeball like Derek Vines?"

Score. That damned irritating, chilly sophistication slipped several notches, and she gaped at him, bristling. "Derek Vines is my client, not that it's any of your business."

"Really? You called him *Derek*, not Mr. Vines," he pointed out, struggling to remain calm. And losing.

"Derek is a family acquaintance, which is *also* none of your business. If you'll excuse me—"

"Cut that asshole loose. Trust me on this."

"Let go of my arm," she hissed, jerking the limb in question.

Blinking, he uncurled his fingers from her sleeve. He hadn't realized he'd grabbed her. "I'm sorry. But please listen," he entreated, injecting his voice with all the sincerity he possessed. Where Vines was concerned, it wasn't difficult. "Vines is extremely dangerous, Grace. You have no idea."

She obviously wanted to leave, but hesitated, anger tempered by curiosity. "How would you know this?"

Oh, God. "Just . . . trust me."

"Not good enough. I don't know you."

"Yeah? Well, you don't know Vines, either, or you'd never have accepted him as a client. You only defend the innocent?" He gave a bitter laugh and wiped a hand down his grimy face. "Jesus Christ, Grace. Even you can't be right in every case, about every person, and you're not right about him."

"How so? Throw me a bone, Salvatore, or I walk."

Salvatore. The pervert is "Derek" and I'm "Salvatore." Great.

What could he tell her when he was shaking apart inside, trying to keep from hitting his knees?

"I grew up in San Antonio, Texas, same as Derek. Suffice it to say he's trouble for everyone unfortunate enough to cross his path. Do some research."

"All right," she said, nodding slightly. "I can do that much."

"Then drop the bastard like yesterday's bad news, because that's what he is."

Anger animated her face again, and he knew he'd never seen a more gorgeous woman. Sucked to have her fury directed at him, but better for her to be aware of the viper in her midst.

"Thank you for the information, however vague, but I'll be the one to decide which clients to take on." A strange expression clouded the anger for a second as she held his gaze; then it vanished. "Good-bye, Julian."

Good-bye. At least she'd used his first name again. Wasn't that a positive sign?

And she'd never actually turned him down, had she?

"Why haven't you just said *no*?" he blurted, inwardly cursing himself for an idiot.

Grace paused, looking over her shoulder, violet eyes cool as ever. The irritation was gone, a ghost of a smile hovering on those plump lips. "Perhaps I just haven't said *yes*."

Jaw clenched, he watched her walk away, small round butt swinging in her tight skirt. *Damn her* for stringing him along.

A hand clamped hard on his shoulder. "Oh, boy. Our Latin lover's got it bad." Six-Pack stepped in front of him, shaking his head. "I've tried to tell you: Forget about her. Grace is as elusive as the wind."

"You're just afraid I'll break your precious sister-in-law's heart."

The lieutenant's expression sobered. "Not anymore, my friend. I'm afraid she'll break yours."

Six-Pack strode away and Julian watched, relieved, as Grace and Derek Vines left in separate cars. Even if she wasn't his business, he cared for her safety. She was representing a monster, and he couldn't make her truly understand.

Not unless he told her everything.

And that was *never* going to happen.

Just like Grace accepting his dinner invite.

He had to let go of this fixation on her. It boiled down to lust. Infatuation. Nothing more.

There were plenty of women who wanted him, even if Grace didn't.

Problem was, giving up and moving on had never hurt so much.

2

Julian wound his way through the press of undulating bodies, the beat of heavy bass hammering his brain cells. Or maybe that was the fourth shot of Patrón.

Thanks to the beauty clinging to his hand, that particular throbbing couldn't compete with the one below his belt. Cindy trailed in his wake, gyrating her voluptuous body to the naughty, hard-driving Nickelback song "Animals."

How appropriate was that?

Yeah, he was planning to get into some major trouble tonight. He loved redheads. Or brunettes. Blondes. Hell, he worshipped them all. Especially tipsy ones in tight, fireengine red dresses with plunging necklines.

He had the exit dead in his sights when his date tugged on his arm, bringing him up short.

"Jules, I want another drink!"

He shot Miss Babe-a-licious his best killer grin and raised his voice to be heard above the din. "Honey, I've got everything you need to quench your thirst. Let's go back to my place and you can take your pick."

Unfortunately, she missed the cue.

She gave him a pretty pout, plumping lips that would be put to better use if she were on her knees. "But I see some people I wanna talk to before we go!" Spinning toward the bar, she waved an arm enthusiastically. "Oh, look, there's Laurie and Will!"

Cindy danced toward her friends, leaving him standing in the middle of the crowd with a raging erection, frustration souring the anticipation of moments ago. The noise of the Friday night crowd, the sweating masses, pressed in on him like a vise, making him feel slightly claustrophobic. A little sick. Why tonight?

Because Derek Vines is somewhere nearby. He's here in Tennessee, your darkest secret, your nightmare in the flesh. Poised to ruin the life you worked so hard to build.

Case in point, this trendy Nashville bar on Second Avenue. It was his bachelor hunting ground, his port in the storm on his nights off from the fire station. Normally he thrived on strobe lights and hard rock, the sultry undercurrents in the room, rife with the promise of sex and other dark pleasures even he didn't dare partake of. An adult playground filled with strangers holding out colorful candy.

Yet his edge had deserted him. Left him adrift and disoriented in a sea of writhing, venomous snakes. A shiver crawled down his spine, as though Derek might emerge from the shadows at any moment. He had to get the fuck out of here, soon.

Shoving his way to the bar, he came to stand behind Cindy, who sat on a barstool chatting with her friends and sipping her third or fourth cosmopolitan. His date turned and blew him a sloppy kiss while her companions shot him a smile, then dismissed him altogether as they continued their own party.

Gritting his teeth, Julian pushed between Cindy and some overweight guy next to her with a mumbled apology and leaned against the bar, assuming a casual pose. The unwanted fifth wheel in a room full of people. Again.

God, he hated this shit. Hated hovering like a fool, holding his dick. He'd give her ten minutes and he was out of here, with or without her. They'd arrived separately, so he wasn't responsible for seeing her home, for which he was now thanking Jesus and the Fabulous Twelve.

He had a feeling that was about all he had going his way tonight.

Squelching the urge to order another shot of Patrón, he filched a cherry out of the cocktail garnish tray, popped it into his mouth, and plucked it from the stem. He chewed the sweet fruit, trying to force himself to relax, and stared across the bar at the patrons lined up on the other side like cattle at a feeding trough—just like his side of the fence.

That's how we look. A slick bunch of losers, people on the make, some cheating, some lying.

Some unbearably lonely.

Not himself, though. No way. Being alone and lonely were two different things. He wasn't sitting around pining over Grace's umpteenth rejection. "Never fix what isn't broken" was a motto that had always served him well.

No, *lonely* was the blond kid sitting directly across from him. Eyes downcast, he picked at the napkin under his beer and laughed halfheartedly at something his older, dark-haired companion said. The kid looked rather unhappy, strained, in fact. Julian wondered whether it was because he was underage and worried about getting caught. If he was one frickin' day over nineteen, Jules was Enrique Iglesias.

"Cody, amigo," Julian called as the bartender started to rush past.

Cody halted and braced his hands on the bar, giving him a mischievous grin. "Am I setting you up again already? Man, if you're still here drinking, you obviously need to come up with a better pickup line than the one about big fire hoses."

"Hey, don't disparage a tried-and-true method. Almost every woman with a pulse, even my eighty-year-old *abuela*, would go home with a firefighter." He arched a brow. "The rest will settle for the bartender, if they must."

Cody barked a short laugh and shook his head. "You want another Patrón, or are you going to just stand there and be an asshole, as usual?"

"Neither. I'm thinking the blond kid behind you should be home watching the Teletubbies."

To his credit, the bartender didn't turn around. He nodded, expression sobering. "Had the same thought, myself. His ID checked out."

"Must've been a damned good fake."

"I'm not a cop, man. You know my take on those nimrods."

"Never one around when you need them." Given his past experience, he'd be the last to argue.

"Right on. Besides, his friend isn't drinking, said he was the designated driver, so I'm not worried. Anything else?"

"Nope. Think I'm going to cruise."

"You need a cab?"

"Nah, I'm good."

Cody slapped a hand on the bar. "Take care, man."

As Cody hurried off to attend to his customers, Julian's attention strayed back to the blond kid and his buddy. The dark-haired man leaned against the bar facing the young guy, his face in profile, features wreathed in shadows. He leaned close, said something in his friend's ear. Laid a hand on the sleeve of the young man's arm in a sensual manner that sent up rainbow flags all around their space.

As he watched their intense body language, that hand lingering on the kid's arm, a chill broke out on Julian's skin. Homosexuality didn't bother him. It was the kid's lost, confused expression.

Exactly as though he didn't really want to leave with the "friend" who wasn't drinking. In a fucking bar, on a Friday night.

His imagination? Probably. Then the man said something else and they rose to leave. As they did, Julian noted the tremble of the kid's hand as he raised the bottle to his lips for one more draw of his beer, the tremor so bad he nearly fumbled it when he set it down on the bar. He stumbled, and his companion caught his arm, steadying him.

God Almighty, he's scared shitless. And drunk?

Or worse—drugged. With that thought Julian was out of his seat, bolting through the crowd after them. Cindy's shout floated behind him, but he pushed on, driven by frantic impulse. He wished he could've gotten a good look at the older man. Maybe he'd catch them outside . . . and then what? Stick his nose where it didn't belong just to appease his own demons? Embarrass them all for no good reason?

He burst outside, scanning up and down the sidewalk. Downtown Nashville on weekend kickoff night was festive at one in the morning. Groups of twenty-somethings hung out, laughing and cutting up, enjoying the spring evening. Some were walking, barhopping their way to oblivion.

Where—? There. Across the street, the pair he sought was climbing into a dark four-door sedan, the older man driving. Damn, he couldn't get a description of the guy. Squinting, he focused on the car instead and made out the metallic glint of the unmistakable Mercedes symbol on the trunk. The license plate, he couldn't see well. *X . . . E . . .* and was that a *P* or a *B*?

The Mercedes backed out and the opportunity was lost. Hell, he couldn't go running after the car like a lunatic. He already felt stupid enough.

"*Dios*, Salvatore, what's wrong with you?" he muttered.

The sedan began to pull away—just as the driver turned his head and looked in Julian's direction.

Other than short, dark hair and broad features, he still couldn't make out the man's face very clearly. He had the fleeting thought that the driver could be staring at any one of the revelers on the sidewalk near Julian. But the man's gaze hit him in the chest like twin laser points.

Julian staggered backward a step, heart tripping, as the Mercedes pulled away, taillights receding into the darkness. It wasn't him. Of course it wasn't.

"Hey, why'd you run off?"

Someone grabbed his arm. He spun to find Cindy next to him, a bemused expression on her face. The same face he'd thought gorgeous four shots ago, and now struck him as garish. A bit harsh, even. His cock, he realized with some surprise, had surrendered hope, and was no longer by any means tempted to come out and play.

Not with Cindy.

"I thought I saw someone I knew," he said, reaching into his pants pocket for his car keys. "I was wrong."

"Oh. So, are we leaving?" Gluing herself to his side like a strip of Velcro, she ran a manicured nail down his chest through the part in his buttoned shirt.

"*I'm* leaving. Alone." Gently, he set her away from him, marveling that he'd almost made the mistake of taking this woman to bed. Giving one of her hands a squeeze, he leaned in and planted a chaste kiss on her cheek. "I had a good time."

"But we were supposed to go to your place!"

"Plans change, honey. That ship has sailed, I'm afraid."

The astonishment on her face was priceless. "You— you're blowing me off?"

"I prefer to call it reconsidering my options." Wisely, he

refrained from pointing out she'd blown him off first. He and his brother hadn't grown up in a houseful of women only to learn squat. "I'll walk you to your car."

Outraged, she slapped his hand away. "Don't bother, prick."

Spinning around, she stalked off, high heels clicking on the pavement in a rapid staccato. He watched her go, the clingy dress painted on her tight, edible body, and sighed.

Yeah, he'd lost his mind.

No doubt, she would've been hotter than a firecracker in July. So why did the idea of a few hours of recreation between consenting adults leave him cold when it never had in the past? Cindy was attractive, willing, and . . . that's all.

She was a virtual stranger. Someone he'd met when Station Five worked a traffic accident last week. She'd slipped him her phone number, and he'd called to arrange a date. Which they'd had. Period.

Julian stood in the middle of the sidewalk, among the milling crowd, and right there had a startling revelation. These clubbers were, by and large, in their early to mid-twenties. On the heels of his thirty-first birthday, those few years of age difference suddenly yawned between them, a chasm as wide and deep as the Royal Gorge. He felt . . . *old.*

What the fuck am I doing here?

He didn't want some stranger.

An image of a certain defense lawyer blindsided him as it had at the restaurant fire, flattening him. The ethereal blond beauty who'd set his body afire and left him to burn.

"Grace," he whispered.

Just like that, the damnable loneliness seeped through his walls of iron. Strangled his breath. *Yeah, you liar—lonely.* He couldn't stand the thought of going home to his empty condo. Slipping between cold sheets, shivering as the horror chased away his sleep.

Only a woman's warm, soft body would ease him tonight. And not just anyone, but one who at least cared for him.

With shaking hands, he took out his cell phone. Speed-dialed the first number on his list. His best—and only—friend's voice answered with a sleepy greeting.

"Hello?"

"Carmelita." He closed his eyes, weary with relief. "*Dulce*, I'm coming over."

The Collector guided the Mercedes away from downtown and glanced at his young passenger. "Did you know that man?" he asked sharply.

The kid, slumped in the leather seat like a limp noodle, rolled his head toward him, the movement loose. His blue eyes were glazed. "Who?"

Good. The GHB was doing its job. Soon, he'd do his.

"Never mind. Just relax and enjoy the ride."

He'd follow his own advice. People who panicked made mistakes, and he'd do well not to make them.

He'd become a skilled hunter, and the best, most vulnerable prey was to be found in places like the bar tonight. Risk versus reward.

The rewards were positively divine.

Recalling the man watching them, however, dampened some of his satisfaction. A skittering along his nerve endings set him on edge, intrusive and unwelcome. He enjoyed being the one to do the observing, not the other way around. And this particular man's observation had been rather . . . intense. He'd been much more focused and purposeful than the oblivious patrons around him.

While he, the Collector, had carefully selected his seat at the bar to remain in shadow, the man had been seated in a pool of light. The stranger's dark eyes had studied them intently, sensual mouth drawn into a frown, brows furrowed. He was Hispanic or maybe Italian, his angular face blessed with classic male beauty belonging on the cover of *GQ*. Raven hair fell in longish wisps over his brow, the length brushing his neck just past his ears.

All these features he memorized out of necessity because it was his business to do so and, goddamn, he could swear he'd seen their pursuer somewhere before. He had an excellent memory, but no matter how he scoured his brain, the man's identity eluded him.

Calm yourself. By God, it would come.

When it did, the Collector would simply have one more loose end to snip.

Julian discarded the condom and rejoined his lover in bed, sated in body if not in spirit. His morose mood wasn't Carmelita's fault. He just couldn't seem to fill the hollow ache in his chest these days, especially after sex. Even great sex with his closest friend.

Still, going home to stare at his empty bedroom was worse. Right?

Flopping onto his back with a sigh, he linked his fingers behind his head. Carmelita wasn't much of a cuddler, at least not with him. Cuddling implied something more than friends with benefits, a stronger bond than either of them wanted or needed. Except lately, he found himself longing for a connection he'd never experienced before. A simple touch not related to sex.

Comfort.

"Julian? What's wrong?"

He turned his head to meet her brown gaze as she rolled to her side, propping her head in one hand. Lush cinnamon hair matching the curls at the apex of her thighs spilled around her shoulders and over her naked breasts.

"Nothing, *dulce*." He grinned, knowing she loved the endearment.

"Don't try to distract me," she fussed. "You haven't been yourself for weeks, my friend."

Months, to be exact, but he saw no need to correct her. "I'm fine. Really. The meeting this afternoon to go over the plan for our captain's intervention was intense. The real thing is going to be brutal."

"I can only imagine. That poor man." Reaching out, she gently brushed a lock of hair out of his eyes, her expression full of compassion. "But I don't think that's all, Jules. Are the ghosts bothering you?"

Ghosts. Her tactful term for those dark days when most teenage boys were discovering the world and Julian had wanted only to die. For the secrets he'd left behind in that other life, the one where his family buried an inconvenient truth along with the corpse of the young man he'd been. The awful mistake Carmelita alone knew about, and even she didn't know the whole story behind why he'd almost thrown his life away. Nobody did, outside his family. No one else would. Ever.

He'd told Grace all he could.

And now tell Carmelita that Derek Vines was here, when she could do nothing except worry about things that couldn't be changed?

"No," he lied. The ghosts never rested. Never would. A partial truth, however, seemed in order to ease her fretting. "I . . . met someone."

Her jaw fell open and her eyes widened. "Really? When?"

"A few months ago." That revelation earned him a punch in the arm. So much for the nice caressing.

"You rat! Why haven't you said anything, and what the heck are you doing *here*, then? Who is she?"

He smiled at his friend. This was why he loved her so much. He could tell her anything, and she never judged him. No inconvenient jealousy, either, to muddle their relationship. "She's a lawyer in Nashville, and I haven't said anything because she doesn't even want to breathe the same air as me."

"Oh. Ouch."

"Yeah, sucks, huh?"

She sighed. "How well I know the feeling."

"That little computer dweeb at work still hasn't gotten a clue?"

Carmelita worked at Fossier, an accounting firm here in Sugarland, not far from his own condo and the fire station, and a short twenty minutes from Nashville. His knockout friend looked like she'd be more at home modeling for Victoria's Secret than crunching numbers, but whatever. Her job sounded like a sexless vacuum slowly draining a person's libido, leaving one in a zombielike state. No wonder she occasionally let off steam in the sack with him, because she sure wasn't getting any from her nerdy pencil pusher.

"He's not a dweeb and my guess is he's definitely not little," she defended. "He's just sort of . . . understimulated."

His brows lifted. "Uh-huh."

"Oh, shut up." She gave him a wistful smile. "We're pathetic. Why didn't we elope years ago?"

He grinned back. That was an old, safe topic of conversation. The question didn't need an answer because they both knew it by heart. He gave one anyway.

"Because I squeeze the toothpaste in the middle, I snore,

I won't trade in my Porsche for a minivan, and I'm always right." There were many more reasons, but those would suffice.

"And I'd smother you in your sleep during a fit of premenstrual rage."

"Prison would clash with your hair and nails."

"So I guess we'll have to remain friends," she said happily.

"With benefits."

"Absolutely."

Her smile took on a predatory quality. She crawled between his spread thighs and his cock reawakened in response to the unspoken demand. He saw no reason to deny them mutual pleasure and spread his legs wider, placing himself at her mercy.

Crouching, she gave the flared crown an experimental flick of her tongue. Her hair tumbled over his groin, tickled his balls. "You want this?" Another lick.

He sucked in a harsh breath. "Shit, yeah."

"Tell me."

"I want your mouth, *dulce*. Suck me."

She did, exactly the way he loved. Hard and deep, laving the ridge underneath his cock while her fingers played with his sac. Relentless, suctioning him with moist heat, bringing his blood to a steady boil.

Second to fucking a woman from behind, this was the finest way to orgasm. To watch his rod disappear between a woman's lips, to enjoy being hers. To feel the awesome tingle, the gathering at the base of his spine. Ready to explode.

Like now. His orgasm rolled his eyeballs back in his head. He let go with a hoarse shout, pumping his cum down her throat. Shuddered as she drank every drop.

At last, she released his softening cock and moved to lie beside him. Not touching, as was the norm.

But tonight, he shivered from the absence of warmth.

"Carmelita?"

"Mmm?"

"Can I . . . hold you?"

She patted his chest, giving him an odd stare. "Sure, for a while. You're like a furnace, you know."

A confusing wave of sadness and unfulfilled desire swelled inside him, smothering any reply as he rolled to his side, spooning her body against him.

As he tried in vain to drift to sleep, a pair of sparkling violet eyes refused to allow him to rest. Mocked him with the inescapable truth.

Wrong as it might be under the circumstances, he burned to have Grace McKenna underneath him. The flames licked at him, hotter than ever before.

Stupid bastard, forget about her.

He had no choice.

Grace didn't want him, had made it perfectly clear she never would. Her loss, he told himself . . . and knew he was lying.

The loss, it appeared, was all his.

Brett awoke to a god-awful pounding in his skull and a grungy taste in his mouth. Like he'd single-handedly attempted to drink the city dry and he shouldn't be awake to relive the experience. "Awww . . . shit."

Agony lanced his brain again, a knife blade burrowing deep into his gray matter to scramble what little was left. He panted, managing not to get sick, but not by much.

The bathroom. Yeah, he needed to crawl there. Splash some water on his face, brush his teeth. Then he'd feel more human.

Cautiously, he uncurled himself from the fetal position and rolled to his hands and knees. He blinked to clear his vision. Frowning, he blinked again. Total darkness. As in can't-see-your-hand-in-front-of-your-face pitch fucking black.

"What the hell?"

That's when he noticed the dirt under his palms. Not linoleum or smelly, beer-drenched carpet as he'd expected. Tentatively, he raked his hand over the surface to confirm his finding—dirt and pebbles.

The stench invaded his awakening senses next. It hung in the stagnant air like a shroud, nearly overtaking the natural, pungent smell of rock and earth, of old minerals and decay. No, a rancid smell like that didn't belong here, wherever *here* was. Didn't belong anywhere. He knew what label to give the stench, but his brain recoiled from going there.

"Hello?"

Brett inched forward, feeling his way, not trusting his surroundings. Falling over the edge of a cliff or something would suck, and he had to get away from here. Find help. He crawled until his fingers brushed something hard and chilly. Wet and a little slimy, too. Instinctively he snatched his hand back, then tried again.

A rock wall. A natural formation, not a man-made structure. A round, small space, he realized as he pushed to his feet and his fingers explored the surface, moving slowly to the right as it curved inward. His shoe kicked something hollow, but he kept going, his mind becoming clearer with every passing moment.

"A cave," he whispered, fear setting in at last. "A freaking cave. What the fuck is going on?"

Willing down the panic, he struggled to remember what he'd done last night—if it *was* last night. He went downtown to party, and his friends took off club-hopping, promising to come back. He'd been content where he was, people-watching, taking up a conversation with a man at the bar.

Who bought him a drink, which he accepted, even though he shouldn't have. But it was free and his fake ID passed muster, so why should he refuse?

What happened after that was a huge, yawning black hole.

Jesus, the bastard must've slipped him a Mickey. *Don't think about it. Just get out.*

Abruptly, the rock face ended—and cold metal took its place. Hands shaking, mind whirling in horrified disbelief, he frantically explored the vertical bars. Kept groping, moving to his right, until he met where the rock resumed on the other side. He stumbled to the left again, rattled the bars.

"Oh, Christ . . . oh, God."

Imprisoned. He'd been locked up in some sort of goddamned cage. Underground. "Hey! Let me out of here!"

Terror overrode the pounding in his skull, the sickness. He yelled, kicked the unyielding bars for several minutes, until he slumped against them, exhausted. "Help, somebody," he moaned.

"Won't do you any good, you know," came a voice from the darkness. A girl's voice, weird and singsongy, making her sound about one card short of a full deck.

"Who are you?" he demanded. "Did you put me in here?"

"Me? No." She giggled as though he'd said something really funny. "No, I'm waiting, just like Joey. Just like you."

Brett gripped the bars, heart knocking against his ribs, certain he'd gone insane. Right down the rabbit hole. "Waiting for what? Who are you, and who's Joey?"

"Joey's next. He doesn't talk anymore." She sounded sad about that.

"Next for what?" The trembling spread from his hands throughout his body. He couldn't stop.

"I'm after Joey. They come back a couple of times, then they don't come back—they don't come back," she sang, the eerie crooning echoing down the chamber. She sounded nearby—perhaps in another cell?

"Who doesn't come back, us or the bad guys?"

"Us. The generator comes on. They scream and scream like Sarah did, like piglets gone to slaughter. Then they don't come back."

Holy Mother of God. *Think, Brett.* "What's your name? Mine's Brett."

"Kendra. Keeen-dra, Keeen-draaa—"

"Listen to me, Kendra," he snapped. "There's got to be a way out of here, right? When the bastard comes, fight, bash him in the face. Just throw him off enough to be able to run, then get away."

"Can't get away when they hold you down, give you the nice drugs, make you float, float. . . ."

So Kendra wasn't just crazy. She was stoned. Out of steam and out of options for now, he slid to the ground and ran a hand down his face, wishing he could see jack shit, but aware he should probably be glad he couldn't.

Down the rabbit hole and straight into a nightmare.

"Hey, Brett? The screaming isn't the worst part," she said, as though making a curious observation.

He barked a laugh, a little hysterical to his own ears. "No shit? Then what is?"

"It's when they stop."

3

Grace McKenna snapped her newspaper closed with a sound of disgust and reached for her mug of coffee. Another missing person, vanished without a trace. The sixth one from the Nashville area in ten months, this time a young man of nineteen with a nice family and his entire future ahead of him. Missing as of one week ago.

No bodies, no leads. Zilch.

Except for a man who wished to remain anonymous claiming to have seen two men leaving a club in downtown Nashville last Friday night, the younger one matching the description of Vanderbilt freshman Brett Charles.

What a sorry-assed, totally messed-up world it was. Sure, the innocent needed a defender, but headlines like these made her burn for the day she would make prosecutor. She'd garnish her Wheaties with the testicles of men who preyed on the weak. Figuratively speaking.

If she weren't attractive, she might've achieved her goal by now. Okay, that sounded like a sexist view, but she had no illusions about the field of law still being a predominantly male, good ole boy environment. It wasn't sour grapes on her part in the least, just simple fact. Not only did she have breasts instead of a penis, but she wasn't one of those mannish, gruff career women who stalked around trying to act as though she sported a pair of balls bigger than her male comrades'.

Her father, who happened to be her boss at McKenna and Associates, the law firm he'd built from the ground up, was fond of saying she possessed a "quiet beauty with a core of inner strength" and was, therefore, exactly where she needed to be—at *his* firm, under *his* supervision. Grace, Champion of the Innocent. She loved her job, but worked hard against being typecast into a role she might never be able to rise above, even if it meant bucking Daddy on occasion. Preconceptions could stall a career.

In any case, she certainly wasn't going to defeat all of the world's bad guys today. She spent an hour reviewing her current cases at the kitchen table, and had just laid aside a mountain of file folders when her cell phone blasted Elton John's "The Bitch Is Back."

She jumped, heart giving a little lurch at hearing the song that usually made her smile. Julian Salvatore hadn't tried to phone her in almost four weeks, even in the wake of their chance meeting last Thursday, so she'd sworn he'd given up. Spying the number on the caller ID, she heaved a sigh of annoyance. And, yes, felt a tiny stab of disappointment, as well. Seemed he'd finally thrown in the towel after all.

This call was *so* not what she needed this morning, family acquaintance or not. Steeling herself, she picked up, forgoing the false, overdone niceties. "Mr. Vines, good morning. How can I help you?"

He laughed. "You're my lawyer, Grace. How do you think?"

She didn't like his tone. Or his presumptuous familiarity, considering she didn't know him very well. "I don't have anything new to tell you. At this point, Mr. Vines, we've barely started on your defense."

For a crime she wasn't entirely certain he hadn't committed. A first for her. Family alliances could be hell on a girl's scruples.

"I thought we were past the formalities. Please, call me Derek like you did the other day. We're family friends, for God's sake. I used to see you every summer when you came to visit your aunt Penny, remember?"

Which was how she'd ended up taking on Derek Vines as a favor, via a bit of pressure from her own father. Warren Vines had phoned Daddy about Derek's trouble a couple of weeks ago, citing Aunt Penny as a reference, to plead his son's case. Penny had vouched for her former neighbors.

And shit, as they say, flows straight downhill. As much as she hated to admit it, she feared Julian might be right about this one.

"Of course I remember." What she didn't recall was being particularly impressed with Mr. and Mrs. Vines or their son. Then again, as a flighty teenager she'd pretty much thought anybody over the age of twenty-one was lame.

In any case, her instincts urged her to maintain a polite, professional distance from this man, even more so than she normally would with a client. Her gut feelings had never steered her wrong. "I called you by your first name because I was introducing you to someone else in a social setting. Again, what can I do for you this morning? Did you have a specific question?"

His pleasant tone evaporated. "I'm being accused of sexual harassment by someone in my own father's company, and I can't refute the charges. Do you have any clue what this is doing to me? How humiliated I am? My God, I'm not even gay!"

Standing, she walked to the sink to rinse out her mug.

"The burden of proof is on Mr. Madison," she reminded him. "He has no video or audio evidence, nor does he have a witness. It's his word against—"

"Tell that to my father." He sighed. "Look, I don't want to discuss this over the phone. Lunch?"

She placed the mug in the dishwasher, then leaned her butt against the counter. This was one part of the job that became exhausting, yet was the very thing she excelled at—holding the frightened client's hand. And though she got paid handsomely to do it, she'd rather suffer the stomach flu than share another meal with Vines.

Be professional. He's paying you and deserves the same quality representation you'd give anyone else. "All right. Meet me in my office at noon?"

"Actually, I don't think I can make it into Nashville today. I have a lot of stuff to do around here. How about that diner on the town square, same time?"

She rolled her eyes. That meant more than two hours carved out of her day, a big chunk she needed to attend to other cases.

On the other hand, driving into Sugarland meant she might run into Julian again.

"Fine. See you later."

Ending the call, she headed off to shower and get ready, shaking her head at her idiocy. She did *not* want to see Jules. Didn't want to hear his smooth, nipple-puckering Spanish accent. Didn't ache to see his sexy smile aimed in her direction.

And she certainly didn't take any extra pains with her appearance.

At all.

Hours later, driving from her office through the gorgeous,

forested hills on the way to Sugarland, she allowed herself to wonder what Julian was doing today. By her calculations, he was off shift, and she knew that only because the guys had been at the fire last Thursday. She wasn't keeping tabs on the man or anything. Was he home, relaxing? Or maybe he'd be in town, running errands. Maybe—

Her cell phone shouted its upbeat greeting again, and her heart did a little two-step as she lifted it from the tray and peered at the screen. Once again, disappointment stabbed her breast, a bit sharper than before. She slipped on the hands-free unit and answered the call.

"Hey, sweet pea. What's up?"

Kat laughed, a musical sound that always made Grace smile. Her sister's irrepressible, outgoing nature was a light-house beacon in stormy weather. To anyone who knew Kat, it was no mystery why Howard's vow of bachelorhood had crumbled to dust.

"Getting the little monsters ready for spring break, and none too soon. I'm so tired of diagnostic testing, I could scream."

This was an old complaint, but Grace heard Kat's love of her job in her voice. "It can't be easy to keep a first grader focused long enough to accomplish them all."

"Yeah, like trying to lasso the wind. But hey, I didn't call to gripe in your ear. I just want to make sure you're coming out to Mom and Dad's for dinner on Sunday." Kat's tone was casual, but held a firm edge Grace didn't hear often.

"Oh? I don't know, honey. I have a ton of work right now."

"Who doesn't? It's on Sunday, for cryin' out loud! Take a break." A pause. "We haven't seen much of each other lately and I miss you," she said softly.

Manipulative brat. Her heart went mushy and she smiled. "All right, count me in. What time?"

"Yay! Around one. Mom says we'll eat around two and not to bring anything except your appetite."

"See you all Sunday, then. Give your hottie a hug for me and I love you."

"I'll give him more than that," she teased. "In the shower, on the kitchen table—"

"Oh, TMI! Lalala, I don't hear you. . . ."

"Love you back. Bye!"

Grace hung up laughing, the warm, happy glow from her sister filling the interior of her car like beams of sunshine. Kat and Howard deserved every joy in their lives, especially after the hell they'd been through. Letting her thoughts drift, she imagined having a man like the lieutenant to come home to her.

An honest-to-God man, all muscles, sweat, and a day's growth of beard from another shift in the trenches saving lives. Tired, but never too exhausted to show his woman just how much he missed her. To set the sheets on fire making love to her, slow and easy. Or fast and hard.

And she was an idiot. Because she had such a man panting after her, right in the palm of her hand. Hers for the taking—if she dared to take a gamble on him.

Did she? Sex with Julian would probably be incredible. The man was tailor-made for sin and she had no doubt he'd deliver. But for how long?

Therein lay the fly in the ointment. Julian didn't strike her as the kind of guy to play with just one woman. He was a ladies' man down to his bones. Oh, she couldn't blame him for that, not when she'd occasionally enjoyed a casual lover to stave off a lonely evening. But while the idea of a marriage, a mortgage, and 2.5 kids left her shaking in her high heels, a strong pair of arms to hold her at night would be lovely. The *same* pair of arms, when they both needed company. Sometime in the last year, she'd moved past the point in her life where she was okay with opening her eyes the morning after to see a man who didn't really care about her.

Did Julian care, or was his smooth charm all an act? And something else about him troubled her. He laughed and joked easily, never seemed to take life too seriously on the outside, but those dark, beautiful eyes . . . they never smiled. They were a bottomless well of sadness, and every time they met, she was torn between taking him in her arms and running like hell.

Grace wasn't wild about hooking up with a man she had to *fix*—her days were monopolized by defending men with numerous personal issues—even if her heart whispered he just might be worth it.

Round and round, no answers in sight. Thinking about Julian was guaranteed to drive her insane.

All too soon, she wheeled her Mercedes into an empty space a few doors down from the busy diner. For a few giddy seconds, she fantasized that Derek Vines had been abducted by aliens and whisked to another planet, before she grabbed her purse and briefcase and slid from the car with a sigh.

Inside, harried waitresses rushed about with steaming platters of burgers and chicken-fried steaks guaranteed to clog the stoutest of arteries. Darned if her mouth didn't water for a big greasy cheeseburger with fries, but the last thing she wanted to do was give Vines the impression she wished to linger.

She spotted him seated in a booth against the wall, and made her way over, hoping to conclude this meeting as quickly as possible. Clutching her briefcase like a shield, she scooted into the booth, then laid it and her purse on the seat.

"Mr. Vines," she said politely, "this isn't—"

"Derek, *please*." Resting his elbows on the table and clasping his hands, he shot her a disarming grin.

His friendly overture didn't move her, but his persistence wore her down. If he was going to make an issue of how she addressed him every time they spoke, their conversations would drag on that much longer.

"Fine, *Derek*. I was about to say that this isn't the ideal place for the discussion you want to have."

Glancing around them, he gave a negligent shrug. "Why not? It's so crowded and noisy, no one will pay us any attention."

The waitress arrived to hand them plastic menus and take their drink orders, halting Grace's frown before it could manifest. After the girl left, Grace pretended to study the lunch selections while perusing Vines instead.

At nearly forty, he was a handsome man in a harsh, rugged way, though in her opinion, his looks couldn't compete with Julian's classic, refined features. He wore his dark, coffee-colored hair in waves to his collar and slicked back from his pale face. His brown eyes were calculating, always assessing.

She closed her menu and set it aside. "Since you're the one paying for my time, why don't you start? I sense you're after more than just an update or a shoulder to lean on."

"I wouldn't turn down the shoulder," he said, placing his menu on top of hers. He pursed his lips as though tasting something sour. "But you're correct. I want this unpleasantness put behind me, and I'm willing to pay to make that happen."

Grace sat up straighter. "You'd settle out of court?"

"To make this go away, yes."

"In spite of your claims of innocence?"

"I *am* innocent, and I'm not into men, despite what fantasies Hayden Madison has cooked up in his head. I adore women and I've never had to bully a lady into bed," he drawled, dropping his gaze to her bosom to emphasize his point.

Grace resisted the urge to cross her arms protectively over said bosom. "I'm going to play devil's advocate here. While settling would certainly expedite the matter, many would view the move as an admission of guilt on your part."

The waitress brought their drinks, iced tea for Vines and Diet Coke for Grace. She ordered a small salad with ranch, tuning out what her client asked for. She couldn't have cared less. After the girl hurried off, Vines leaned forward, expression intense.

"What you said is true, but I'm being maligned *now*, and so is my father. A few weeks or months of fighting Madison on a quid pro quo sexual harassment charge won't change that fact, and could very well do more harm than good in the end."

"Whether or not you're guilty." It wasn't a question; she was feeling him out, thinking out loud. She took a sip of her soda, then fiddled with the straw. "A man with money is accused, the plaintiff threatens to take the case all the way to its nasty conclusion, and the defendant settles. It's played out that way before, with people in the hot seat who have much more to lose than you, careerwise. Actors, musicians, politicians, you name it."

"What are you getting at?"

"As you said, you're already feeling the heat from Madison's charges. So why not fight? If you're innocent, he can't prove otherwise and to hell with what other people think. Your father owns the company, so it's not like you'll lose your job." *If you're innocent.* A Freudian slip, but he didn't seem to notice.

"Is that your official advice? That I fight?"

"I'm presenting you with your options and encouraging you to make a careful decision. The choice is yours."

Mentally, she gave the honest angel on her shoulder a swift kick in the ass. She'd probably just advised her way into having to deal with him for months. Ugh.

What's more, something was off. And not just with his noise about settling, which quite honestly would suit her fine. No, it was his attempt to appear interested in her as a woman. His leer felt flat, no real lust or emotion behind his expression. Immediately, she recalled Julian's dark, soulful eyes caressing her body from head to toe. The pure, undisguised need written in their depths—and the disappointment in them when she continued to avoid his overtures.

Oh, yes, she knew what a man looked like when he truly craved a woman. In that area, Julian left Vines eating dirt.

Which begged the question, *Why would Vines pretend unless he's guilty as hell?*

Their food arrived and Vines dug into his club sandwich, the topic apparently not affecting his appetite. Grace picked at her salad, ready to dispense with this meeting and pick up that cheeseburger on her way back to the office. She might be slender, but she could eat like a sailor on shore leave, something that never failed to amuse her family.

After scarfing a second section of his sandwich, Vines waved a fry in her direction. "Let's make Madison an offer."

"If that's what you want," she said, struggling to keep the profound relief off her face. Laying down her fork, she opened her briefcase and dug out the file. Vines chewed silently while she scanned her notes. "He's claiming your unwanted advances have made working at W. H. Vines impossible and is asking for wages lost plus punitive damages. One hundred fifty thousand."

"Ridiculous," he scoffed.

Not if he's telling the truth. Wisely, she refrained from saying so.

He ate the fry and continued. "The little shit barely pulls in sixty grand a year. Offer him seventy with the stipulation that the amount, including the extra money, is simply a gesture of goodwill from me and W. H. Vines. We wish him the best and so forth."

"They'll counter, and so will I. What's your bottom line?"

"One hundred grand, not a cent more."

Interesting. Gathering the file, she shoved it into her briefcase, dug a ten out of her wallet, and tossed it next to her salad plate.

"Leaving so soon? You've hardly eaten."

"Big breakfast," she lied, willing her stomach not to growl. "I have to run, but I'll let you know as soon as I hear from his attorney." She scrambled from the seat, poised to make good her escape.

"Grace?" The earnestness in his tone stopped her.

"Yes?"

"Would you have dinner with me one night? After all of this is cleared up, I mean."

I'd sooner have my bottom lip stapled to my forehead, thanks.

"Um, I'm kind of seeing someone right now." Whoops, two lies in a row. She tried for a sympathetic smile, but it felt as fake as his ogling had been earlier. Why on earth would he ask her out? "I'm sorry."

Smiling, he shook his head. "Hey, I had to try."

In the safety of her car, she blew out a tense breath. Going out with Julian, enjoying his company—more and more the idea held vast appeal.

Grace wondered whether she'd really lied after all.

Derek finished his sandwich, the picture of perfect calm. Inside, his guts roiled with rage and frustration. Fear. He was not going down on Madison's charges, the goddamned weasel. He didn't need the public scrutiny.

He had more to lose than the high-and-mighty Grace McKenna could ever dream.

Julian fucking Salvatore.

After the Collector's phone call last Friday describing the witness, Derek had put it all together. The man Grace had introduced him to. The boy from fifteen years ago. They were the same. And now he'd seen the Collector. Derek had rushed straight to his bathroom and thrown up his gin and tonic. Desperate, he'd considered cleaning out his accounts and skipping the country, but discounted it almost immediately. There wasn't a corner of the earth where he could hide that he wouldn't be found. The stranglehold around his neck was absolute, and unforgiving.

His cell phone chirped and he glanced at the display. Gruber. That call could mean only one thing, and Derek hated what must be done. "Yes?"

"I found Salvatore. He works for the Sugarland Fire Department, Station Five. You want to tell the boss or shall I?"

"I'll deal with that end," he snapped. "You just take care of *him*, and the other one, as well."

"Already on it."

The bastard hung up without asking how Derek would prefer the deed to be carried out. The man was always so in control, unflappable to his rotten core.

Derek placed a call of his own and waited, stomach cramping, and wished he hadn't yet eaten.

"Tell me you have good news," the smooth voice said calmly.

"I do. He's been located."

"I trust the Collector is taking care of him? I don't appreciate your loose ends."

I've never done anything to please you, regardless of how hard I try.

"Of course he is. By this time next week, the problem will no longer exist."

"Good. When it's successfully completed, you'll be rewarded."

Derek knew what that meant, and his cock hardened even as the knowledge horrified him. The predator in him anticipated toying with his new gift, much like a cat holding a mouse under his paw. Watching them squirm, writhe in fear, knowing his power over them was absolute, their flesh his to savor, aroused him beyond endurance. They were beautiful in their final surrender, precious to him, and his arguments to keep them always fell on deaf ears.

Knowing how his angels must end made him sad, but he was a slave to his own desires. Derek wasn't the one calling the shots or making the rules—only with full compliance did he receive his rewards—and his tormentor never failed to remind him of his weakness.

"Thank you," he whispered, his voice betraying his misery. His need.

"Just don't forget who keeps you safe and loved," the boss said gently. "I'm the only one who understands, Derek. We look out for each other, because no one else will."

"I know." He hung up and stared at his half-eaten food, more than a little sick. Again he dreamed of running, hiding somewhere far away. Living in his own skin, on someone else's terms, was a repeating, perpetual nightmare. Survival shouldn't be this difficult.

Innocent people shouldn't have to die even if, by the end, they were begging for release from hell.

At least in death they were given the peace Derek could only wish for.

4

Grace pulled her car into her parents' driveway beside Howard's mammoth black Ford truck and shut off the ignition, sparing a glance for the car parked on the street, one she didn't recognize. Puzzled, she wondered who else their folks had invited over, and came up empty. Sunday dinner was usually just a casual family gathering, a time to catch up and reconnect.

Curious, she grabbed her purse and hurried up the flagstone sidewalk. The heavy front door stood open and through the glass storm door, Grace heard the sounds of several adult voices raised in merry laughter. Maybe she should've worn something nicer than jeans and a cotton blouse. No help for it now.

She stepped inside, calling out to the group lounging in the den. "Hey, I'm here! Better late than never, huh?"

"But better never late," her father quipped, setting aside his glass of wine and rising from his easy chair. He enveloped her in a hug, then relinquished her to her mother for more of the same.

"Something smells terrific," she said, releasing her mom. "Roast?"

"With all the trimmings. I have to fatten you up, since your father seems determined to work you to death!" She shot a frown at her fair, handsome husband, who widened his blue eyes in mock innocence.

Grace chuckled at their banter and turned to greet their guests, who were busy talking animatedly with Kat and Howard. A small, delicate bird of a woman sat next to Kat on the sofa. Howard was sitting on the other side of her sister, holding her hand and grinning like a luck-struck fool. A big man who was an older version of Howard sat close to him in a chair. Grace had met the lieutenant's parents only a handful of times—most recently at Howard and Kat's wedding at the end of January—and seeing them here threw her for a moment.

"Chief Mitchell, Georgie, it's so good to see you!" She bent and gave hugs to Mrs. Mitchell, Kat, and Howard, then found herself wrapped in Bentley's bone-crunching embrace. Like his son, Sugarland's fire chief was a large, fine-looking man, though his face had a few character lines and his brown hair had gone salt-and-pepper with age. Quite a contrast to her own dad, who was tall, lean, and blond, like herself.

"Good to see you, too, honey," he said, pressing a kiss to her cheek. "Mary says you're working too hard; is that right?"

Grace pulled out of his embrace, shaking her head. "Mom worries too much." Especially after Daddy's heart attack last year, but she didn't add that part. "It's just business as usual around the office. I'm sure you know how it is."

The chief nodded, folding his arms over his chest. "Not for much longer, if I have anything to say about it. I'm thinking of retiring at the end of June, before our Alaskan cruise."

"Oh, that's wonderful! Congratulations. I'm sure Georgie must be thrilled." Georgie beamed and chimed in her agreement. Howard, on the other hand, stared at his lap, smile dimming some. Grace knew from her sister's and brother-in-law's stories how every firefighter in the department idolized

Bentley, so it was no wonder Howard would be a little bummed at the change.

"Thanks, so am I. I'm looking forward to spending more time with my gorgeous wife." The chief smiled. "And with my son."

Howard perked up at that, meeting his father's gaze, his happiness plain. After what they'd been through these past few months, they were both eager to make up for lost time.

Howard and Kat exchanged a meaningful look. "I think that's probably a great place to share, don't you?" he murmured, brushing her lips in a gentle kiss.

"I agree." The room went quiet while her sister paused, making sure she had everyone's attention. "We have some great news. Howard and I . . . well, we're pregnant!"

The room erupted in squeals from the moms and laughter from the men. Georgie wrapped Kat in a tight squeeze, followed by her own mom. Howard stood, trading backslaps with the men, beaming as though no other guy had ever accomplished such a manly feat. Then the parents switched for another round of effusive well-wishes. Through it all, Grace waited her turn, feeling pretty much the way she'd felt in the fourth grade when Jimmy Fredrick beaned her at recess with a line drive to the forehead—knocked flat on her ass.

Thank God nobody noticed. They were too busy peppering the radiant couple with questions to wonder at Grace's silence.

Georgie settled back into her spot next to Kat. "When's the baby due?"

"The week of Christmas, poor thing," Kat said, green eyes shining. "Bam, double presents, and then nothing the rest of the year."

Daddy laughed. "Oh, right! Like the kid won't be spoiled at all."

"Mary, we'll have to take our girl shopping for the nursery. She's going to need, well, everything!" Georgie said, squeezing Kat's hand. She smiled at Grace. "Of course, you'll go with us, dear."

"I'd love to." Grace smiled back, hoping her expression wasn't as strained as it felt. A whirlwind of emotions battered her from all sides, not the least of which was annoyance at being included as an afterthought. Or was that really the problem?

No, Georgie was a sweet lady, as overjoyed as everyone else, and Grace was ashamed of her own petty thoughts.

What's wrong with me?

Mom clapped her hands in excitement. "Ooh, there's that new factory outlet in Nashville! I heard they've got furniture, bedding, clothes. . . ."

As she chattered away, the men cringed, and the chief arched a brow at Howard.

"Might as well just hand over your wallet now, son. Fighting the Estrogen Squad will do you no good."

Howard put on a mournful face, but chuckled when his wife elbowed him in the ribs. Kat held up a hand, addressing the group at large.

"All of that sounds like fun, but we're going to wait until my first trimester is past before we start feathering the nest." She laid a hand on her husband's big, muscular thigh. "It's all a little too good to be true. It didn't take us nearly as long to conceive as we thought it would, and we don't anticipate any problems, but still . . ."

Her sister's common sense tempered the joy some, but not by much. Despite the poor odds surrounding Howard's ability to father children, they'd created a tiny life together without having to resort to more-aggressive measures. Grace couldn't be happier for them. Really.

So why did she feel like sneaking off for a good cry?

Grace had never thought of herself as the maternal type, had never experienced a single twinge of anticipation or envy when others mentioned their children. Babies cried, pooped, peed, and got sick. They required one hundred percent of their parents' attention for the next twenty or thirty years.

Diapers, bottles, nipples, baby smells.

Loose teeth, growing pains, parent conferences.

Dating, joyriding, prom.

Thanks, but no thanks.

And yet a weird sort of funk settled about her shoulders as they trooped in to dinner. Jovial, upbeat conversation swirled around her, little of it requiring her input, which was fine. Or maybe not. It gave her far too much time to brood. Everyone in the room seemed to be moving forward into a new phase of their lives. *Except me.*

Slowly, she lowered her fork, the revelation like a slap in the face. Good God, when had she begun to feel stuck in her own life, spinning her wheels? How had that *happened*?

A hand touched her arm. "Hey, you're awfully quiet," Kat observed. "Something wrong?"

Grace blinked at her sister. "No, I just . . . I think I'm going to call him."

"What? Call who?" Kat's pretty face scrunched into a puzzled frown.

Grace lowered her voice, shooting Howard a meaningful look. "You *know.*"

Her sister's eyes widened. "Oh! Oh, wow. He's finally getting to you, huh?" She grinned like an imp, the little bitch.

"Well, there's no harm in making a new friend," she said, too casually.

Kat giggled. "Friend. Right. Let me know how that works out."

"Let's keep this between us, for now."

"Sure, but *he's* going to find out anyway, eventually," Kat whispered, rolling her eyes toward her husband. Though the lieutenant was a steady rock who loved his team like brothers, it was no secret that Julian tried his patience more than most. According to Kat, he'd even gone so far as to warn the gregarious ladies' man away from Grace months ago, before the chief's birthday party.

That Howard had reportedly hurt Julian's feelings in doing so bothered Grace more than she cared to admit. "I know, but I don't want this to seem like a big deal and get his nose all out of joint. Because it isn't."

"Okay."

"I'm not looking to hook up with this guy."

"Whatever you say."

Studying her sister's smug expression, she decided it was time for another tack. "Hey, I'm really thrilled for you two. I can't think of anyone who deserves happiness more."

"Thanks . . . but I can."

Well, damn. Tears pricked her eyes and she glanced away, willing down the sudden rush of emotion. "I *am* happy, honest."

Kat gazed at her curiously and she gave her sister's hand a reassuring squeeze. She had built a successful career, enjoyed a luxury car and a healthy savings account. She was happy.

And until today, she could've sworn to a jury that it was the absolute truth.

Man, what a pissy, soggy mess of a day. Julian didn't mind the rain so much, but people taking idiotic chances *plus* rain? There you had a recipe for a shift loaded with calls for traffic accidents, on top of the usual shit.

Mr. Stafford had forgotten to take his insulin again, two young boys had decided to find out if putting dry ice in a plastic bottle will cause the container to explode—it *so* fucking does—earning the miscreants a trip to the ER, and a student at a local elementary had suffered a severe asthma attack. And the damned shift was barely eight hours old.

Julian slogged into the station house after the others, butt dragging, soaked and chilled to the bone despite his heavy clothing. It might be spring, but you couldn't work out in that crap all day without feeling the effects. Right about now, he figured his balls were shriveled to the size of raisins.

"Man, all we need right now is to have to do a water rescue in this shit," Tommy said, stripping off his coat and regulation navy polo.

"Don't tempt the gods—they might hear you," Eve replied drily, eyeing his bare chest. "And for Christ's sake, put on a shirt before we eat. I'm out of Tums."

Tommy grinned, flexing a bit. "What's the matter, Evie? Am I finally getting to you, making you all hot and bothered?"

Eve snorted, engaging in their usual banter. "Yep. I decided just last week to take up cradle robbing."

"Yeah? Best news I've heard all day." Tommy gave her an exaggerated, come-hither pout, which looked disgustingly cool on his movie-star-handsome mug. He stalked toward her slowly, waggling his brows, making her and everyone else laugh. Julian grinned, shaking his head. The kid loved teasing her and Eve never seemed to mind.

"Let's go put out a fire, huh? I've got the equipment you need—"

"Knock it off, Skyler," Sean said, stepping into his path, expression black. Tommy froze, blue eyes wide. After a tense few seconds of silence, the captain waved a hand at his team. "Go change and let's eat while we can. Who's responsible for dinner?"

"I am," Tommy muttered. "I'll start as soon as I get dry." Turning on his heel, he headed in the direction of the room he shared with Zack.

Okay, so not everyone had been amused. Feeling bad for the guy, Julian caught up with him in the hallway and slapped a hand on his shoulder. "What's on the menu? Chili dogs? *Dios*, I'm starving." He usually gave the kid hell about his limited culinary skills, but he figured now was not a great time to poke fun.

Tommy glanced at him, brightening a little. "Me, too, but no dogs today. I'm expanding my horizons to homemade lasagna. Well, not totally homemade, because who has all friggin' day? But I found these great noodles that you don't have to boil. Just stick them in the oven and they poof out—how freaky is that?" At Julian's dubious look, he grinned. "Relax, I already tried the recipe on my family last week and they gave it two thumbs-up."

Julian's stomach rumbled. "Sounds good. Want some help?"

"Sure, thanks," he said, his tone appreciative, yet a little hesitant. "You can fix the salad and garlic bread, if that's okay."

"Works for me." Julian ducked into the room he shared with the lieutenant, skirted the wall of lockers separating their beds, and began to strip. Howard was already inside, yanking on a dry shirt and tucking the tail into clean pants.

"I heard what you said to Skyler. That was decent of you."

"What, like I never offered to help with grub duty before?" First Tommy appeared surprised at the offer, now this from the man he admired most. *Am I really such an asshole that he feels the need to point out when I'm not?*

"I'm talking about distracting him from his embarrassment over being snapped at by Sean. You're good at that sort of thing. . . . You know, bringing calm or humor to a tough situation."

The unexpected praise rooted him in place, warming a cold spot inside him. Grabbing a clean towel from his locker, he fumbled with his response as cynicism warred with the painful bloom of hope. Like maybe, for once, he was moving into the circle, rather than on the outside looking in—

Cristo. Wouldn't do to let his insecurities, his yearning for acceptance, flap naked in the breeze, so in the end he just said, "Um, thanks."

From the other side of the lockers, Six-Pack said, "I'm gonna go make sure the ambulance is stocked."

Then, thank God, the man shuffled out, leaving Julian to his business. Quickly, he dried off, got dressed, and headed to the kitchen to help Tommy. Bagged salad and frozen bread he could do. A simple, mindless task to quiet his brain, keep it from wandering down the same old treacherous path to the reason for the glass bubble separating himself from the world.

His fear of never breaking the barrier.

His terror of rattling the skeletons by trying.

Blowing out a breath, he ripped open the bag of lettuce and glanced over to where Tommy stood at the counter a few feet away, mixing the white, goopy ricotta. "God, how can something that looks so nasty taste so good?"

"No shit. Kinda like oysters, huh?"

"I'll take your word for it."

Tommy grinned. "Hey, they're supposed to be an aphrodisiac."

"So are rhinoceros horns, but you won't see me chowing down on one." Studying the younger man, he decided to go out on a limb. "I wouldn't think you'd need any help in that department these days. Aren't you seeing that cute friend of Cori's? What's her name?"

"Shea Ford." He lifted a shoulder in a negligent gesture. "We've been out a couple of times. No biggie."

Coming from Tommy, the cool response was interesting. With his blond, Brad Pitt looks, sunny personality, and family straight out of a TV sitcom, the former high school star quarterback was so perfect it was nauseating. Seeing him off his game was rare. "You're not into a doll like her?"

"Correction—*she's* not into *me*." He laughed, the sound a little forced. "She thinks I'm too young for her. I'm out all goddamned day, breaking my back pulling people out of mangled cars, cleaning up their messes—I walk into fucking burning buildings—yet I'm a *kid*. I'm not good enough for her. But hey, like I said, no sweat. I don't need a woman with balls bigger than mine, you copy?"

Julian blinked at Skyler's vehemence and made a mental note to himself—*Stop calling the guy a kid, even in your head.* "Yeah. Damn, that's . . . I'm sorry. If it's any consolation, I'm in the same boat."

The younger man glanced up from layering the ingredients in the pan. "Yeah? You got a lady yanking your chain?"

"Yanking, hell. She's got the chain wrapped around my neck choking the life out of me. Christ, she won't even let me close enough to know what she's thinking, so you're way ahead of me there."

"Sucks, man."

"No lie."

"Are we bonding here, Jules?"

"No way, I've got an image to protect. I go all warm and

fuzzy and people might start to mistake me for a sonofabitch who cares." He smiled, waited. For once, would someone take the joke as he intended?

Tommy's lips curved upward, those pale blue eyes dancing with humor. "Good to know. Who needs friends, anyhow?"

Something strange and nice unfurled in Julian's middle, warming the chill even more, and a knot of tension he hadn't even realized was there eased from his neck and shoulders. "My thoughts exactly."

They worked in comfortable silence for a few minutes, Julian adding some cheese and vegetables to the salad and laying out the garlic bread on a baking sheet, Tommy sliding the lasagna in the oven. After a while, Julian's curiosity got the better of him and he leaned his butt against the counter, studying the other man thoughtfully.

"Didn't I hear once that you started out playing college football right after high school?" The sudden, stark flash of grief across Tommy's face instantly made him regret the question. "Forget it, I—"

"No, it's okay. I played for the Alabama Crimson Tide my freshman year. Saw some game time, had a great season, was on top of the world and looking forward to my sophomore year. I'd gotten a little buzz from the press and was flying about as high as any nineteen-year-old could be. But I had to drop out of school." He stared at a point over Julian's shoulder, remembering. When he spoke again, his voice was quiet. Sad.

"My older brother, Donnie, was killed in Iraq and I came home. End of story."

Not by a long shot, but Julian was sensitive enough not to question Tommy further on the painful subject.

"Madre de Dios." Julian scrambled for the right words,

unable to imagine how he'd feel if one day he received the dreaded call about Tonio, a narcotics officer who lived every single day on the edge. He couldn't, so he settled for honesty. "I'm so sorry. I can't begin to understand what you and your family went through."

"We survived," Tommy said softly, turning to wipe the counter, offering nothing more.

Julian was hit with another strange, unfamiliar emotion— shame. A few moments ago, had he actually compared this man's personal life to a TV sitcom? God, everyone at the station probably knew about Tommy's brother, and the rest of the story he had yet to tell Julian—like why he ditched his plans to play college and pro ball and threw away his education. And on the heels of that thought, a startling epiphany shifted the ground under his feet.

For so long, he'd felt like the outsider on this team, carried a chip on his shoulder the size of LP Field. He'd resented the closeness the others shared, felt like none of them gave a damn about knowing him other than being able to count on his skills as a firefighter/paramedic.

Until this very moment, it had never occurred to him that the others might feel the same way about him.

When had he bothered to take a personal interest in anyone else's life? *No wonder Grace doesn't want anything to do with me.*

Jesus Christ, self-realization sucked.

As the aroma of baking lasagna drifted through the station, the rest of the team filed into the kitchen to hover like a pack of starving dogs. Fortifying his nerves, Julian made an extra effort to try to say something, hell, *cheerful* to each of them—with mixed results.

"Hey, Eve! So . . . are you still seeing that nice guy you brought to the Waterin' Hole a while back? The teacher?"

Pausing in the act of filching a slice of cucumber from the salad bowl, she eyed him with suspicion. "Why do you ask?"

"Just making conversation. You two made a good-looking couple."

"Uh, thanks. But Drake and I are just friends," she said, cutting a quick look at the captain, who strolled in right at that moment.

Sean zeroed in on Eve, scowling. "You and who are just friends?"

"Drake. The teacher I was seeing." She shrugged, a blush coloring her bronzed cheeks.

"Oh? You've never mentioned dating anyone," he said irritably.

"You met him, for God's sake. Oh, wait—you must've been too toasted to remember." Eve rolled her eyes and moved away, but Sean followed, the unhappy pair arguing in quiet whispers, leaving Julian staring after them.

O-kay. What the devil was up with that?

Zack strolled in next, running a hand through his short black hair, spiking the damp strands in every direction. Julian sent him a smile, putting as much sincerity into it and his tone as humanly possible. "So, how's Cori? Everything still great with you guys?"

Zack rested an arm on the counter, cocking his head. "She's fine and so are we. Why?"

Shit, I really must be a jerk. "I'm happy for you, that's all. Is the lady going to make an honest man out of you?"

The tensing of the other man's shoulders was subtle, but clear. "We're tying the knot the fourth Saturday in July, before she starts showing too much. Everyone knows invites are going out this week, and so would you if you cared enough to pay attention."

Ouch. The hurt, although deserved, speared deep. "I cared enough to continue CPR on you long after even Six-Pack believed we should call it," he said quietly.

Zack's reserve crumbled, and he glanced away. "I know, man. I owe you my life, and there's no way to thank you enough for that kind of gift."

"You owe me nothing. Just . . . give me a chance. Please."

"To do what?" Confusion and wariness battled in his laser-blue eyes.

"To prove I'm not a shithead."

Zack shook his head. "No one thinks you're a shithead, Jules. You just waffle between trying too hard or not at all. You're fantastic at your job, but personally? You need to ease up some, give people a chance if you expect them to give you one."

"That's what I'm doing. I want to try."

"I hope so, because you're among friends here, if only you'd see it."

Tommy, bless him, cleared his throat and interrupted their heart-to-heart. "Who's hungry?"

Six-Pack joined them and they settled at the table, digging into the food. They were so famished boot leather would've tasted like filet mignon, but the lasagna was really good and Julian told Tommy so, the sentiments echoed by the rest of the team. By some miracle, they were actually able to finish their meal before the three loud tones on the intercom system shattered the blessed peace and warmth.

Another frigging traffic accident. In the rain. But by now, he welcomed the chance to escape the close confines of the station and the tumult in his own head. Out on a call was the one place he didn't have to question where he fit in the world, where people were glad to see his face. Where his existence had meaning. A man could live off that high for weeks. Years.

A man could forget.

The wreck was on I-49, always a bitch to work because the two-lane highway snaked through the hills, surrounded by forest and numerous sheer drops into valleys that Tennessee natives like the lieutenant called "hollers." And wouldn't you know, the accident was situated on a curve, oncoming traffic unable to see the activity until they were almost on top of it.

Zack pulled the quint in behind the two vehicles, as far onto the shoulder as possible. Six-Pack drove the ambulance around the whole mess, parking in front of the cars. They could see more of the oncoming lane from here, at least.

"Just a fender bender," the lieutenant said, his relief apparent. "The car in front must've hit the brakes for an animal or something."

"Yeah, we'll be out of here in a few." Julian swung out of the ambulance to see the captain speaking with the occupants of the two cars, moderating a heated discussion on who was at fault. Zack and Tommy were at his back, ready to intervene if need be.

Julian shot Six-Pack a faint smile as water began to drip from the brim of his own hat. "No injuries, then; just waiting on the police to get here."

"I'll check to be sure. Why don't you help Eve set out the cones?"

"Sure thing." He jogged to the back of the quint and grabbed a stack, then returned to the front of the ambulance. He spaced out the cones at regular intervals in an arc from the shoulder to the center stripe as a warning to the eastbound vehicles.

A warning drivers sometimes chose not to heed. Like the truck coming on way too fast for conditions, barreling straight for them all. Julian turned, shouting, waving his arms.

"Eve, get out of the road!"

Looking up, she frowned in his direction. "What?"

"Move!" Shit, she couldn't see the truck from her angle, looking up the rise. And a glance backward as he took off toward her told him the guy wasn't slowing down.

Julian raced for her, heart in his mouth. He heard the whine of the truck's engine, tires on the rain-slicked pavement, bearing down. Heard Eve's scream as he shoved her toward the shoulder. He spun, planted his feet to run.

And saw nothing but grille.

The glancing blow caught the right side of his body with a sickening thud, sent him airborne. Flailing, helpless, over the edge of the gully. Falling.

He hit the steep slope on his back, so hard the air rushed from his lungs, and tumbled, ass over elbows. Down, down. Limbs and brush scratched at his protective clothing, his face. His head slammed into something hard, his hat long gone.

Gradually, the incline leveled off and he slid the remaining few feet on his stomach . . . and stopped. The whole thing was over in seconds.

Alive. The patter of rain on the foliage sounded so normal and incongruous with what had just happened. The rich, pungent scent of the earth invaded his senses, and he dug his fingers into the leaves and mud. *You're fine; get up.*

Gathering his strength, he lifted his head—and agony exploded behind his eyes, crashed through his chest and hip. Blinding pain, so bad his brain spun, the forest floor whirling around him. His gut heaved and he vomited, unable to prevent it and not particularly giving a fuck at the moment.

Okay. Moving? Not a good plan. Voices sought him, calling his name from somewhere up the gully. How far had he fallen? Weird how the shouts seemed to be getting farther away instead of closer. But the crunch of boots reached his ears, and the urgency in the voices told him that he'd been spotted.

"Julian? Can you hear me?" Sean barked, sharp and worried.

"Yeah, I—" His stomach rolled and he got sick again, closing his eyes against the misery. "God, my head . . . everything hurts," he rasped.

Careful fingers probed his scalp, searching for the wound. "Here," Tommy said, parting his hair near the back of his head. "Damn, that's going to need stitches."

Julian swallowed hard. "Eve," he managed.

"She's fine, thanks to you. Don't try to talk anymore," Six-Pack said, low and soothing. "Let us do all the work. Your biggest job is to stay awake, okay?"

They turned him over, gently, onto a backboard. Working together, they opened his coat to check the rest of his injuries, jostling him as little as possible, though the movement was still too much. He fought down the nausea as pain shot through every nerve ending. "Oh—oh, Jesus."

Tommy laid a hand on his shoulder. "Easy does it. We're getting you out of here. Just don't go to sleep, buddy. Julian?"

God knew he tried to obey. The buzzing in his ears drowned out their insistent voices as he struggled against the cloak of darkness.

And lost.

5

Call him, you lily-livered chicken.

Four days. Well, five if you counted Sunday. Most of the week wasted by procrastinating, telling herself she'd been busy. Which was the truth, but she hadn't been too swamped to pick up the phone and hold out the olive branch.

"You've never been a coward before," Grace told her reflection in the bathroom mirror. "Nothing's changed."

Except for the object of her interest being just a little too dangerous. A bit of a bad boy.

Part of her wanted too much to be, for once in her well-ordered life, a very bad girl.

With a sigh, she pinned her hair up into a twist, not because it looked elegant, but because it annoyed her less this way when she was working. She eyed her crisp, pale blue power suit, dissatisfied. "You look like a buttoned-up bore."

Why couldn't she be more free and fun-loving like Kat? Just take a chance, roar off on a motorcycle with the hottie of her dreams, and find a love to last a lifetime?

The phone rang, interrupting her pity party, and she strode into the bedroom. Nobody ever called this early, unless . . . leaning over, she peered at the caller ID and a rueful laugh escaped, her secret hopes dashed. Not the hottie of her own dreams, but her sister.

She picked up. "Hey, Sis. What's up?"

"I'm sorry to call so early. I know you're getting ready to leave," Kat said, sounding strange. Using *that tone*, the one with the quiet edge loved ones can't help but project when something is terribly wrong.

Grace's fingers gripped the receiver, all sorts of horrible thoughts flooding her mind. "What's wrong? Is it Daddy? Do you need me there?"

"No! No, nothing like that. Daddy's fine." Kat hesitated. "Sweetie, did you ever call Julian this week?"

Grace frowned in confusion. "Not yet, but I was planning to. Why? Oh, wait," she said, sitting on the edge of her bed. "Let me guess—he got tired of waiting around on a lost cause like me, and Howard told you he's dating someone else."

The idea made her want to strangle someone. Very unsettling to feel like doing violence to another person.

"No, I . . . Grace, Julian was hurt last night. They were working an accident on I-49 and he was struck by a car," she said quietly.

The air left Grace's body, cold washing over her in a rush. She gazed at the tasteful watercolor on her bedroom wall, trying to comprehend her sister's words. Julian. The beautiful, charming rogue who'd pursued her for months, hurt. Or worse. "Oh, my God. How bad is he?" Was that her own voice, hoarse and choked with tears?

"He'll be okay," her sister assured her quickly. "Howard said he's pretty banged up, though. His right side, mostly his chest and hip, caught most of the brunt of the impact. Nothing's broken or bleeding internally, but he hit his head on something when he rolled down a gully for about forty yards. He's got a nasty concussion and an even worse disposition. Seems he threw up for hours and they kept him overnight for observation, even though his CAT scan came back clear."

Grace pressed shaking fingers to her temple. "Thank God. About the tests being good, I mean." Why was this hitting her so hard, as though she'd been socked in the gut? She knew the man only casually, and she found her strong reaction baffling. "Is he still in the hospital?"

"Not for much longer. He's at Sterling, but they're releasing him today—hang on a sec." Kat muffled the receiver, responding to something her husband interjected. After a few seconds, she came back on the line. "Howard says they won't release him unless he's got someone to watch over him for a couple of days. The problem is, he refuses to let anyone babysit him, to rephrase his protests mildly."

"Stubborn idiot," she muttered.

"Tell me about it. Howard offered to bring him here, let him stay in our guest room, but that went over like a turd in a punch bowl."

"Gross, Katherine Frances."

"Well, I'm just saying!"

Grace blew out a breath, too out of sorts to rise to her sister's bait. "Is he in a regular room?"

Kat spoke to Howard again. "Yes, they admitted him. He's in room 609."

"All right." Damn, she had to call her office.

"Are you going to see him?"

"What do you think?"

"No clue. You're the one who's been avoiding him like he's a fatal disease."

"What? And who's been encouraging me to stay on the other side of the county from him?" Another thought occurred to her, and she grimaced. "So much for keeping this thing with Julian—whatever it is—from your hubby. I'd hoped to lie low a while longer before you spilled."

"I didn't say a word—it was Howard's idea to call to let you know what happened."

Grace digested this. "Why the change of heart?"

"I haven't had a chance to ask him yet. So, you going?"

"You know I am, you little witch," she snapped, without any real heat.

"I know you too well." The smug satisfaction was evident in her sister's voice. "You always think everything to death before you act. So this once, don't."

"You must've read my mind," she said, smiling. "I was having the same thought earlier. You know, while I was thinking it to death."

"Ugh! You're impossible. Call me later and give me the scoop."

"I will. Bye, sweet pea."

After calling her secretary with a directive to cancel her morning appointment, Grace was on her way. The twenty-minute drive to Sugarland ended up being forty with the morning traffic, and she was ready to chew nails when she finally arrived and pounced on a parking spot. She hurried inside, took the elevator to the sixth floor, and rushed to Julian's room.

To find it empty.

She stood blinking at the mussed, empty bed, wondering where on earth he could've gone. A quick check of the bathroom revealed it to be unoccupied, as well. Lord, what if something awful had happened?

Worried, she marched back to the nurses' station she'd passed on the way in, and cleared her throat to gain the attention of a woman behind the counter. "Excuse me."

"Oh, I'm sorry, I didn't see you there." The nurse sent her a pleasant smile. "How may I help you?"

"The man in room 609, Julian Salvatore—is he all right? Has something happened?" What if his injuries were worse than they'd believed? The idea caused her to go weak in the knees.

The nurse's serene expression vanished and she pursed her lips to the size of a raisin. "Mr. Salvatore decided our services were no longer required."

"What?"

"In short, he left. Without the doctor's okay, I might add."

Grace sagged against the counter, the wind taken out of her sails. "Unbelievable. Stupid, stubborn man."

"Most are, dear. I assume you're a friend of his?"

"I . . . yes," she said, suddenly hoping it was true.

"Then maybe you can talk some sense into the man, or make certain he rests, at the very least."

She nodded, resolve stiffening her spine. "I will."

Thanking the nurse, she left. Outside, she used her cell phone to call her sister back, but Howard answered instead.

"Hey, Gracie! Kat's gone to work. Did you already see Jules?"

"I got here to find out he went AWOL. Can you believe that?"

"No freakin' way." A sound of disbelief drifted from his end. "Damn, the guy goes miles out of his way to create more trouble for himself than anybody I've ever known."

"And here I am chasing his tail." She colored at how that sounded and pushed on. "Anyway, I wondered if you had his address handy. I'd rather drop by than give him the chance to hang up on me."

"I doubt he'd do that to you, but sure. Hang on and I'll peek in our address book." After a few seconds of rustling, he spoke again. "Got it. Ready?"

She slid into her car and dug in the glove box for a scrap

of paper and a pen. "Okay." She scribbled furiously, then repeated the information back to him.

"Yep, that's it. I'll be home, so call if you need me to come over and beat him to a pulp," he joked. "Won't take much effort, considering."

"I happen to know some wicked self-defense moves, but thanks for the offer. Smooches," she sang by way of good-bye.

Her brother-in-law chuckled as they disconnected. And drat, she'd forgotten to ask him why he was no longer grousing about her getting closer to Julian. An intriguing puzzle, since Howard was as steady as a mountain and ten times as immovable when he set his mind for or against something, or someone.

In short order, Grace turned into Julian's complex and located the correct building with little difficulty. The buildings were set back in the trees, older and not as fancy as her own, but the landscaping was very well sculpted, trimmed, and neat. Parking a couple of spots down from his lower-level unit, she hoped she wasn't taking up anyone's assigned space. Maybe she should move.

"Quit stalling," she muttered to herself, grabbing her purse. What was the worst he could do? Shut the door in her face? Wasn't as if it hadn't happened before, although it had been with clients and witnesses, never with friends or lovers.

What am I doing here? He wasn't really a friend and wasn't likely to ever be more. They had nothing at all in common.

Save for one lovely kiss on a beautiful fall night, months ago.

Even so, she found herself knocking on his door, fidgeting with her purse strap, breathless with anticipation like a silly fifteen-year-old girl. The seconds crawled, became a minute and more, as she bounced between concern and the urge to flee. Glancing at the cars parked in the closest spots, she realized she didn't know what he drove. Had he made it home yet? What if he was inside, sick or unconscious because he'd left the hospital too soon—

Then the lock scraped and the door opened to reveal Julian standing on the threshold, gaping at her, scratched, bruised, rumpled.

And half-naked.

The man was just over six glorious feet of taut, tanned skin stretched over cords of lean muscle. Her gaze slid down his strong throat to the beautiful gold cross resting on his smooth chest, to the dark, pebbled male nipples, to the impressive ridges of his abdomen, south to the drawstring cotton sleep pants hanging way low—holy shit, no underwear—on slim hips that she'd bet her life savings could make a woman scream when in full Elvis rotation.

"You want to talk to me, my face is up here, *querida*," he said in amusement, his accented voice smooth as hot butter. "Unless it's not conversation you have in mind?"

Good God! Her cheeks heated and she forced herself to meet his eyes squarely. And oh, what gorgeous eyes they were, so dark brown they appeared almost black, vibrant, dancing with mischief. As though he knew a delicious secret and couldn't wait to share, perhaps over a glass of wine. Gathering her wits, she reached for the cool sophistication she wore like a shield. Too bad she croaked like a frog with emphysema.

"I just came by to make sure you're all right. I hope you don't mind my dropping in on you like this."

He lifted an eloquent brow and dipped his head a bit, causing a fall of raven hair to tumble into those mesmerizing eyes. "This isn't exactly in the neighborhood for you, Grace.

Forgive my rudeness, but I'm surprised to see you here. What do you care what happens to me?"

Flummoxed, she stared into his striking face. What *did* she care? Too much, she knew. After all these months of pursuit, his white flag of surrender was an icy slap of reality. No man would make a fool of himself forever, and she wanted this one in her life. "May I come in?"

He shrugged, stepping back and holding the door wide. "Sure."

She walked inside, casting a furtive glance at his bruises. His entire right side—chest, arm, ribs, and hip—was a deep shade of purplish black and looked horribly painful. He led her inside and she noted his slow, halting shuffle. His back was spotted with bruises, as well, though not as widespread. Only his face sported some raw scrapes on his chin and cheekbone, and she guessed his heavy clothing had protected his skin from further damage.

In the living room, he lowered himself to a chocolate brown leather sofa with a miserable groan and propped his bare feet on the glass coffee table. "Have a seat, please," he said, waving a hand. "Tell me why you're really here. I mean, if Six-Pack told you about my accident, he also told you that I'm fine, so you had no need to come here."

"You're *not* fine," she pressed, avoiding his perceptive question. "You left the hospital with a severe concussion, you idiot!"

He gave her a tired smile, flashing a set of straight white teeth against his bronzed face, and the effect was devastating to her senses. "I can mope here as well as there, and in greater comfort. What's the point?"

"You could've hurt yourself worse! You could have brain damage, swelling or something." She perched on the other end of the sofa and set her purse on the coffee table, scowling at him. "What if you'd come home and passed out? Had a seizure?"

"I'm a paramedic," he reminded her gently. "After the CAT scan, I knew I was okay. Plus, I know the symptoms if I start to feel worse."

"But what if you're so sick you can't call for help?"

"What do you want me to say? I left, I'm not going back, and I'm not sorry." Julian scrutinized her for a long moment, dark eyes drinking her in. "I hate being physically confined, okay?"

Physically confined. The way he'd said it, low and hollow, as though death were preferable, made her pause. "Are you claustrophobic?"

"Not on the job, crawling through tight spaces and stuff, but yeah. You could say that."

"Sounds more like a fear of being helpless than claustrophobia. What would *you* say?"

He flinched, a shadow passing over his expression, there and gone in an instant. "That I'm dying of curiosity you've yet to satisfy."

Confounding, aggravating man. "Is it such a big mystery why I'm here, given how you've been on my heels like a bloodhound?"

"I haven't called you in weeks." He looked far too smug for comfort. "Yet here you are, just as I'd decided to throw in the towel. Why is that? I wonder."

Great. Now he was going to have fun nettling her. "I'm here because I want to be, and I don't have a better psychoanalysis for you than that." She sighed. "This isn't really the way I'd planned to accept your dinner invitation. If it's still open."

His sensual lips curved into a small smile, but he didn't

precisely leap for joy. He appeared guarded. Of course, he wasn't going to make this easy, and she didn't blame him.

"Did your well of rich lawyers run dry? Is that why you're here, for easy pickings?"

Don't get angry. What's he supposed to think? "I don't date other attorneys. In fact, I don't date much at all. No time."

"But you'll make time for me." His tone, rife with self-deprecating humor, betrayed his doubt.

"I'm not proposing marriage, just accepting an invite to dinner as friends."

"You want to be friends." He studied her from under a thick fringe of lashes, expression warm.

"I'd like that very much," she said, scooting next to him to lay a hand on his left thigh. Lord, his muscles were so tight under her palm, his body heat scorching her through the thin material and radiating up her arm. "I think we could be good friends. I know I almost lost the opportunity to find out, because of my indecision. But I'd like to try. What do you say? Is it worth a shot?"

She knew the answer the exact moment the warmth in his dark eyes became a low-burning fire. His breath seemed to catch as he looked down at her hand, so slender against the bulk of his leg, and covered it with his own. He brushed his thumb lightly over the delicate skin of the back of her hand, his calluses rough and, to her surprise, more than pleasant. A working man's hands, humming with sure, solid strength. But his voice, when he spoke, was quiet and vulnerable.

"Do you weigh every single decision in that brilliant lawyer's brain as if the fate of the universe rests on it? Or am I really so hard to like?"

Guilt speared her breast at the sudden, startling notion that she'd misjudged this man from the beginning, based on assumption and bias. Now she strongly suspected that the grinning, careless devil he presented to those around him was nothing more than a bold cover for an aching, lonely soul.

Which completely melted her inside.

And made him even more dangerous than before.

"Guilty as charged on the first question. 'Hunting a hair in the soup' is an ingrained trait my sister is constantly trying to nag out of me. Oh, it's great in the courtroom, but hell on personal relationships." Turning her hand, she curled her fingers around his. "As to the second . . . no. You're far too easy to like, Julian, and I guess it scares me a little."

He gazed at their linked hands. "You, afraid of anything? I find that difficult to swallow."

"You know what you said about physical confinement? Well, I suppose you could say the same for me, emotionally. I'm independent to a fault, and the idea of tying myself to another person, depending on him for love and security, a sense of well-being? Frightening."

He cocked his head, looking genuinely interested. "Where does that come from?"

She gave him a rueful smile. "I have no clue. I had a normal upbringing, no skeletons, nothing. It's just me, I guess."

He brought her fingers to his lips, brushed a kiss across them. "I say the only way to conquer a fear is to face it."

"Like you did by leaving tread marks on the way out of the hospital?" God, his mouth. Pure magic.

"Touché," he said, laughing. The deep, masculine rumble sent shivers down her spine. "Maybe we both need more practice in expanding our comfort zones."

Before she could form a reply, Julian pressed her palm to his chest, over his heart. Then he cupped her cheek and urged her close, hesitating a fraction of an instant before settling his mouth over hers.

Oh. Oh, God. Magic?

No, much more. Overwhelming, wicked sensuality.

His tongue swept between her lips to tangle with her own. Explored her moist heat in a slow, gentle seduction. His heartbeat thrummed under her palm, his skin so soft, so hot. He smelled like earth, rain, and a hint of spicy cologne. More potently male than any man she'd ever known.

She melted against him and one arm went around her waist, cradling her close as he deepened his kiss. Not demanding, but giving. Opening all of himself to her, not forcing his attention, but simply enjoying this moment together.

An awakening.

Her entire body blossomed to life. Her nipples, the insistent throb between her thighs. So long since she'd been held, pleasured. And he was solid and good underneath her, his erection pressing against her hip through her skirt. Hard and ready, yet taking his cues from her. Not rushing.

Greedy, she wanted *more*. She wriggled against him, eliciting a moan. Encouraged, she raked one hand through the longish strands of his silky black hair, cupped the back of his head to draw him closer. Deeper.

Julian broke their kiss with a gasp, pulling back and screwing his eyes shut with a sharp curse in Spanish. Dazed, she blinked at him for a second before realizing what she'd done.

"Your head! I touched your wound, didn't I?" The gray cast to his tanned cheeks, the lines around his mouth as he panted in pain, were answer enough. "Oh, honey, I'm so sorry!"

"It—it's okay."

"And your poor bruises! You're hurting and I'm lying half on top of you." Carefully, she levered herself off him, reached out, and brushed his hair out of his eyes. "Show me where the injury is so I can check to make sure I didn't make it worse."

Without arguing, he gingerly touched a spot near the back of his head. "Here."

Leaning over him, she parted his hair, searching until she found a neat row of stitches, about an inch in length. "The cut's not bleeding," she said, relieved. "But that's some knot you have there. No wonder you were sick for hours."

He cracked an eye open, breathing a little easier now. "Ever had the flu?" She nodded. "With a knock like the one I took, multiply the nausea and disorientation by ten. For a while, I figured dying would be kinder."

She shuddered. "Don't even joke about that."

"I wasn't."

She moved over to give him some room, and he sat up, gritting his teeth. Part of her was disappointed she'd ruined their interlude, but the return of common sense was for the best. They were going to be *friends*. Anything more was a complication neither of them needed.

Even if they sparked like dry kindling and a torch.

Even if desire for completion with him left her breathless and shaky.

Julian seemed to sense her withdrawal, and didn't press. Nor did he get angry or sullen. He just smiled and flicked a hand at his state of undress—and unsatisfied arousal. "I'd put on some jeans or something to, um, make you more comfortable, but to be honest, moving around to get dressed hurts too much."

She shook her head, amazed. Who knew this man was such a gentleman? "I won't be scarred for life at the sight of a little skin." Well, a lot of yummy skin. "Besides, this is your home and I barged in. Are you sure you're all right?"

"I will be, don't worry. It's not like I haven't had a concussion before."

"Don't remind me." Several months ago, Julian had been caught in the explosion that had nearly killed Howard. Two good men almost lost at the hands of a maniac. Deftly, she steered the topic from that subject. "How'd you get home from the hospital, anyway?"

"Called a cab. My car is at the station, so Tommy's stopping by to give me a ride when I return to work next Wednesday."

"Isn't six days after you were struck awfully soon to go back?" She didn't like to think of his pushing himself too hard, too fast.

"Naw, I heal fast. I might still be a little sore, but nothing I can't handle."

What a bunch of macho baloney. Thinking of her dad, she decided stubbornness must be burned into a man's DNA. She started to tell him so. Then another thought occurred to her. "Did the police catch the driver who hit you?"

Julian sighed. "Nope. Hit-and-run, didn't even slow down. Zack said the truck's rear license plate was missing, too, so we don't have much to go on."

The back of Grace's neck prickled. "That means either the driver or someone else removed the plates."

"So?"

"Doesn't that bother you? It makes your accident sound like not such an accident after all."

He dimpled a grin at her. "Oh, come on. Who'd want to hurt me on purpose?" His grin faded along with his rhetorical question, and he looked away, eyes widening.

Alarmed, she laid a hand on his arm. "What is it?"

"What? Nothing, *bella*," he said, giving her his full attention once more. "I'm just wiped out."

"Oh. Well, I should go—"

"Please don't. Stay for a while and—" He broke off with a soft laugh, the sound wistful. "Listen to me. You probably have a million things to do that don't include keeping me company."

She did. But suddenly, there was nothing she'd like more. "Are you hungry at all? Because I can scramble a mean egg, if your stomach is up to it."

The surprise—and happiness—on his sexy face was well worth the impulsive decision. The first she'd made in a really long time.

"I could eat something," he admitted.

"Good. You sit right there and rest, and I'll take care of everything."

The slow, lopsided grin sent a jolt to her toes. "I have no doubt of that whatsoever."

Lord, she was in big trouble.

6

Grace was here. In his kitchen.

In his life.

Last evening, when he'd tumbled to the bottom of the ravine, he hadn't been sure he'd have a life to resume. And now the woman of his dreams was skipping work to take care of him. Somehow, someway, he must've done something to please the saints. From his spot on the sofa, he fingered the cross around his neck and listened to Grace's melodic voice as she hummed, fishing eggs out of the fridge.

Unreal. No one had cared for him since he'd left home, years ago. A houseful of sisters fussing over him and Tonio couldn't compare with the attention of a gorgeous woman like Grace, here on her own because she'd chosen to be, not out of obligation.

Friends. Okay, he had to admit he didn't like the distance she wanted to keep between them. But companionship was a place to start and he could work with it. He should be grateful for what she offered. Right?

Tell that to his raging libido. God, just those few moments when her guard had come down and she'd kissed him as though he were the only man on earth, pressed into him, her body soft and pliant . . .

But she'd pulled back afterward, leaving him hard and aching for more.

Who was he kidding? He must be ten kinds of a masochist to long for what he could never have. He'd known he wasn't a keeper the day he'd walked out of Mama's house for good. After all the heartbreak he'd put his family through, all the secrets and lies, as much as they loved him, they'd been relieved to see him go. How could he blame them?

Let us never speak of it again.

No, Mama.

Vaya con Dios, hijo.

"Toast?" Grace called.

The sweet sound of her voice chased away the past, and he could swear the room seemed brighter. The aroma of scrambled eggs teased his nose and made his stomach rumble, and he thought he might be able to keep them down. Toast would help. "Please."

"Where do you keep your plates?"

"The cabinet to the left of the sink. Silverware is in the drawer to the right of the dishwasher."

He heard her push the lever down on the toaster and rummage for a plate and fork. Next, she scraped the eggs out of the skillet, set it in the sink with a clatter, then got something else out of the fridge.

"Can you make it to the table, or do you want to eat on the couch, where you're more comfortable?"

I'd rather feast on you. "I'll go sit at the table," he said with more confidence than sense. Whatever he'd hoped to gain by a manly display to prove he was feeling great had backfired. As he pushed to his feet, his abused body screamed in protest and his head swam. He reached for something to steady himself and found Grace already at his side.

"Good grief, why do men have to be so stubborn?" Putting an arm around his waist, she helped him over to the small dining table while he tried not to lean on her too much.

"I'm not stubborn. I'm a pussycat." He lowered himself into his chair with a pained groan, figuring it best not to add that all she'd have to do was stroke him the right way and he'd purr.

"Ha! More like a saber-toothed tiger." Before he could reply, she disappeared into the kitchen again. The toast popped up and after a few moments, she returned with his plate, a fork, and a glass of orange juice. She set the items in front of him and took a seat across the table.

"Thanks. This looks good. Hey, aren't you fixing anything for yourself?" Frowning, he eyed her empty spot.

She shook her head, some of the white blond tendrils escaping the clip at her nape to hang in wisps at her cheeks. "No, I'm not hungry. I'm not in the habit of eating a big breakfast because I'm usually in too big of a hurry in the mornings to bother."

"You wouldn't skip meals if you worked with us," he said, spearing some scrambled egg. "We burn so much energy, we eat three squares a day with plenty of carbs. Can't perform a rescue if we're running on fumes."

He dug into his food, thinking that for a simple meal he'd never tasted anything finer. Probably because Grace had cooked it for him. Looking at her, he admired the delicate structure of her face, the arch of her pale brows over stunning violet eyes. Full, pink lips he knew firsthand were made for pleasure, the slender column of her pale throat. Naturally, his gaze dipped a bit farther south to the vee of her blouse, which no doubt hid small breasts that would fit just right in his palms.

He forced his attention back to her face and found her expression curious. She leaned forward on her elbows, voice animated.

"What sorts of rescues have you done?"

He smiled, unable to help the surge of pride it gave him that Grace was interested in what he did for a living. "It might be easier to list what we haven't done. There's the usual— traffic accidents, medical emergencies in the home. Those calls make up roughly ninety-seven percent of what we work, and most of the medical emergencies involve the elderly. Calls to fires are rare, contrary to what most folks believe."

Dammit! He hadn't meant to remind her of the horrors the lieutenant and her sister had faced last fall. *Cristo*, he should cut out his tongue.

But she merely nodded, appearing unaffected by the blunder, and encouraged him to continue. "What's the hardest rescue you've ever performed?"

"Physically?" He gave it some thought. "I'd have to say the father who tried to cross a flooded road in his truck with his two children inside. The truck stalled and got caught in the rushing current. We had to run a line from one side of the road to the other, secure both ends, and use it to guide our boat to their vehicle and back to safety. We had to make two trips because the boat wouldn't hold them all, so we got the kids first."

Grace's eyes rounded. "I've seen rescues like that on TV, and they always look impossible."

Taking a bite of toast, he barked a laugh. "Ever tried to put a screeching kid into a rubber boat in the middle of raging floodwaters during a storm? Try forcing a scalded cat into a burlap sack, one-handed, and you'll have an idea how much fun it is."

"It's amazing you got them all to safety!"

"No kidding. They were terrified to leave their dad. As it was, we barely managed to get him into the boat before his truck rolled and was swept away."

Remembering how the vehicle lurched and disappeared just as they hauled the man into their craft still gave him chills.

"Well, my job isn't nearly so dangerous or exciting," she said, giving him a grin. "That might change when I make district attorney."

"Gonna lock up the bad guys and throw away the key? Good for you."

"It's a goal, anyway. I don't see myself working under my father for the next twenty or thirty years only to be stuck running the firm." She sighed, her tone wistful. "It would kill him to hear me say that, when he's worked long and hard to build up a legacy to leave to his family."

"Oh, you'd be surprised. Parents are more resilient than we give them credit for, bouncing back from disappointment." He should know.

"Speaking of parents, are yours still in San Antonio?"

He tensed at the normal, innocent question, but tried not to let his discomfort show. "My mother is. Everyone but me. My four older sisters and a younger brother."

"Kat and I used to spend a week there every summer, visiting our aunt, but it was just us and her. No cousins. Must be nice to have a large, close family." His noncommittal shrug did nothing to dissuade her interest in his background. "If it's not too personal, I'd wondered. . . . You speak Spanish, but your last name is Italian."

He cocked his head, studying her. "Not many people notice, or if they do, they don't bother to ask. My father was from Italy, and my mother's people are from Mexico City. They met in the States after my dad moved to Texas, and he adapted to her culture. All of us were raised in the Hispanic community."

Grace looked absolutely fascinated. "Which one do you resemble most, your mother or father?"

"My father, but I only know that from his pictures and what my sisters tell me. He died when I was young and my brother was a baby, killed in a drive-by shooting as he left a gas station," he said, relating the story by rote. Hard to grieve for a man in a photograph, though he'd felt the loss acutely as a teenager who desperately needed a father's strong shoulders.

"Oh, Julian," she breathed. "I'm sorry. That must've been horrible for your family."

He poked at the remnants of his breakfast, appetite deserting him. "I don't think Mama ever got over his death. She never remarried, and God knows she could've used a husband's love and support through the years."

Especially after what I did.

Dios, he was tired. Laying his fork on his plate, he stood, a tortured curse escaping before he could stop it. Tidal waves of pain washed over him, but at least he didn't feel nauseated. Bad enough being incapacitated in front of her— even if his mishap did bring her to his door—but to get sick? Not happening.

Immediately, Grace was at his side. "Okay, let's do this once more. Get to the couch, stretch out, and rest, you hear?"

"Yes, *bella*." Her soft laugh, the welcome TLC, thawed places that hadn't felt warmth in a long, long time. Chipped the ice from a particular cold place in his chest that had been barren for as long as he could recall.

"What does that mean? *Bay-yah?*"

"Beautiful, because that's what you are." As he limped to the sofa, he glanced at her rosy cheeks in satisfaction.

"Oh. Well, I'm not, but that's sweet of you to say. Here you go."

"It's the truth," he said, grimacing as he eased himself down. After taking a few deep breaths, letting the pain subside, he pinned her with his gaze, completely serious. "I'd never lie to a woman about her beauty, inside and out."

"But you'd lie about other things? Just teasing," she said, cutting off the denial that sprang to his lips. "You're blind, is all. I'm too tall, too skinny, and I have no chest."

"You're perfect to me, Grace."

For a long moment, she fell silent, studying him with an intensity that must compel her clients to blurt full confessions in under a minute. "Close your eyes while I clean up the kitchen," she said quietly.

Then she left him there, wondering what had just transpired between them. And feeling foolish as hell.

Chingado! What's the matter with you? Haven't you learned by now to keep your trap shut?

Be glad she's here, dumbass, and accept what she's offering. Don't push, and for Christ's sake, don't drive her away.

A real challenge for him. Either he acted like he didn't care or he pushed too hard, as Zack had so tactfully pointed out. Exhausted, he lay down on his left side, the only position that didn't hurt too much, and closed his eyes. Right away, he began to drift, last night catching up with him despite his resolve to stay awake and keep Grace company.

Just a few minutes . . .

Gradually, the muted sounds of canned laughter seeped into his brain. Weird, the quiet noise tearing at the cobwebs in his head, prodding him to consciousness when he wanted to stay buried. But he surfaced anyway, finally recognizing a verbal tennis match coming from the television, courtesy of Lucy and Ricky.

Cracking an eye open, he blinked, trying to focus his vision. As it cleared, he noted the sun filtering through the curtains near the TV had dimmed, the angle lengthened, and shadows were encroaching. Late afternoon? And what was that smell?

Something savory cooking. That got him motivated to move when nothing else could, except the thought of seeing Grace. He couldn't believe she was still there.

Sitting up with a groan, he was amazed it was possible to feel more stiff and sore than he'd been before. His body felt like he'd been beaten half to death by the Titans' defensive line. And shit on for good measure.

"Grace?" he croaked.

Apparently he sounded pathetic enough to bring her in a hurry, a worried frown furrowing her brow. "Hey, there. I was afraid I was going to have to light a stick of dynamite underneath you." Perching next to him on the sofa, she brushed her fingers over his forehead. "How do you feel?"

"My head doesn't feel too bad, but the rest of me? I'm ready to trade in for a new model."

Her lips curved up, eyes twinkling. "Sorry, but you're stuck with this one until it heals."

"I can't believe you stayed." Crap, he hadn't meant to blurt it like that.

"You thought I'd just leave after you pretty much passed out?"

"Well, no, I just . . ."

"You went down hard," she said, patting his knee. "I'll leave when I'm sure you're okay, or when you get sick of my company and ask me to go."

He snorted. "Hope you brought a toothbrush." God, he loved her smile.

"You never give up, do you?"

"That's the quickest, surest way to lose."

"Then it seems we have something in common after all." She gave his knee a squeeze before letting him go. "Hungry?"

"Starving." *For you to keep touching me, and never stop.*

Standing, she offered him a hand. "Good! Let's eat."

He let her help him up, and as he followed her to the table, he noticed how the prim skirt hugged her round little butt. The flow of white blond silk down her back, the clip gone. He cleared his throat, willing down one very uninjured part of himself. "After three? You shouldn't have let me sleep so long."

"Why? Got a hot date?" She gave him an odd look before ducking into the kitchen.

"Nope. The only date I want is right here, even if I had to get smacked like a cue ball to get your attention." Pulling out a chair, he sat gingerly.

"Oh, you've had my attention," she said, carrying in a dish and placing it on a hot pad in the center of the table. "Though apparently I'm not the only one you have on a string."

"What do you mean?"

"A very enthusiastic lady friend called for you earlier. Someone named Carmelita." She made a couple of trips, setting a bowl of peas and two glasses of iced tea in front of them, as Julian struggled with how to respond.

Shit, shit. The thought of Grace hearing something she shouldn't, and getting the wrong impression about his relationship with his old friend, made his stomach sink.

"What did she say?"

"I didn't speak to her. She left a message for 'Jules, baby' to call her back, and hung up."

Damn. He gave Grace a weak smile. "Okay, thanks. I'll call her later. She's just a friend—"

"I wasn't asking. Peas, *Jules*, *baby*?" She grabbed the serving spoon, giving him a droll stare and silently daring him to refuse.

"You bet. I love peas." He hated them. Bought them only in a moment of madness because they were on sale. Of course, he took a healthy portion, along with a bacon-wrapped chicken breast smothered in some sort of white cream sauce. "This looks really good, Grace. Thank you."

"No sweat," she said, waving a hand, then dishing up some for herself. "You need some real food in your stomach, and thankfully for you, I'm a much better cook than my sister."

Dutifully, he cut off a piece of chicken and took a bite—and groaned in appreciation. "This is awesome. You can come over and work your magic on my frozen meat any time you want." Grinning, he winked at her, hoping she didn't take offense.

She smiled back. "Don't think this counts as our first dinner date, buddy. I fully expect to be wined, dined, and otherwise spoiled until your wallet screams for mercy."

He laughed. The first real, honest laugh he could remember enjoying in ages. It felt foreign. And good. "I think I can handle that. Should we pin down the day before you change your mind? Next Friday, one week from today?" He hated to wait so long, but he wanted to plan a special evening, to be fully functional again and show her a good time. Nothing was going to spoil this, if he had any say.

"Next Friday, then. Sounds good."

"Great! I'll pick you up around seven and we'll go from

there." After Sean's intervention, almost guaranteed to be a bad scene, he'd be more than ready to spend an evening relaxing with Grace.

They ate in comfortable silence for a few minutes, Julian basking in the warm glow of his shift of fortune. If he was a superstitious man, he'd think the reversal almost scary. Which was why her next question threw him, though he probably should've anticipated it.

"Tell me something. . . . Why did you go off on me about Derek Vines that day?"

Oh, God. Not now. Couldn't the man just fall off the face of the earth? "Grace—"

"I want to know. Your reaction to seeing him was disconcerting, to say the least. I haven't been able to get it out of my mind and I haven't turned up any damning information on the man. Frankly, it's made me uneasy in my dealings with him. Never a good way to feel around a client."

A giant, unseen fist grabbed his gut and twisted, and a chill blasted through his body. "Have you asked *him* what my problem is?"

"No. With my clients, I only discuss what pertains to their case. I try to avoid getting into personal issues unless they have a direct effect on my ability to provide a fair defense." She took a sip of her tea and waited.

Sitting back, he laid his hands in his lap to hide their shaking. "I don't know what more you want me to say," he managed. "My opinion of Vines wasn't welcome the first time around, so I can't imagine what's changed."

"I care about you, that's what," she said quietly. "And after I got over being angry with you for trying to interfere, I realized you must have good reason. But it's hard for me to understand where you're coming from when you won't explain."

She's reaching out, he realized. *She's worried about me more than about having to defend him.* But he couldn't tell her, or anyone, the truth. No, that secret would die with him.

And with Derek Vines.

What if Grace was right, and his being hit wasn't an accident?

"Get rid of him, Grace," he said hoarsely. "Pass him to another attorney, quit altogether, or shove him off the nearest cliff. Wash him out of your hair like the parasite he is, and you'll be safer, trust me."

"That's harsh," she observed. There was no accusation in her tone, only concern.

"I wouldn't piss on the man if he were on fire, and that's the truth."

She stared at him a long moment, as though weighing whether to keep prying until he cracked. For whatever miraculous reason, the normally tenacious woman let it go— for now.

"I'll take what you said seriously, and as we get to know one another, I hope you'll feel more comfortable leveling with me."

To that, he had no answer. "Do me a favor and don't mention my name to him, okay?"

"I haven't, and I wouldn't." She leaned forward, a half smile on her lips. "All right, I probably shouldn't even say this much, but I'll toss you a line—Vines won't be my problem much longer. Whatever he's done, past or present, doesn't matter, because my dealings with him are almost concluded."

"I hope that's true, because the man is a cancer and I hate the idea of his being near you," he said, jaw clenching. He wanted badly to ask her what Vines was accused of, not to mention how he'd managed to maneuver his sorry ass out of trouble yet again, but suspected she couldn't or wouldn't be any more forthcoming than he'd been.

She nodded. "Count on it. No worries, okay?"

She looked so beautiful sitting there, gazing at him as though she really did care and, if he wasn't mistaken, with a certain amount of heat.

"No worries, *querida.*"

And maybe it was true. Maybe a man could outrun his past, find love and happiness, and live the rest of his life in peace.

Surely a man wouldn't be doomed to lose everything twice in one lifetime.

Julian strolled down the sidewalk toward the Diamond Cadillac with a slight limp, damned glad to be out of the condo. Even though he'd gone back to work the previous day, the calls had been light and there hadn't been much to do.

He didn't do convalescence well, hated being forced to lounge around for days, the only perk being Grace's three visits; she'd returned Saturday and Sunday to check on him, bring him something to eat, and keep him company for a few hours. But since Monday, she'd been busy at work, and he'd been bored out of his mind.

He missed her. He'd gotten spoiled by her laughter, her sunny smiles, the way she seemed to fill all the empty spaces with joy. Not the bubbly, bouncy, over-the-top kind of joy, but the quiet sort. Like her name, she was as calm and steady as the Cumberland River on a lazy Sunday. Strong, self-assured.

Unattainable.

She'd kept him at arm's length, driving him mad with the need to taste her lips again, to press his body to hers. To roll her underneath him as he longed to do, spread her legs, and lose control—

His cell phone chirped and he snatched it from his shirt pocket, half-expecting it to be Carmelita searching for yet another excuse to chew him out—as if raking him over the coals for not calling to tell her about his mishap wasn't enough. Yeah, she was pissed that he'd waited two days to return her call from Friday and let her know.

A glance at the caller ID, however, sent his heart into overdrive. Not Carmelita. Flipping the phone open without breaking stride, he didn't bother to try to hide his pleasure.

"Hello, *bella*."

"Hey, you! I called your place to see about driving over and got no answer. I suppose you're feeling better if you're out and about, but I hope you're not overdoing it."

Regret lanced through him that he'd missed Grace's call. He hadn't expected her to even consider making the drive to his condo, especially when they'd see each other tomorrow night. "Well, if I can work, I can certainly go for a walk. I'm much better and I was going stir-crazy at home." An idea occurred to him, and he brightened. "What if I come over to your place instead? I won't overstay my welcome, since you have to work tomorrow, but we could, you know, hang out for a while."

"Um, sure," she said, sounding a little hesitant. Then her voice warmed. "I'd like that. Ready for directions?"

"I'm not in my car right now, and I don't have a pen or paper. I've got an errand to run, but as soon as I'm done, I'll call you back. Shouldn't take me more than half an hour. Work for you?"

"Sounds good. Talk to you soon."

"Absolutely." He snapped the phone shut. "Yes!"

A couple passed him on the sidewalk, giving him a funny

look, but he couldn't care less. Grace's visits while he'd been recovering had been nice, but this had an altogether different vibe. *She wants to see me. As a man, not because she feels sorry for me.*

Any plans he might've had to linger at the bar and drown his loneliness took a flying leap. He did have a specific reason for going back there, and now he'd simply satisfy this inner voice nagging at him, and get going.

Inside, he made his way to the bar with ease. The hour was prime for the after-work barflies, yet too early for the die-hard party crowd. He'd counted on a quieter atmosphere so he could speak with the bartender without shouting.

When he sidled up to the bar and took a stool, however, the bartender on duty wasn't the one he sought. The guy ambled over and slapped a napkin on the wood in front of him.

"What's your poison, my man?"

"Jack and cola," he said, glad he hadn't needed one of his powerful painkillers today.

"Long day?" the big man inquired jovially, flipping a highball glass in his hand and reaching for the bottle.

"Long fucking week." And how.

"Heard that."

"Say, I was wondering if Cody's here. I'd really like to talk to him."

The bartender gave him a sharp look from under bushy brows, never slowing in his task. He topped off the Jack with cola, stuck a wedge of lime on the lip and a thin straw inside, then slid the glass toward Julian. "What would you be needin' to speak to Cody for?"

He'd rehearsed this, just in case, and decided a portion of the truth was the best policy. "I'd like to talk to him about something strange that happened in here about three weeks ago."

The man stilled, braced one burly forearm on the bar, and leaned over, his voice for Julian's ears. "Yeah? You and every other frickin' guy who's come in here."

"What . . . what do you mean?"

"I mean you ain't the only one who's been real interested in talking to Cody in the last few weeks."

Julian paused, unsure what to make of that information and the bartender's sudden tense body language. "Oh. Well, I just want to speak with him about something we saw. I'm sure he'll remember, so if you could maybe pass him a message—"

"Sorry, man. He don't have nothin' to say to anybody."

"But—"

"Listen up good," he said in a low voice, glancing around them to be certain no one heard. "Cody's dead."

7

Grace surveyed her place with a critical eye. She'd tidied a few magazines on the coffee table, thrown out the empty cartons from her frozen dinner, and put on a pot of coffee. She'd also run the vacuum and swiped the woolly duster thing over the furniture, though the touch-ups really weren't needed—the apartment was a moderate size and easy to keep clean.

Last, she ducked into the bathroom to check her appearance. Not that she was eager to look fabulous for Julian or anything. She wasn't. There was nothing exciting about worn, faded jeans and a soft cotton blouse, hair loose and in need of taming. Automatically, she reached for her brush, and tried to quell her puzzling case of nerves.

She hadn't felt this unsettled when she'd dropped by to visit Julian this past weekend. She'd looked forward to seeing him, sure. Despite his being laid up with his injuries, they'd had a good time watching movies, eating pizza, talking. Snuggling on his couch, sharing a few stolen kisses. To her delight, she'd found him to be funny and genuine. Julian was a wonderful companion and she hadn't been nearly this frazzled. Why now?

Setting aside the brush, she stared at herself in the mirror, thinking of his phone call. How her stomach had flipped when he suggested coming here. For a couple of seconds, she'd considered putting him off with some sort of excuse, or simply telling him no. This place was her cave, her refuge. Allowing him inside seemed much more intimate than her visits with an injured friend. Like she was agreeing to something deeper between them, when she wasn't.

So why hadn't her refusal formed?

The soft knock at her door made her jump despite the fact that she'd been expecting it, and her hand went to her chest. Her heart knocked against her palm and she heaved a breath. This was just Julian. Her friend.

Her charming, roguish, very sexy *friend*.

Nothing more.

Which didn't account for her rubbery knees as she hurried through the living room, the little thrill zipping to every sensitive spot in her body as she put her hand on the knob, pretty sure who stood on the other side.

A quick squint through the peephole confirmed her visitor's identity, and she opened the door with a cheerful greeting. "Come on in! I see you didn't have any problems with the directions."

Julian moved inside and turned as she closed and locked the door behind them. "None at all." Stepping up to her, he took her hands and brushed her lips with a kiss. "This is a nice complex, a security gate and everything. I'm impressed."

"Huh? Oh, thanks." Her brain was still on the kiss—a sweet gesture of hello that could've been more if she'd taken his cue. Tingling all over, she studied him from head to toe. Good Lord, the man looked fantastic!

He wore a dark blue button-up shirt tucked into nice jeans that emphasized his narrow waist, cupped his sex nicely, and hugged legs that went on forever. Good enough to eat.

Abruptly aware of ogling him, she jerked her gaze to his

face and noted the lines of strain around his fine mouth, the haunted look in his dark eyes.

"Your hands are cold when it's over seventy degrees outside. You were in such good spirits when I phoned earlier and now you seem upset about something," she said quietly. "What's wrong?"

"Me? Upset? No, no, I'm great. Wow, is that coffee I smell?" A weak smile curved his lips as he sniffed the air, his attempt to make light of her concern falling flat.

"You are so transparent, I hope you don't play high-stakes poker. Sit down and get comfy while I get us a mug," she ordered, waving at the couch. "Then you're going to tell me what's going on."

He complied with a heavy sigh, offering no argument or witty comeback. For Julian, that was telling. And a little scary. She poured two mugs of coffee and called out to him. "How do you take yours?"

"Cream if you have any. No sugar."

"Got it." She poured cream in both, adding a liberal dose of sugar to hers, then carried them to the living room.

"Thanks," he said, taking his. "God knows I don't need more alcohol tonight."

She frowned as she sat next to him. "You didn't have too much before you drove, did you?"

"What? No, I just meant . . . never mind."

"Uh-uh. You're not getting off that easy," she said, tucking her legs up on the couch next to him. "Let's have it. What's happened since we spoke to make you look like you've lost your best friend?"

Settling back into the cushions, he ran a hand down his face. "I don't suppose you'd just let it go, would you?"

"Nope. Not when it would sit there between us all evening whether you tell me or not. So you might as well get it off your chest," she reasoned.

"Why do women always have to be right?"

"Because we usually are."

"Spoken like a true lawyer." He paused, apparently considering where to start. "Have you read in the paper or seen the story on the news about these young adults who've disappeared in the past few months?"

"I'm not sure—oh, wait. Yes, I have." She thought back. "I read something about a college student who vanished from a club downtown. I can't remember his name."

"Brett Charles. He went to Vanderbilt."

"That's the one. Someone saw him leaving the club with a man, and was probably the last one to see him alive. But what does that have to do with you?"

"I . . . I'm the unidentified witness," he said quietly.

Grace stared at Julian, the import of his revelation washing over her like a bucket of ice. "But . . . that means you're the only link to a serial kidnapper and possibly a murderer."

"Maybe." His shoulders slumped. "Yeah, probably."

"My God, Julian." Her anxiety ratcheted up several notches, along with a spark of anger. "So when I asked you whether your hit-and-run might not be an accident, you lied—"

"I didn't mean to mislead you. How could I lie when I didn't even know what to think myself?"

Okay, calm down. He's right. "Point taken. What's changed, then?"

"I wasn't the only witness, just the only one to talk to the police. But apparently, that didn't matter to the evil bastard who's behind this," he said, looking away, expression miserable.

She reached for his hand, squeezed it gently. "I don't understand."

"Someone besides me noticed Brett Charles leaving with the strange guy—Cody, the bartender who always waited on me whenever I came in. We talked about the two of them, about the weird vibe they gave off. The kid seemed out of it, but the older guy hadn't been drinking. Told Cody he was the designated driver. The two of them left shortly after that."

Grace shook her head in confusion. "Since he had the same concerns you did, how do you know Cody didn't go to the police, that he wasn't the witness the paper referred to, and not you?"

Julian gave a bitter laugh. "He didn't have much faith in cops, thought they were a bunch of dickheads, but he never told me why. Guess he wasn't so far off base."

"Julian—"

"Cody's dead. Oh, *Dios*." Bending over, he buried his face in his hands. "He's dead, Grace."

Dead. The only other man who'd spoken to a possible kidnapper was dead. And Julian had survived a close brush with death just one week ago. "When? How?"

He sat up, gazing at her with sorrow. "That's where I went after I talked to you. I dropped by the club to talk to Cody, see if the older man had been in there again. Another bartender told me Cody fell off a ladder and broke his neck while fixing the rain gutters on his house—the day before I was hit by the truck. There were no witnesses and the authorities ruled it an accident."

"Wait. When Brett Charles disappeared, didn't you tell the police about your conversation with Cody?"

"Yes, but with the way Cody felt about cops, he probably didn't make it easy for them to catch up with him for an interview. And I doubt they connected his so-called accident with a missing-persons case. Shit, it's possible the cops working the disappearances don't even know Cody's dead."

"But you're going to tell them," she guessed.

"Hell, yes. I'm going back to the police station tomorrow to talk to the detectives about all of this. It might not make a difference, but they need to know."

Seeing his tortured expression, Grace wondered how she ever could've typecast Julian as a man who didn't take life seriously. How could she have misjudged him so badly? "Then you're doing all you can. Give yourself a break, okay?"

He shook his head. "How can I? I went after them when they left the club and got part of the license plate of the guy's Mercedes. But I didn't chase them down. Not a day has gone by when I haven't asked myself, what if I had? What if I'd trusted my instincts and caught up to them, confronted the older man? If I had, that kid might still be alive and I—" His voice cracked and he looked away.

"Hey, look at me," she said softly, cupping his face in her hands. She waited until he reluctantly met her gaze before she continued. "You don't know he's not alive. And perhaps he left of his own free will and doesn't want to be found—have you thought of that? Either way, the police could still locate him, honey."

"I told myself that at first. But after Cody and I both have accidents? *Bella*, my gut tells me this is bad and I'm in the middle of it—"

Grace kissed him. Gently at first, because it was the only thing she could think of to take away his anguish. Then deeper, more demanding. Because she couldn't stop.

She had to taste him, savor him. He met her exploration, tangling his tongue with hers, stroking. The tension in his shoulders gradually dissolved and he buried a hand in her hair, taking charge.

The woman in her thrilled at the shift of power even as the steadfast lawyer quivered at giving it over to him. But, oh, had anything ever felt so wonderful as the slide of his palms down her back? Had any man ever smelled so masculine, so potent, his hard, muscular body fitting to hers perfectly?

Nimble fingers inched under the edge of her shirt, skimmed her side, eased upward. Searching. They caressed the swell of her breasts and she arched into his touch. "Julian . . ."

Reason fled when he plucked one nipple through the sheer fabric of her bra, sending mini bolts of pleasure to every nerve ending. She gasped as he rolled the peak between his thumb and forefinger, pinching, skirting the edge of pain, shredding her resistance.

He nibbled along the curve of her jaw and pushed up her shirt, treating the other nipple to the same attention. "Tell me what you want."

What she wanted? Her brain could form only one word.

"More," she breathed.

His throaty laugh sent tendrils of heat curling through her insides. "Your wish . . ."

Slowly, he pulled her shirt over her head, dropped it to the floor. Her bra went next, Julian reaching around her to unclasp it, draw it forward. Down and off, exposing her to his hungry gaze, the nubs tightening as the air teased them.

"More lovely than I dreamed," he said reverently.

Then he bent his head, flicking one with his tongue, teasing just the tip. She raked her fingers through his hair, helpless not to touch him, wondering which of them held the power now. Or whether it mattered. He seemed as enthralled in his endeavor as she, suckling one peak, then the other, heightening her arousal to a near-unbearable level. She squirmed, seeking relief for the ache between her thighs, asking without words.

He raised his head, eyes dark and hot, one hand sliding to the button of her jeans. "More?"

"Yes! Julian, *please*."

He wasted no time unfastening and unzipping them, sliding them off her hips along with her panties, but neither did he rush. He slid them off and tossed them aside, and she had a brief flash of relief that she'd shaved her legs that morning. Silly, but the notion fled as he spread her thighs, hooked his arms under her knees, and urged her forward.

"Like this, *querida*," he murmured. "All the way over the edge so I can taste you."

Leaning over her, he kissed and rubbed her tummy gently, almost lovingly. His fingers trailed over her pale blond curls, then dipped low to stroke her slit. His touch ignited a flame that coursed through her sex, her belly, to every limb. She moaned and her knees fell open wider, inviting him to take what he wanted. Past caring about the wisdom of doing this.

"So beautiful, my sweet Grace."

His tongue replaced his fingers, licking at the tender folds. So hot, wet, and wicked. He stroked and teased her needy flesh, toyed with her throbbing clit, swirling the bud until she thought she might lose control.

As though sensing she was getting close, he changed tactics and cupped his hands under her bottom, lifting her off the cushions, to his mouth. A feast, his for the sampling. His tongue stabbed into her core like a cock, sliding deep, stroking and lapping. In and out, tongue-fucking her with single-minded determination.

Writhing, she clutched at his hair, desperate to take him deeper, give him everything. Let him take her. "Oh! Oh, God, yes! I want—I need—"

"Tell me." Lick. "What do you need?"

"I—don't stop!"

"Don't stop what? Say it."

"Eat me," she cried, pulling at him.

He complied with enthusiasm, fastening his mouth to her sex, sucking her clit. Relentless, like a starving man savoring his last dessert. Driving her higher . . .

At last she unraveled, shattered, hips bucking, shouting, heedless of the neighbors who might hear. On and on until the last of the orgasm subsided, leaving her lying there like a limp noodle. Completely sated.

And physically vulnerable, though the position itself didn't bother her at all compared with the vulnerability of having given in to . . . intimacy. Not uncomplicated sex. Not with this man. She shook her head to clear the disturbing notion.

"Wasn't that good for you?"

She blinked into his earnest eyes, covering her confused thoughts. "Are you kidding? I think I disintegrated."

"Ah," he said, a satisfied grin curling his lips. "Success, then."

"Oh, yes." She smiled, smoothing his hair out of his face. "In spades. But what about you? I'd like to return the favor."

An odd expression flickered across his face, and was gone. "I'm good, *bella*. That was for you," he said softly. "Because I wanted to, not because I expected anything in return."

"But—"

"Shh, no worries." Reaching down, he fished around for something, then handed over her shirt.

She took it from him and pulled it on, more confused than ever. Since when did a lover not expect his attentions to be reciprocated? The idea caused a warm flutter in her middle.

Why did Julian have to be so damned gallant?

Nothing about the man was what she'd expected so far. Quite the contrary. She'd never felt so off-balance around a man, and she wasn't sure she liked it.

She pulled on her jeans, as well, at a loss as to what to do or say next. *My fucking God, what a fabulous orgasm! More coffee?*

"Thank you." Feeling ridiculous, she crossed her arms, watching as he stood, smiling.

"For you, anything."

"You really mean that, don't you?"

His smile softened, his dark eyes warm as he laid his palms on her shoulders. "I never say anything I don't mean."

"No man has ever put my wishes first," she said, and felt a blush stain her face. What on earth made her admit that to him?

"I'll always put you first, Grace. No matter where our relationship goes."

"Is that what you want? A relationship?" Her stomach fluttered. Was it possible she wasn't just a challenge to him? A prize to be captured because he got a thrill out of the chase?

"After all these months, can you really not know the answer to that question?" Pausing, he pinned her with an intense look she'd never seen before. "But what happens is up to you. I won't risk driving you away; you said you wanted to be friends and I believe we are. Nothing more develops unless you want it to. You're that important to me."

His words, spoken with complete honesty, struck her to the core. Turned her conception of him inside out yet again. A hard lump formed in her throat.

"I . . . I don't know what to say." Crossing the short distance between them, she reached for him, entwined his fingers with hers. "Except thank you. And you're right—we are friends. I love having you around. A lot." She knew he wanted her to make more of a declaration about where she saw them going, but she just couldn't.

She didn't trust this strange new feeling in her chest, chafing her emotions raw. It scared her more than a little.

If he was disappointed, he didn't let it show. Lifting her hand, he brushed his lips over her fingers. "Me, too. When I get to see you, it's the best part of my day."

The protective shell around her heart cracked. "That's the sweetest thing any man has ever said to me."

"Better get used to it," he said hoarsely. Letting go of her hand, he started backing toward the door, as though escaping while he held a small advantage. "Still on for dinner tomorrow night?"

"Of course," she said, a weird pang lancing her chest at the idea of letting him go. "I'm really looking forward to it."

He grinned, a lock of black hair falling into his eyes, making him look every inch the sexy devil. He was certainly leaving in a better mood than when he'd arrived. "Not as much as I am, *bella*. Seven o'clock."

"I'll be ready."

"And, Grace?"

"Yes?"

"About the other . . . thanks for listening."

"Anytime," she said sincerely.

He nodded and in seconds he was gone, leaving a vast emptiness in his wake.

He hadn't once touched his coffee.

Julian followed an officer through the small, busy rabbit warren of the Sugarland Police Department building, glad for any distraction to take his mind off the ache in his heart. Even this one, being escorted to see Detective Shane Ford in homicide rather than the detectives he'd spoken with before.

Homicide. Holy shit, what did that mean? He didn't have long to speculate.

Ford sat behind his desk, perusing a pile of paperwork, an expression of intense concentration on his face. At Julian's knock, the brown-haired man looked up and gave him a distracted, but pleasant, greeting.

"Mr. Salvatore?"

"Julian, please."

Ford waved him inside and stood to shake his hand. "Come in. I've been meaning to give you a call and follow up, but the shit has sort of hit the fan around this place. It's just as well you're here," he said in a soft drawl.

Julian shook his hand, studying the tall, lean cowboy dressed in jeans with a gold buckle. The guy looked tired, like he'd pulled an all-nighter. "Why's that?"

"What, the shit hitting the fan or that it's good you're here?" Sitting down again, he leaned back in his chair.

"Both, I suppose." Julian decided he could see why the lieutenant liked the guy. Ford's friendly demeanor and honest face reminded him of the detective's twin sister, Shea, whom he'd met at the Waterin' Hole with Tommy.

The detective picked up a pencil with a mangled eraser and tapped it on the desk as he spoke, probably a habit. "All right. Why don't we begin with you. Even though you told the other detectives what you witnessed at the club the night Brett Charles disappeared, I'd like to hear it from you." Ford was silent a moment as he opened a file and flipped to a page of notes.

"You came into the station two days after Charles vanished because you caught the story on the evening news, saw his picture, and were sure he was the man you'd seen, correct?"

"That's right."

"Tell me."

Taking a fortifying breath, Julian did as Ford asked, relating every detail he could recall. The two men, their odd interaction at the bar, Julian and Cody remarking on them, his following the men outside.

"Where you said they got into a dark, four-door Mercedes."

"Yes. License plate *X*, *E*, and either a *P* or *B*. I couldn't read the rest."

"That's quite a memory now, much less that night, when you'd been out drinking with your date."

"I didn't have that much to drink. And I have excellent recall, especially when something bothers me as much as this did."

Ford pinned him with an assessing stare. "Because of the weird vibe between the men." There was no sarcasm in his voice, only speculation—as though he sensed Julian was holding something back.

And he'd be right.

The memory made his skin clammy with old terror and shame.

"Let me ask you. . . . Cody corroborated everything I said, didn't he?" Now maybe he'd learn whether the police ever spoke with the bartender.

"The detectives tried a few times, but he was 'too busy' at work and never home. I'll have to pay him a visit, not that I don't believe you. It's better to have more than one person relate the same details."

Damn. "Detective, there's no good way to say this, but Cody's dead."

Ford's eyes widened. "What?"

"I just found out last night. Another bartender at the Cadillac told me he fell off a ladder outside his house while fixing his rain gutters."

The detective threw down his pencil in disgust. "Well, sonofabitch."

"The kicker is, he was killed last Wednesday, the day before my hit-and-run."

"Your *what*?"

"Shit, nobody told you about that, either?" He shook his head, studying the cop, who appeared pretty pissed. "Unbelievable. We were working a minor traffic accident out on I-49 when some asshole in a pickup tried to turn me into a pavement patty. I had a concussion and just got the stitches out yesterday."

"Sounds like you're damned lucky to be alive."

"Yep, and get this—the truck had no plates."

Ford's expression darkened. "I can't fucking believe I wasn't informed about any of this."

"Considering you might've had both of your only witnesses accidentally killed within twenty-four hours of each other? Me, either." He paused, wondering whether to push, but curiosity got the best of him. "You said the shit hit the fan. Care to explain?"

"You had the news on last night or this morning?"

"Haven't had a chance." Oh, this was going to be bad.

"These disappearances, officially they've been elevated in status from missing persons to kidnappings. We've got remains of two bodies, one male and one female, found beside a washed-out bank along the Cumberland. Runoff from the rain unearthed them."

The blood drained from Julian's face. "Brett Charles?"

"No, these were earlier victims. In fact, they were the first ones to disappear ten months ago. Their names are Samuel Yantis and Patricia Marston, ages nineteen and twenty. The medical examiner says they probably haven't been dead for very long. Five or six months at the most."

"But that means . . ."

"Yeah. They were held somewhere, kept alive and tortured, and murdered months later. In short, we've got ourselves a serial killer."

Automatically, Julian clutched at his cross and whispered a brief prayer in Spanish. "*Dios*, that's insane. Monstrous."

"It is. But it also gives us hope that we have time to find the other victims before they suffer the same tragic end."

"How—"

"You don't want to know. Trust me."

No, he didn't. It sickened him to imagine what those poor kids had been through before they died. Years ago, he'd been damned lucky—

The idea shook him. In truth, had been stewing all along.

Was it even remotely possible?

How could what happened in Texas a lifetime ago possibly be related to here and now, more than six hundred miles away?

You know how. But since you didn't go to the police back then, will anyone believe you?

"I've told you what I know," he said, trying to shove the ghosts out of his head. He stood. "If anything else comes up, you know where to find me."

"Likewise." Ford got to his feet and shook his hand once more. "Do us all a favor and watch your back."

"You know it."

Julian made his way out of the station, his mental ramblings turning to this afternoon.

This day was bound to get a helluva lot worse before it improved.

Brett sat hunched against the cold rock, knees drawn up, and clutched his tattered, filthy shirt. He shook with terror, wide gaze fixed on the dim light coming from somewhere far down the passage.

They'd come, taken Joey. He knew for sure when they called him by name, murmuring words of false comfort, of praise. Sickening.

Then the generator came alive with a deep hum that reverberated along the cavern walls, some awful beast with gaping jaws, hungry to prey upon its next meal.

Kendra sang, a maddening, nonsensical tune that had him pulling at his hair, ready to yell at her to shut the fuck up.

And then, the screaming.

Shrill, animal screams of fear and horror. On and on, in staccato bursts, digging into his brain. Shredding his soul. He clapped his hands over his ears, desperate to shut out the wails, the demented singing that went on forever. No amount of drugs would ever be enough to do the job.

When it all stopped, the silence cut to the bone. Left a black hole in his middle that nothing would ever fill again. Not even if he got out of here alive.

Tears ran unchecked down his face as he realized Kendra was right. Nothing was worse than when the screaming ended.

Because that meant someone else was next.

8

"All right, out with it. What's so dire that you had to descend on me the second I got home, on a *Friday*, after a long week with my little tyrants?" Kat smiled at her sister with affection, taking the sting out of her words, letting her know she didn't really mind the impromptu visit. "And why is my workaholic sibling off work so early, anyway? Friday afternoon blues?"

"Something like that." Grace swirled the glass of Chardonnay Kat had poured for her, took a grateful sip. "Oh, this is good. I just wanted to check on my baby sis—is that a crime?"

"Of course not. I'm basking in the glow of all this attention like the diva I am," she said, picking up her glass of milk. "Howard won't let me carry anything heavier than my book bag loaded with the kids' work sheets, and he even complains about that."

"And you're not even showing yet, you brat," she teased.

"You don't think so?" Looking down, she smoothed one hand over her tummy. "Oh, well. It won't be long."

Grace snorted, unable to resist nettling her. "Exactly, which means you'd better appreciate that cute, curvy little bod while you have it. Before long, you'll be lying on your back and realize your boobs have gone on strike and now permanently point east and west instead of north."

"Oh! Bitch!" Kat hurled a throw pillow at her sister, making them both giggle. "You are *so* evil!"

"Is Grace being mean to you, baby?" Howard walked into the living room, sweaty and shirtless, dressed in torn jeans, a hammer in one hand. He bent and gave Kat a sound, sizzling kiss.

Grace couldn't help but stare. Her brother-in-law was one prime chunk of real estate, no matter how you sliced it. More than that, he loved her sister to distraction and treated her as if she were a princess, which in Grace's eyes made him a god. When he laid a big, gentle hand on Kat's belly, Grace's throat burned with an unexpected wash of emotion and she had to look away.

"I think she's just PMS-ing," Kat said, giving her husband an exaggerated pout. "She said you'd better get ready for saggy boobs."

Howard straightened with a put-upon groan. "Oh, jeez. Days like this, I'm glad to be an only child. Ladies, the new deck is calling me."

With that, he spun and made himself scarce. Grace and Kat shared a grin, then laughed as one of the back doors banged shut. Grace tucked her legs up on the sofa and studied the happy glow on her sister's face.

"He's a good man, sweet pea."

"Yes, he is. I'm not sure how I got so lucky." Kat toyed with her glass, arching a brow. "Now tell me what's wrong."

"Nothing's wrong, I just—" She faltered, feeling the weight of loneliness crashing down. Wished she'd managed to come back with some witty retort or bullshit story to divert her sister. One look told her neither of those tactics was going to work, and she sighed. "How did you know Howard was *the one*?"

Kat stared at her in surprise, appearing caught between making a joke and answering honestly. To Grace's relief, she opted for the latter.

"I think I knew the second we met. But I didn't *know* I knew, if that makes sense, until after our first date, when he revived that little girl who fell in the river. Seeing this big, strong man almost go to pieces over saving a baby? That was the clincher."

"I'm sure it would be," she said, thinking of Julian. He did those same sorts of heroic things, every day. "But wasn't there ever a time when you second-guessed yourself? Asked yourself whether this was what you really wanted?"

"We had some definite issues to work past, but no. Howard was the one who had to figure stuff out. I knew I wanted my man and I'd do just about anything to get him."

"I envy you that sort of confidence," she said quietly. "I always have."

Kat blinked. "What the heck are you talking about? You've always been the one with the ironclad life plan, marching toward success and prestige, taking no prisoners."

"Yes, but you're referring to work, not personal relationships."

"So, what? You're having, like, an identity crisis or something? You're not confident with men, in knowing what you want?" She posed the last question as though the idea were inconceivable.

"I *thought* I was, and I believed I did. I've had relationships. Nice, uncomplicated, casual affairs."

"I hear a big fat *but* hanging there."

"But . . . what if a woman doesn't know whether he's *the*

one? What if the guy wants more than a fling? I don't know if I'm ready for complications. I don't want to—to hurt him. Or to get hurt."

Scooting closer, Kat laid a hand on her arm. "This doesn't sound like my poised, self-assured sister. This is about Julian—am I warm?"

"Burning. The man is . . . charming, hardworking, sexy—"

"Skilled?" Kat waggled her brows.

"I wouldn't know," she said, a tad too quickly. At her sister's knowing smirk, she relented somewhat. "Well, all right, yes! But we haven't slept together, and believe it or not, he's a total gentleman who puts the lady first."

"Wow, who would've thought?"

Grace bristled, some strange urge to defend him heating her blood. "Why is that so surprising? He's a kindhearted, wonderful man, and I don't think anybody has ever really taken the time to get to know him."

"Whoa, it's not me you have to convince! You're the one worrying yourself in circles where the man is concerned."

"I'm not—" She clamped her mouth shut. Okay, so she was. Perplexed, she took a healthy draw of her wine. "What's wrong with me, Sis?"

"Honey, I think you have an idea," she said, lips curving in a soft smile. "But it's your bridge to cross, in your own time. Not everyone is magically ready and willing to make the final leap at the first sign of lusty-ever-after, and you shouldn't feel bad about being cautious. You want to know what I think?"

"Of course I do, or I wouldn't be here."

"I think that deep down you know this attraction with Julian won't be just a satisfying fling. I think you're fighting it because he doesn't fit your well-ordered life plan. In Grace's schema, passion equals losing control, and commitment equals loss of freedom—and both scare the crap out of you. How am I doing so far?"

Grace's eyes widened as she stared at her sister. "Damn, you're good. How'd you get so smart?"

Her sister pressed on, ignoring her question. "I also think you know in your heart there's something worth exploring between you. Your reaction when you found out he'd been hurt proved it like nothing else could have."

"You think I should go for it."

"The question is, what do *you* want?"

"I want my well-ordered life plan to go back to following its boring little path," she blurted. And knew she'd lied.

From the sparkle in Kat's green eyes, she knew, too. "Uh-huh. Good luck with that."

"You're all heart."

"I still owe you for the comment about the saggy boobs. We're nowhere close to even."

"And then there's the stretch marks—"

"Danger," Kat said in a low, menacing voice. "Hormonal, pregnant, homicidal maniac at nine o'clock."

Grace laughed with her sister, the familiar banter comforting, unconditional love grounding her, steady and solid. She studied Kat for a few seconds, the mirth fading. "Sis?"

"Hmm?"

"How do you know you're in love with *him*, not just with the *idea* of being in love?"

Kat sobered, too, and looked her straight in the eye. "That one's easy. You'll know when you mess around until he walks away, and takes your heart with him."

Julian parked down the road from Howard and Kat's new place as directed, dread curdling in his gut. He didn't give a fuck what any fancy intervention book claimed. An intensely private man like Sean would feel embarrassed and betrayed, and no amount of hand-holding or singing "Kumbaya" was going to send him skipping off to rehab with a tearful promise to get sober. Julian had told them as much during their planning session.

His opinion hadn't been welcome.

After the captain heard what they had to say, God help them all in the face of his white-hot anger, then the glacial freeze that would make A-shift about as much fun as boot camp in Siberia. One boot in particular was about to kick their collective asses. Of course, he could be wrong. But he didn't think so.

Kat opened the front door before Julian could even knock, and showed him inside. "I'm glad you're here," she said, giving him a brief hug. "The others are in the living room. They're just waiting on Howard and Sean."

"What did Six-Pack end up telling him about where they were going?" he asked as he stepped inside. One key to a successful intervention, they'd learned, was the importance of keeping the plans a secret and handling the situation with delicacy. *Sort of like defusing a bomb without knowing which color wire to snip first, if you ask me.* Which nobody did.

The normally bubbly blonde was about as serious as he'd ever seen her. "Howard didn't have the heart to lie to Sean, so he told him they were coming over here and that he'd have to trust him."

And if this didn't go well, that would probably be the last time Sean ever did, but he refrained from saying so. Just barely. He trailed Kat into the living room, waved, and returned the hellos from Eve, Zack, Tommy, Clay Montana, here to represent both B- and C-shifts, and Chief Bentley Mitchell. Julian had worried that the chief's presence would make this seem to Sean more like an official warning from the fire department rather than the giant group lovefest it was supposed to be, but everyone else felt he needed to know he had the chief's support.

Bentley was more than a boss to Sean; he was a father figure, a good friend. They'd known each other for the better part of twenty years, and the chief had been there right alongside Howard, literally holding Sean up, when his wife and children died. Despite Julian's initial misgivings, he had to concede now that the day had come, he felt better having the older man present. Nobody respected the chief more than Sean.

"I'm going to make myself scarce," Kat said, patting Julian's arm. "Can I get you anything first, water or soda?"

"Nothing, thanks." This wasn't a social visit. He hoped like hell they wouldn't be entrenched here long enough to need refreshments.

"Okay. If you guys need anything, let me know." Kat turned to leave, then hesitated, looking back at him with a slight frown. "Julian?"

"Yes?"

The oddest expression settled on her face and she opened her mouth to say something. Changing her mind, however, she shook her head. "Forget it. It's none of my business."

Well, it didn't take a genius to figure out what was bothering her. "Let me guess—if I break Grace's heart, you have a fishing pole and you know how to use it." He enjoyed watching her face turn beet red.

"Does everybody at the station know that story?"

"Yep. Sorry, but it's a classic." And boy had Six-Pack learned his lesson about even breathing in another woman's direction.

"Just so you know, I've been practicing my swing."

"I'll remember that," he promised, struggling not to grin.

After she disappeared to another part of the house and he took a seat on a folding chair, his amusement fled. He doubted it would matter that they'd kept the size of the group within the parameters suggested by the experts. They'd planned for weeks, right down to the meticulous details of making a reservation at a treatment facility and covering his absence. No, those were the sorts of things a man appreciated down the road. Miles down.

Two car doors slammed outside and all conversation died. Julian glanced at each of the others, the wariness in the room warring with hope, some fidgeting, some checking their pockets subconsciously and fingering the letters they'd written to read aloud. If Sean stayed long enough to hear them.

The two men came in the front door, Sean in the lead. Obviously not yet having a clue, he strode into the living room with a half smile. His face was gaunt, collarbones too pronounced through his dark T-shirt, jeans loose on his hips. He settled his John Deere baseball cap back on his head, and Julian noted how much the gray at his temples had begun to spread into the brown strands. He appeared exhausted, worn, but not in bad spirits.

"Hey, guys. Where's the snacks and beer? Was I supposed to bring something?"

A round of murmured greetings ensued. Bentley rose and shook his hand, then resumed his seat, prompting the other men to follow suit. Eve hung back until last, giving Sean a fierce hug when her turn came. His arms came around her slim shoulders and his bottle green eyes closed for a few seconds, as though that embrace were a life preserver in a storm. When Eve let go, Julian wondered whether anyone else caught

Sean's reluctance to relinquish his hold—or the flash of longing on his face, quickly squelched.

"This isn't that kind of get-together. Why don't you have a seat, buddy," Howard said, clasping his friend's shoulder gently. A firm order, not a request.

"Oh. Okay." He took the empty seat next to Bentley and his gaze traveled around the circle. "Where's everybody's cars?"

"Most are at the neighbor's house down the road, son," the chief said in a low voice.

"But . . . why?" he asked in confusion.

Howard took the last vacant seat on the other side of his friend. Since they'd voted him spokesperson, he went first. "Sean, it's important for you to understand we're here because we love you. We—"

"Oh, my God," Sean whispered, his face white. "You're all . . . Th-this is an ambush."

Julian winced at his choice of words, knowing he'd feel the same way if the tables were turned. Seeing the captain's confusion morph to shock, the lost look in his eyes, made his heart bleed for the guy.

"No, we're not here to attack you," Howard continued, his voice calm, steady, as he went through the introduction he'd rehearsed. "Every single person in this room is here because they love you and they care what happens to you. Because we care, we can't sit back any longer and watch you slowly kill yourself with alcohol. Your problems are too big to handle alone, and that's why we're here. We know your drinking stems from grief and that made it understandable at first, certainly not unexpected or surprising. But we're all guilty of letting you struggle for far too long without stepping forward to lend a real hand to a friend and leader we value."

"Value? I can't believe you're doing this to me," he rasped, fists clenching in his lap. Denial and misery oozed from every pore, and twin flags of red on his cheeks betrayed his humiliation.

He looked like a cornered wolf, Julian thought. Feral, ready to tear out the throats of his tormentors.

Howard shook his head, undeterred from finishing his statement. "We're here for you, but something else you need to understand is that besides hurting your health, your problem is starting to affect those around you. We're scared, Sean. Watching you self-destruct is making us all feel helpless. It's like you're on the top floor of a burning high-rise and there's no way to get to you. Only there is a way, if you'll let us."

"You're full of shit," Sean hissed, desperate. "I have never, ever been drunk on duty! How can you claim what I do on my personal time is affecting anyone else?"

"We're getting to that now. For over a year, we've all seen frightening changes in you, both physically and emotionally. You don't see them, but we do. Look at these people, Sean." He waited a few beats while the captain scanned the faces present, wild-eyed. "These are good folks. You know that because, except for the chief, you hired most of them. These are your friends, the people who've stuck by you through every type of bad shit imaginable. Do you honestly believe they'd come here like this to jerk you around? To participate in something so dead serious if it weren't absolutely necessary?"

Sean swallowed hard. "No," he answered, his voice barely audible. "But I can handle this on my own. I can."

"Before you make that decision—and regardless of how it appears, it *is* your decision—you're going to listen to what your friends have to say. They've all gone to a great deal of effort to put their thoughts in writing; they're completely sincere, and as tough as it will be, we'd like for you to listen with an open mind. Can you do that?"

Clearly past speech, Sean nodded. At his affirmation, everyone pulled out their papers. From the captain's expression, you'd have thought they'd brandished rifles instead. All the poor guy needed to complete the picture was a blindfold and a cigarette.

At that very moment, any remaining anger Julian might've been nursing toward his captain turned to ash. The inescapable truth was, this man wasn't in control of his life. His engines had failed and he was caught in a death spiral, plummeting toward the earth. And he had to be stopped before he took out not only himself but all the innocents on the ground below.

Bentley, to Sean's right, went first, his part being the shortest. He spoke of his great respect for Sean, but also his concerns. His worry for his firefighters and the lives hanging in the balance during every call, at Sean's command. He had complete faith the captain would recover, if he truly devoted himself. Being ensconced at the city offices, he didn't have close-up and personal day-to-day concerns, but the others had plenty.

One by one, each of them reiterated what Bentley said, adding their own experiences with Sean over the past year. They told different anecdotes, but the theme was the same—their captain wasn't the same kind, patient, and happy person he'd been before. That man had disappeared and in his place was a rude, surly stranger who didn't seem to value their efforts or their friendship, one who was wasting away before their eyes. Reading his own letter was the hardest thing Julian had ever done.

Howard went last. "I miss you," he began simply, and let the quiet statement hang as the paper shook in his hands.

Sean rested his elbows on his spread knees and hung his head, face hidden. Clear droplets plopped to the hardwood floor between his feet.

Howard saw, and his voice quavered. "All I want to say is, you've been my best friend for almost half my life. You've been there for me more times than I can count, whether laughing together or when everything was going straight to hell. You're the brother I always wished for, and you ought to know by now I'd do anything to make you whole again. Let me, us, help you."

Several heartbeats passed. "How?"

"I've made you a reservation at a really nice facility in Nashville," Howard said, hope shining in his eyes. "They'll counsel you, help you get sober, get your life back. This place is on our insurance plan, the station is covered, and I've packed a bag. All you have to do is get in the car with me and go."

Julian waited, tense, unsure about all his dire predictions. So far, this had gone better than he'd thought. No vile spewing of temper, no lashing out. Just one broken man facing the music in front of his friends, trapped and floundering.

After what seemed an eternity, Sean raised his head, wiped his face. "No."

Everyone froze except Howard, who looked like his best friend had just pulled a gun and shot him at point-blank range. Somehow, he found his voice. "What?"

"I said no." Sean stood, swaying a bit, his words tumbling out in a rush. "I'll do this myself or not at all. I don't need strangers poking in my head, telling me what I ought to feel and how to live my life. I'm going home."

Howard pushed to his feet. "Sean, please—"

"Hear me, and respect my wishes, old friend," he said softly. "I appreciate what you and what everyone else has done, and I heard what you have to say. I listened. I want you all to know this means a lot to me, but I'm leaving. I'll deal with my problems my own way, in my own time. I'll see you all at work and . . . thank you."

With that, he strode out. The front door shut with an ominous click and everyone stared at one another, stunned and unsure what to say. Julian noted the devastation on Howard's face and was compelled to say something to make him feel better.

"Six-Pack, listen," he began. "This went so much smoother than I thought it would. I believe he really did listen like he said—I just don't think he's ready to face getting help. But you know what? I bet once he lets all of this digest, he *will*. You'll see." Others chimed in their agreement.

Howard stared at him for a long moment before heaving a tired breath. "I hope you're right."

"I am."

"The question is, will he seek treatment before he hurts himself or someone else?"

Nobody had an answer for that one.

"I'd better go after him, get him home," Howard said, running a hand through his short, spiky hair. "If he's still listening, I'll work on him."

The others stood, as well, the mood a little shell-shocked. Julian felt as if his brain were made of raw hamburger, his emotions treading the razor's edge. There was only one thing he could think of that would come close to easing the pain of this afternoon.

Grace's beautiful smile.

With her serene face in mind, he excused himself. Once out on the road, he let the horses run on his way to one last stop before he saw Grace, willing the tension from his neck and shoulders. Everyone had their baggage, some more than others, but Julian had to concede that Sean's horrible loss and subsequent fall made his own problems pale in comparison.

And, unlike Sean, tonight he would be in the company of a lovely, delightful, challenging woman.

Julian, for the first time in a long damned while, had absolutely no complaints.

9

Julian parked in a lot beside W. H. Vines and whistled softly. Even when they'd lived in San Antonio, the Vines family hadn't laid claim to this level of wealth, at least as far as his memory served. As a teenage boy hired to mow their expansive lawn that fateful summer, he remembered being awed at their upper-middle-class minimansion. But Warren's old company building in downtown San Antonio had been crumbling, somewhat run-down.

This building, situated in an area of new development near the river, was nothing short of palatial. Rolling landscaped hills surrounded the property, a jewel green carpet leading to the broad double glass doors. Jesus, they'd come up in the world.

Probably by stomping right over the backs of anyone standing in their way.

Julian sat for a few moments, palms gripping the steering wheel, breath hitching with the force of rage he thought he'd mastered long ago. *Cool it.* He needed to wind down a little if he hoped to confront Warren, get the answers he sought.

One thing Julian was dead certain of: The man knew the truth about the day that had ruined Julian's life—and he'd threatened Mama to keep it buried.

"I'm coming, you sonofabitch."

In all honesty, this confrontation had been simmering since he'd recovered from the shock of seeing Derek with Grace at the restaurant. Derek may have committed the horrible act so many years ago, but Warren was the real power in the family. He'd made sure his son walked away scot-free, and Julian had fallen into a downward spiral that almost killed him.

But I'm not a helpless kid anymore, someone he and his sleazy son can treat like garbage. I survived, and it's time they know it.

Whatever Warren had to say, Julian would at least get closure.

He got out of the car and jogged up the wide steps. In the lobby, he inquired about which floor housed Warren's office. "I'm an old friend from San Antonio," he said, flashing his most engaging smile.

Eyeing him, the reluctant receptionist picked up her phone. "Name, please?"

"Julian Salvatore." Let the old bastard chew on that.

The woman spoke briefly to someone, then hung up and gave him a slight nod. "Mr. Vines will see you as soon as he's available."

A tiny jolt of anticipation made his pulse leap. He hadn't expected gaining admittance to be so simple. Moments later, he stepped off the elevator into another reception area, belatedly wondering whether he should have let someone know he was coming here. Unease crept along his skin, but his need to see this through was greater.

After giving his name to the second receptionist, he took a seat in a fat leather chair and forced himself not to fidget. He wished he hadn't had to give his name and lose the element of surprise. He would've loved to see Warren's unguarded expression when he realized who Julian was. But this seemed the most likely—and safest—place to catch the man.

The receptionist's phone buzzed several minutes later. She picked up the handset, gave an affirmative answer, and hung up, looking at Julian. "Mr. Vines said to send you in. Take this hallway behind me, last door on your left."

He sprang to his feet. "Thank you."

As he hurried down the corridor, Julian wasn't aware of holding his breath until the door opened. Whatever he'd been expecting, the sophisticated, petite beauty with the dark blond hair took him by surprise.

"Mrs. Vines, it's been a long time," he said, aware of her big, dark-haired husband looming behind his desk.

Some women became more desirable with age and maturity. Studying Zoe Vines fifteen years after he'd last glimpsed her, he found this was definitely the case. The woman had to be pushing sixty, yet due to great genes and possibly an even better plastic surgeon, she didn't look a day over forty-five.

Her lips turned up and she addressed him, a tad cool as she returned his scrutiny. "Mr. Salvatore, I'm afraid you have me and my husband at a disadvantage since we couldn't place your name. We left few friends behind in San Antonio and none who would travel all this way to visit."

Was she lying about not remembering him? If so, she hid it well. Julian's gaze shot to Warren, who stood stony and mute, one hand braced on his desk. A flicker of something that might've been recognition—or malice—flared in those watchful eyes, there and gone.

He knows. Julian's hands tightened into fists.

Having to face both of them at once shifted the odds for him, and he fought to regain his mental footing. Addressing both of them, he kept his tone even, carefully devoid of anger. "Mr. and Mrs. Vines, I mowed your lawn one summer fifteen years ago, when you lived in San Antonio."

Her smile deepened and she shut the office door, gesturing to a seat across from her husband. "Sit down, please."

He did, though it made him uncomfortable to have them standing over him.

Zoe went on, perching on the corner of her husband's desk and crossing her arms. "We've employed a lot of temporary help over the years. They come and go, so you'll forgive us for not recalling you when you couldn't have been more than a boy."

"I was almost sixteen," he said quietly, blanching at the sudden flood of disjointed, horrible memories.

"Well, you're certainly not a boy now and I don't have all day to play guessing games," Warren said gruffly, gaze narrowing. Slowly, he lowered himself to his chair. "Why don't you tell us who you are and why you're here?"

"I'm a firefighter with the Sugarland Fire Department, and my reason for being here dates back to that summer I was employed by your wife. First, I want answers. Specifically, I want to know why you allowed your son to get away with molesting me."

Zoe paled. Warren's rugged face flushed a deep crimson and he gaped like a landed trout. Evidently, the man wasn't expecting such a direct challenge.

"Wh-what's the goddamned meaning of this?" the older man sputtered. "Where do you get off barging in here making ridiculous accusations like those?"

"It's not an accusation. It's history." Julian returned the man's hard stare. "Do us both a favor and drop the pretense. A grown son getting into trouble for fondling a teenaged boy isn't something a parent is likely to forget."

For several long moments, Julian thought the man might lunge across the desk and strangle him. Zoe studied the floor, rubbing the arms of her silk blouse, her face a mask of regret. While her husband appeared on the verge of a stroke, it was Zoe who spoke gently.

"You're right, and I apologize for not recognizing you before. Why don't you share with us what you remember?" She raised her head and looked at him expectantly.

Grateful for a rational ear, he took a deep breath and began. "Derek was always kind to me that summer, stopping to chat, bringing me something cold to drink when I was parched from working." Breathing and talking at the same time became a little difficult, his nerves trying to get the best of him.

"He was in his early twenties, rich, and on his way to success. Of course, you know that. But I think I idolized him somewhat, my being a poor, impressionable teenaged boy from the wrong side of the tracks, reveling in the attention he gave me, like an older brother I'd always wanted. You see, I had all older sisters, and my little brother was just a bratty kid to me at the time. Derek *talked* to me when no one else in my family could be bothered."

Zoe's full mouth curved into a small smile. "My son is, and has always been, very outgoing. He has a kind heart and a way with young people."

Julian gave a bitter laugh. "I thought so, too. Until the day he slipped me a Mickey and I woke up naked in his bed."

Zoe and Warren stared at him. For several seconds, he anticipated more angry denial, the venom to spew from both of them. Instead, Zoe surprised him by relaxing and heaving a sigh. "My God, I can't believe no one ever told you."

"What are you talking about?"

"After all of this time, to realize you thought . . . this is incredible. Julian—if I may call you by your name—I think I can put your mind at ease. You actually passed out from heat exhaustion."

"What?" He glanced between Zoe and Warren.

Warren cleared his throat, his defensive attitude calming somewhat. "It's true."

"Derek brought you to his room," Zoe said. "He only removed your clothing because you were overheated, and he was trying to get you cool. I know all about it because Derek came to get me."

"No," he said hoarsely. "I remember being touched. All over."

Hands, sliding over every inch of skin, but he couldn't focus. Couldn't fight. He felt sick, wanted to go home, but couldn't speak.

Zoe's husky voice brought him back to the present. "Derek was very worried, even bathed you with a damp cloth before fetching me. I was concerned and we set about trying to figure out how to get your mother's phone number because we'd been stupid and had never considered needing it for an emergency."

He blinked at her. "You? You were there?" he asked, what she said finally registering. He scoured his memory and . . . nothing. He couldn't place her there, but then again, he didn't remember much. Except the touches and feeling trapped in his own body. Could it be he'd been wrong? Was the new hope he felt because he *wanted* to be wrong?

He could confront Derek, but his entire being rejected the idea. Just as he didn't want Grace anywhere near the man, the same held true for himself. Besides, he didn't want Derek to realize Grace's friend was the boy from all those years ago.

"Of course I was. I assure you, Derek did nothing inappropriate. You were very ill and we tried to help you. By the time we located your mother's number and went back to check on you, you'd awakened and left. I called your mother, who wouldn't say anything except you'd no longer be working for us. I was confused, as I'm sure you can imagine, but decided to let it go." Reaching over, she squeezed his knee in a gesture of comfort, gazing at him in sympathy. "I'm so sorry you've carried the wrong idea with you all these years."

"I told Mama what happened and she never said anything about you phoning or me getting heatstroke." His head pounded with this new, startling information. Could it be true? Had his feverish brain taken a completely innocent kindness and made it into something frightening?

You were only a kid, and she sounds sincere.

"I told your mother what happened, but I see she refused to hear my explanation. Why would she, with you being so upset and not thinking straight? Your mother obviously wanted to support you, whether she believed your story or not. Would knowing I was worried have made things any better or changed your mind about what you thought happened at the time?"

"No," he admitted. "I don't think it would have. I just can't understand how I could've been so wrong."

A seed Zoe planted took root and began to grow, despite his effort to dislodge it. *Dios*, had Mama not believed him? Is that *really* why she swept the entire incident away, told him to forget?

"The human mind plays all sorts of nasty tricks on us, especially when we aren't well," she concluded.

Yes, it could. As a paramedic he knew the symptoms of heat exhaustion. Summer in San Antonio was like beachfront property in hell, and he'd been doing hard manual work all afternoon that day. He had been dizzy, a bit of a headache coming on, and the drink Derek provided could have been too little, too late. He'd passed out, become disoriented.

The rest could've happened exactly as Zoe said. All very reasonable.

But then— No. Impossible.

He fixed Warren with a cold stare. "If that were true, then why did you threaten my mother into making sure I kept quiet about Derek?"

Warren's amused bark of laughter rang hollow. "You can't be serious."

"She didn't say it in so many words, but I know she was afraid of repercussions from you. She was terrified of what you might do to our family if I told the police."

"Bullshit! Yes, she phoned me and I raised my voice, but I only defended my son from her wild accusations the same as any father would do! Any verbal threat she perceived was in the way of legal action on my part should your story prove just that, nothing more."

"Then you don't deny attempting to intimidate a single mother of six, a woman on a fixed income." For that alone, he could kill Warren Vines.

"I merely protected my family," Vines hissed. "Even now, you can't recall what happened, and you might have destroyed our lives. What would you have done in my place?"

Julian's anger didn't dissipate, nor did the sick dread in his gut. They'd rendered him as helpless as he'd been fifteen years ago. Watching the man wipe a bead of sweat off his brow, Julian knew he had no proof they weren't telling the absolute truth.

He wasn't sure what he'd accomplished, coming here this way—aside from serving notice to the patriarch.

"Aren't you glad to have such a horrible misconception

put to rest? I, for one, am glad you stopped by," Zoe said, sliding from her seat on the desk. Again, Warren subsided. Obviously, she was used to acting as a buffer for her husband's temper.

Julian took his cue to leave, and rose. "Misconception. What a tame word for the crime that ruined my youth. That's right, *crime*," he emphasized, cutting off their protests. "Because it will take a lot more evidence to make me buy what you're selling."

Warren started out of his seat. "Now, wait just a damned minute—"

"No, you wait. Sit there and wonder whether I'll discover you're lying out your ass," he said, low and dangerous. "And if I do? I'll make you both wish you were dead."

Turning on his heel, he strode out, half expecting a curse—or a sharp knife—to be hurled at his back.

Neither came.

In his car, he fumbled for his keys and started the ignition, hands shaking. Not from fear, but from the rush. He'd done it. Faced Warren and called him on his actions regarding Mama. Let him know the scared kid was gone, a man in his place.

As he drove away, however, an oily feeling slithered over his body.

Like maybe he should have let the past rest in peace.

Grace jumped at the knock on her door at five minutes before seven. She'd been jittery as a schoolgirl awaiting his arrival all afternoon, her talk with Kat doing a number on her head. The closer she got to a certain tall, dark, and handsome man, the more out of control she felt.

Ruthlessly squashing her nerves, she opened the door—

and the sight of him dressed in dark pants and a sport coat, starched white shirt underneath, sucked out her brains.

His smile lit up like a beacon and those dark eyes danced, leaving no doubt how pleased he was at seeing her. He breathed something in a reverent tone in Spanish, too quickly for her to catch.

"What did you just say?"

He dipped his head in an almost shy gesture, then raised his gaze to hers again. "I said you'll outshine the stars tonight."

Touched, she reached for his hand, twined her fingers in his. "Thank you. I must say you look pretty darned handsome yourself."

One cheek revealed a fetching dimple as he plucked at his jacket. "I clean up okay, I suppose. Beats smoke and grime, anyway. Ready?"

"You bet. Let me grab my purse and lock up."

Taking care of it quickly, she joined him and they started down the sidewalk together, hand in hand. Funny how something as simple as holding hands could ground a person, make her feel as though all were right in the world. She enjoyed how everything about him was bigger, stronger, and being able to let down her guard was a nice feeling. His physical presence was intoxicating, and she wanted more. Wanted him closer, to crawl inside him and—

Her thoughts ground to a halt as he hit the button on his key-ring device to unlock his car. "You drive a *Porsche*?"

He grinned, obviously pleased that he'd surprised her. "You expected me to be some poor city grunt driving a ratted-out El Camino?"

"I—of course not, but . . ." She waved a hand, practically drooling over the sleek, metallic dark gray Porsche Cayman. "This is gorgeous."

Opening the passenger's door for her, he cocked an eyebrow. "And you're dying to know how I can afford it."

"No! I'd never ask such a rude question." But he was right, dammit. She was too darned nosy for her own good.

Closing her door, he walked around and slid in the driver's side, stuck the key in the ignition, and fired it up. The engine idled with a throaty, sexy purr—not unlike its owner's.

"I've been a firefighter for almost ten years," he said, pulling out of the parking space. "I've never been married. I've lived well without going overboard, worked extra shifts, saved my money. I mean, until now, I've never had anyone to splurge on."

As he pulled onto the street, he shot her a look that could've melted iron at a hundred yards, leaving no doubt about his meaning. He intended to splurge now, on her.

She grinned, warming inside, deciding to tease him. "Well, in that case, I'm happy to help you out. I'm so hungry you may have to buy me dinner *and* dessert."

Glancing at her, he laughed, a rich, throaty sound that made every nerve ending tingle in delight. As she studied his beautiful profile with his straight nose and high cheekbones, longish locks of raven hair falling over his forehead and brushing against his neck, her belly fluttered. She could easily become addicted to this man.

"You could've been a model," she blurted, and immediately felt foolish. Good grief, she was getting as bad as her sister, spouting whatever silly observation was on her tongue.

"I don't think so," he said easily enough. But a hint of darkness crept into his tone. Pulling onto the highway, he merged with traffic. "Actually, that was suggested to me more than once when I was younger. The idea of using my body to make money left me cold."

"I can understand that. I didn't mean to offend you."

"You didn't, *bella*."

The smooth accent made her shiver. God, she was hopeless. "I'm glad, because I meant it as a compliment."

"I know, and thank you."

"You're welcome." She paused, wondering at the sudden reserve she sensed in him. "You've told me some about your job, but not why you chose the profession. Did you always know you wanted to be a firefighter?" she asked, steering them toward safer ground.

He smiled, a bit wistful. "Not originally. I wanted to be a cop, but Mama begged me not to. After several arguments, I finally gave in and decided becoming a firefighter would fulfill my desire to help people. Mama still wasn't happy, though, since my job can be every bit as dangerous as a cop's."

"Which is why I'll bet you didn't call and let her know you got hurt, did you?"

"Are you kidding? She doesn't know about me getting knocked out during the explosion a few months ago, either. The last thing I needed was Mama taking root at my place indefinitely, fussing and worrying herself half to death. She's got enough on her plate being afraid for my brother on a daily basis."

"I remember you mentioning him. What does he do that she'd worry so much?"

"Mama lost the argument with my hardheaded sibling. Tonio's a narcotics officer for the San Antonio PD," he said, love and pride evident in his voice. "He works undercover with the most dangerous criminals in the city. Mama's not the only one who worries, but he's a grown man, so what can you do?"

"You could always encourage him to transfer to Sugarland. I'm guessing they don't have nearly the crime rate San Antonio does," she said. "Just a thought."

"You know, I posed that very suggestion to him a couple of months ago, when he took a knife in the side from a dealer."

"Oh, no! Was he badly hurt?"

"The wound wasn't too deep, thank God. The ER patched him up and after a week of rest, he was back on the job, the idiot. Anyway, he said he'd think about moving here. Kind of depends on how Mama will react to the idea of her only other son moving hundreds of miles away."

"After what happened, I'm sure she'd rather have him working in a safer environment. Besides, she survived your move, right?"

Julian sighed. "Yeah, I suppose she did."

Okay, what was with the hint of sadness? "Why *did* you move here?" The tension in his face, around his mouth, told her she'd struck a nerve. "I'm sorry. It's none of my business. It's just that . . . you obviously love your family very much, and from what I've gathered, you're the only one who left home and moved so far away."

He was silent for so long, she didn't think he'd answer. When he did, his voice was quiet. Reflective. "Have you ever made a series of decisions based on a misconception, only to find out too late you may have been completely wrong? That this ghost who owned your soul possibly never existed at all, except in your head?"

She considered this, and nodded. "Yes, but only on a small scale, day-to-day stuff like a family squabble or a misunderstanding at work. Sounds like you're referring to a major, life-altering event—and whatever it was drove you far from the only home you'd ever known."

"Oh, Grace, you have no idea." He shook his head and put on a casual front. "But hey, let's not talk about this now. I promised you a nice evening, and that's what you're going to get."

"But—"

"Later, *querida*."

Grace snapped her mouth shut. The lawyer in her knew when to hold her tongue and wait, and she sensed Julian was about ready to crack. He wouldn't be pushed on this, and when he needed her, she'd be there for him.

Twenty minutes later, they arrived at a nice steak and seafood restaurant on the outskirts of Nashville. Julian had chosen well. She'd been here once before, and she knew the place was fairly expensive, more for special occasions than everyday dining. He was out to impress with his thoughtful selection, and succeeded.

After being shown to a quiet, dimly lit corner, they ordered two glasses of wine and studied each other over the tops of their menus while pretending to consider the food. Instinctively, Grace decided against ordering the least expensive item on the menu because he'd get the wrong idea, and she didn't want to insult him. She settled on grilled salmon and shrimp, then closed her menu and gratefully took a sip of her Merlot.

The waiter appeared, set down a basket of fresh bread, took their orders, and left them alone to eye each other. Julian propped his elbows on the table and rested his chin on his clasped hands, meeting her gaze from under a fringe of sinfully long, black lashes.

"How was your Friday?" he asked.

"Busy, but not too bad. And you?"

"I've had better, but tonight makes up for the entire day. No, scratch that—the whole month."

"You're too sweet," she said with a little laugh. One side of his mouth quirked upward.

"I'm not sweet at all," he murmured. "Or perhaps you need another demonstration?"

Hooo-boy! Her blood pressure skyrocketed and the sultry look on his sexy face gave her rock-hard party nipples. The memory of exactly how bad he could be, especially when applying that sensual, talented mouth, nearly sent her into hyperdrive.

Willing her jackhammering pulse to calm, she sent him a heated parry of her own. "I might at that. Sometimes I can be a slow learner and require a bit of a reminder."

What are you doing? Friends, friends! That's what you told him, Grace Marie!

"Invite me in for a nightcap, and I'm sure I can bring it all back to you," he said, taking her hand and stroking it with his thumb.

In the face of the all-out sensual gauntlet he'd tossed down, she faltered. Never had a man gotten to her this way. He was the poster boy for blatant sexuality and promised untold satisfaction for the woman who snared him. She longed to experience all of him, but a niggling voice told her once she did, she'd be reluctant to let him go.

The thought was terrifying.

But her lips formed her reply independent of common sense. "Do you like Buttery Nipples?" *Take that, stud.*

He choked in the act of taking a drink of his wine. "What?"

She couldn't help but chuckle at his surprise. "Buttery Nipple shots. You know, Baileys and Buttershots?"

"Oh. Right. I, uh, never tried them."

His reaction was so cute—she suspected if his skin weren't naturally bronzed, he'd be blushing. "Well, you're in for a real treat! That is, if you're game later on, at my place."

His recovery time was remarkable. He gave her a slow grin. "I'm game for whatever you have in mind, *bella.*"

She'd just bet he was!

Grace settled in for a wonderful dinner, trying to recall

when she'd enjoyed a man's company this much. The answer was swift and simple.

Never.

He'd said the progression of their relationship was up to her, and she was comfortable in that knowledge. She trusted Julian.

It was her own mind—giddy, scared, and confused by turns—she wasn't so sure of.

10

Julian shifted in his seat, mentally cursing the hard-on that plagued him all through dinner. This sensual, playful side of Grace breaking through her normal reserve had his blood boiling, his entire body coiled to pounce.

He wanted his lovely lady on her hands and knees as he thrust into her from behind, down and dirty. Maybe slow and easy next, her wrists bound as she writhed, at the mercy of his mouth and cock. He wanted to watch her shatter, her inner fire no longer hidden, but his to command.

And by God, she would be his. No other woman would ever challenge him, stimulate him, as Grace did.

But first, he'd have to come clean with her about his past, and about his visit to Warren's office today. O-kay, that particular memory went a long way toward deflating his current problem. With new relationships came the baggage, and he was afraid his might be too heavy for Grace.

"If you think any harder, you're going to short out your brain," Grace said, waving her fork at him. "Wanna share?"

"Sorry. Just contemplating leopards and spots." He gave her a lopsided grin he hoped masked his anxiety, and let her tranquil beauty wash over him anew. Not just physical beauty, but the inner light he wasn't even sure she was aware of.

"Hmm. You know a leopard who's looking to become a house cat?" Her violet eyes bored into his, growing pensive.

"Something along those lines. What do you believe? Can a leopard change his spots?"

"Maybe, but either way he's still a beast at heart. He'd be much better off if he simply learns to love what he is, feral nature and all."

They both knew they weren't discussing cats. The invitation in her eyes was unmistakable, and his arousal threatened to return full force.

"Dessert, *querida*?" he asked hoarsely.

"I've got something sweet for us at my place, if you'll recall."

Ah, shit! He signaled the waiter for the check and in five minutes, they were walking to his car. He rested his hand at the small of her slim back, amazed at how right it felt. Like it belonged there. Like a real *beginning*. Did she feel it, too, or was he just a sappy fool?

When they reached his car, instead of opening the door for Grace, he took her arm and gently turned her to face him. Pressing close, he backed her against the side of the car, making his desire clear. He cupped her cheeks and stared into big eyes he wanted to drown in, had no prayer of escaping, and brought his lips within a millimeter of hers.

"I was right."

"About?"

"You do outshine the stars," he whispered.

And kissed her. Long, deep, and thoroughly. She responded with a needy little whimper that shot straight to his balls, and he raked his fingers through her hair, loving how the silky white blond strands slipped through them. Loving her lithe frame pushing into him, seeking more, pert breasts crushed against his chest.

He finally forced himself to pull back before he wound up bending her over the hood of the Porsche. The image nearly made him come in his pants, and he vowed to find a way to make the fantasy a reality. All his fantasies, with her.

"I've never done this before," he said, tracing her lips with his thumb.

"Been on a date?"

"Would that surprise you?"

"Shock would be a better word, if I bought it. Which I don't." She stroked his chest absently where his shirt parted, making him tremble with need.

Shaking his head, he reached for his nerve. "No, I don't suppose you would. What I'm trying to say is, tonight, with you, is different than anything I've ever experienced before. Being with you feels good and right. I've never cared this much, never wanted to please a woman the way I want to please you."

She looked away, silent for a few moments. "In bed or out?"

"I'm not going to lie. I'm ready to take this to the next level, but I meant what I said the other night about moving things at your pace." Grasping her chin, he coaxed her to look at him. "What matters most is that being with you makes me happy, Grace. Whatever we're doing, you're what's important to me."

"And if what makes *me* happy is sharing my bed with one very special man, enjoying his friendship, while maintaining my independence? What then?"

The stab to his gut was swift, painful. He couldn't take being a convenient lover. Not anymore. Not with Grace. "You'd give me everything but your heart? You ask a lot of a man, *bella*."

"Yes, I guess I am, at least for now. Am I worth the risk? Are we?"

"Yes," he answered without hesitation. Her words "for now" gave his spirits a lift. "Are you willing to let this be what it is between us, not close yourself off to the possibilities? Am *I* worth the risk? I have some things to tell you, so you might want to wait to answer."

"I don't have to wait," she said, brushing his lips with hers. "I know you're worth it. The problem is me, not you."

The sick dread in his stomach eased a bit. She wasn't closing any doors on what they might have together. He could live with that, for her sake.

For a while, as long as his heart could take the punishment.

"I do want to hear what you have to tell me, though," she continued with a smile. "Take me home?"

"My pleasure." He pressed one more kiss to her mouth, then helped her into the car.

Even with what he had to say looming on the horizon, his soul had lightened somewhat by the time he was back on the highway. What complaints did he really have? This *was* a new beginning, and if he wanted this woman's love, he'd have to earn it the old-fashioned way—by winning her.

Love? *Dios mío, I'm falling for her.*

He had been falling for months, ever since the very first time she tilted up her regal nose and shut him down. And look how far they'd come since then! She'd known he had some growing up to do, and he liked to think he'd succeeded, for the most part. She was here, wasn't she? With him, and no one else.

Bolstered by his inner pep talk, he settled back and basked in her nearness in the dark. In her light, fresh scent he wanted to rub all over his body and let soak into his skin. Damn, it was like he'd been bitten by some sort of exotic bug and she was the only cure for his fever.

At her complex, he parked beside her car and they went inside, a live wire of sexual tension sparking between them. Heaving a deep breath, he called upon every ounce of restraint he possessed to behave as a gentleman should—until he received the signal from her to do otherwise. Which he would. Gladly.

Grace switched on a floor lamp, bathing the living room in a soft, comfy glow, and tossed her purse and keys on the bar. "Can I get you something to drink? Beer or wine?"

"Depends on whether I have to drive any time soon."

"Not unless you want to make a clean getaway." She cocked one hip, giving him a sultry look.

"Honey, when you're ready for me to leave, you'll have to push me out."

"Good. Don't count on escaping too soon." Kicking off her shoes, she padded into the small kitchen. "Let's see, I've got Corona, Merlot, or Chardonnay—"

"How about one of those shots you mentioned?"

"Ah, a man after my own heart. Two Buttery Nipples coming up!" She rummaged around in a cabinet, grabbing two bottles and two shot glasses. "These are more like dessert than anything."

"With a kick."

"Not at first, but they sort of sneak up on you if you're not careful."

Grace joined him, setting the bottles and glasses on the coffee table. "These are really easy to make. Just pour equal parts. You like butterscotch candy?"

"Sure," he said, watching her fix them. She handed one over and he held it up. "A toast to us and whatever the future brings."

"To us!"

They clinked glasses and he took an experimental sip. "Smooth, buttery, and sweet, just like it sounds. It's good. But I'll bet no straight guy would order one of these in a bar."

She giggled. "Probably not. But your rep is safe here, with me."

"Then I'll just have to indulge, won't I?"

"All you'd like. We have all night." She took another sip, studying him for a few seconds, weighing her next words. "Will you tell me now what's on your mind? There's never a great time to share something difficult, and if you don't, it will sit between us until you do."

This was it. He gazed at her expression, and found only concern and caring. He had to believe she'd stand by him. And if he didn't believe in someone, he'd never have peace. "This is really hard. I haven't told anyone this story in almost sixteen years, and the one time I did . . . Let's just say it didn't go well."

"I'm here, and we have booze," she said, attempting to make him smile.

It worked. He toyed with his glass, giving her a grateful look, lips turning up briefly. "Hope you have a good stash. There's no easy way to say this, so I'll just come out with it—when I was fifteen years old, I was molested."

If he'd hit her, he couldn't have shocked her more. "Oh, my God!"

"By Derek Vines," he said softly.

"Oh . . . oh, no," she gasped, hand flying to her mouth. "That's why—sweetie, I'm so sorry. I never would've represented the slimeball if I'd known, and on a sexual harassment charge, no less!"

"Sexual harassment . . . *Cristo*." Coincidence? From his position, it didn't seem likely.

"Why is the asshole still free and not in prison?"

Despite the topic, he couldn't help but be amused by Grace's colorful language. He'd never seen her so undone. "I can't speak for what he's been doing in the years since I knew him, but in my case, the police were never informed."

"What? Why the hell not?"

"I told Mama and my oldest sister, Maria, what I remembered, and they believed me. But we were poor and the Vines family was rich, connected. Mama was alone and afraid of them, with good reason; Warren Vines threatened her to keep me quiet. It also didn't help that Mama was raised to believe that if you ignore a problem, it goes away."

"Only it didn't—not for you," she guessed.

"Not by a long shot." Pausing, he realized Grace believed him. What's more, he had her support. Her strength fortified his own. "It really messed me up. I became depressed, got into drugs. I caused my mother a lot of grief, not to mention a load of guilt."

"Because she felt like she'd let you down?"

"Exactly, and I guess, deep down, part of me wanted to punish her as well as myself. When I was sixteen, I overdosed on enough cocaine to kill a man twice my size. God knows why I didn't die, and for years I resented that I hadn't."

Reaching out, she clasped his hand tightly, squeezed hard. "You were meant to save lives, like the man caught in the flood with his kids that day. That's why you didn't."

Damned if tears didn't sting his eyes. He blinked them back. "It's comforting to think so."

"This is horribly personal and perhaps even a conflict of interest for me to ask, but . . . what happened between you and Derek? If you don't want to get into it, I understand."

"No, it's all right. I really need to tell someone about this because I got a different version of the story today, and I'm damned confused."

She frowned. "From Derek? Tell me you didn't confront him."

"No, from his mother. I went to see Warren at his office today and his wife was there. I told them both what I remembered."

"Good Lord, you didn't! Julian—"

"Yeah, I know. I probably shouldn't have done it, but holding the anger inside was making me sick. Knowing Warren and Derek were here, going about their lives as though they'd never destroyed mine . . . it finally got to me. Warren almost had an aneurysm." He sighed. "I'll admit, I got a certain amount of satisfaction from seeing him almost come unglued."

"You took a risk, Julian." Worry darkened her gaze. "From my dealings with Warren he strikes me as a dangerous man. Someone you don't cross. He's such a control freak, he sat in on the first meeting I had with Derek and he's even phoned me for updates."

"I don't like you being around either of them," he said tightly.

"So you've said, but now I understand why. Go ahead, finish your story."

Julian blew out a breath. "Anyway, while Warren was about two seconds from detonation, his wife was the calm one. What she said threw me for a loop, though it shouldn't have. I mean, what else was she supposed to say but give me a totally innocent explanation for Derek's behavior that day?"

"She was there?"

"So she claims."

Grace paused. "This is what you meant earlier when you said you might have lived your life based on a misconception."

"Yeah. What his mother told me really screwed with my head."

"Why don't you tell me your version first?"

He did, leaving nothing out. Working in the hot summer sun all afternoon, being dizzy with a slight headache. Derek bringing him a cold drink. Blackness.

Awakening naked in Derek's bed, to hands roaming his body.

Grace shuddered. "My God. You don't recall a face, specifically?"

"No. In spite of what Zoe said, I believe he slipped me something. Have you ever been high? Or falling-down drunk to the point that everything seems amplified times twenty? Then the next day your recollections are hazy and disjointed?"

"I was drunk like that in college once. It's an experience I don't ever care to repeat."

"That's how it was for me. I recall touching I swear was inappropriate, and voices. Maybe more than one. I'm positive I wasn't hallucinating—my privates were fondled until I . . . Christ." He hung his head, willing down the awful memory. "Anyway, I finally came to enough to yank on my clothes and stumble home. I remember the doorbell rang, so Derek must've gone to answer it. I took the opportunity to escape while I could."

He paused and when Grace remained silent, he glanced over to see her brow furrowed in thought. "What?"

"I just . . . nothing. Whatever teased my brain is gone," she said, kissing his cheek. "I can't imagine how terrible it must've been. How helpless you felt."

"I've lived with this every day for the past fifteen years, running it over and over in my head, and I'm telling you there's just no way it happened how Zoe claimed."

"So, what was her version?"

"She claimed I passed out from heat exhaustion, and Derek took off my clothing, applied damp cloths to help cool me down. She said I was sick and my brain must've conjured the whole thing."

Grace snorted. "That's ridiculous! I'm glad you didn't buy her stupid story."

"Well, I have to admit she made it sound pretty credible while I was talking to her. But that's probably because I was thrown by her being there, and by how sincere she sounded."

"She could be lying to protect Derek."

They finished their shots and he waited, seeing her chewing on something. Her next question was gentle. Hesitant.

"You've never spoken about this with anyone outside your family, even as an adult? Professionally, I mean."

"A shrink?" He gave a humorless laugh. "No. Not happening."

She patted his hand, glancing down as she rubbed her thumb over the back of it. "Why am I not surprised? I just can't help but wonder . . . no. Never mind."

"What?"

"No, it's none of my business."

"You can ask me anything, Grace." He meant it.

She met his gaze evenly. "I can't help but wonder how this has affected your sexuality."

"I—I'm not sure I follow." But really, he was afraid he did.

Her cheeks flushed a rosy shade. "You've been with a lot of women, and it would make sense that you were trying to . . ."

"Compensate? Prove my masculinity because of what happened to me?"

"Yes, I guess so."

Damn. "To be honest, I suppose a therapist might've said that. And there might even be some truth to it."

"But?"

"I've never been a saint and I won't pretend otherwise," he said, shrugging. "I love sex, and to have a woman underneath me is the most wonderful and natural thing in the world, and I don't think that has a thing to do with any hidden need to prove myself. I like it often and varied."

"Varied how?" She eyed him, truly curious.

"*Bella*," he said with a groan. He was glad to move the topic away from the subject of his trauma, but this? Her eager curiosity wrapped around his balls, enticing his erection to throbbing life.

"Come on, tell me," she coaxed, scooting into his side.

"You're killing me here." He shot her a smile. "All right. I like it slow and easy, or fast and hard, a little rough sometimes if she's willing. I love a little danger, and I'm a bit of an exhibitionist. Do any of these bother you?"

"Not at all—well, except for the rough part. I'm not sure pain sounds like fun."

"There's a fine line between pleasure and pain," he said, trailing one finger down her throat. "And there's nothing like allowing yourself to lose control with a lover you trust implicitly." She arched toward him, pupils large. He could practically smell her arousal mingling with her natural sweet scent.

"Seems I've led a very boring, missionary life. Sounds like you might have the cure."

"I might. Why don't we find out?"

"I don't like to lose control."

"Let me change your mind," he whispered against her lips. He brushed them with a kiss, nibbled her jaw.

"Make love to me, Julian."

"*Dios*, yes." Standing, he pulled Grace to her feet and led her the short distance to her bedroom. When she began to work on the buttons of her blouse, he stepped up and pushed her hands away. "Let me."

She opened her mouth to protest, but nodded instead, watching his face. He planned to strip her barriers, layer by pretty layer.

Parting her blouse, he pushed it off her shoulders. She let it slide to the floor, but his attention was on removing the lacy little scrap of a bra. He flicked the clasp and drew the straps off her shoulders, tossed it down to join the blouse. Next, he unzipped her pants, drawing them over her hips along with her panties, down her legs.

She stepped out of her clothes and he sucked in an appreciative breath. "Beautiful, just like I remember."

"Good thing you're blind."

"You're perfect to me, every inch of you."

His gaze swept from the halo of blond hair flowing loose down her back, to her trim waist and hips, down her slim, coltish legs. True, she wasn't the stacked, curvy bombshell type he'd gone for in the past.

But this was his Grace, and no woman could ever be fit to breathe the same air.

"My turn." Advancing on him, she relieved him of his jacket and shirt. She made short work of his belt, unfastened his pants, and returned the favor, quickly getting him naked.

His erection sprang free, jutting proudly toward her, begging for attention. With a low sound of approval, she reached out and cupped his balls, manipulating them. Groaning, he brushed a hand through her long hair, canting his hips, eager for more. Clever fingers traced his length, dabbed the precum on the cap.

"God, that feels so good," he hissed.

"You are one gorgeous man, Salvatore. Get on the bed and let me taste you."

Lord help him, he did exactly as she said, aware that, for the moment, she'd taken control. For now, he was happy to let her. He spread his legs and she crawled between them, stalking him, amethyst eyes glittering. He thought he'd die of anticipation before she finally licked the head of his cock, and when his shaft was surrounded by her hot, wet mouth, he was certain he would.

"Ahh, shit. Yes, baby . . ."

The glorious suction sent bolts of heaven through his balls, to every limb. Her tongue swirled around him, bathed his cock, laved the sensitive ridge underneath. His breaths were hitching in short gasps, and he knew he'd unravel soon.

"Baby, stop or I'm going to come," he managed.

Crouching over him, she smirked. "Isn't that the idea?"

"Not yet. I want to be inside you, take us there together." Body aching in protest, he sat up and gestured to the middle of the bed. "Get on your hands and knees, *querida*."

She blinked at him, but after a brief hesitation, she complied. Moving into place, she arched her back and spread her knees, poking her tight, round rear into the air.

His cock jumped at the sight, and he moved behind her, smoothing a palm over one creamy globe of her ass as she shivered. Oh, yes. Before he was finished, he'd have her writhing and begging for him. "Stay just like this."

Quickly, he dug a couple of condoms out of his wallet and returned to her, pitching them on the bed beside him. Resting a hand on one butt cheek, he dipped his fingers into her sex, pleased to find her already wet.

"Good girl," he murmured, his tone low, seductive. He began to rub her slit, spreading her cream, loving how she went liquid for him. "You like this, don't you?"

"Y-yes."

"Spread your knees wider. That's it." Gently, he inserted two fingers into her moist channel. Began to pump her, making sure to tease her clit with each stroke. "Tell me how this feels."

"Good," she moaned, wriggling on his hand. "So good."

"Want me to stop? All you have to do is say the word."

"No! Please . . ."

"Please, what? Do you want my cock?"

"Yes! I need you inside me."

Removing his fingers from her sheath, he teased the tender nub of her clit. "Not yet."

She shook her head. "Now! Julian . . ."

"Soon." Crouching, he nuzzled her sex. At her whimper, he gave her slit a long, slow lick, savoring her juices. She shuddered, and he knew then that he'd own her body and soul. He suckled the slick folds, nibbled and flicked. "You're burning up, baby. Ready for me?"

"Hurry," she panted, quivering.

Wetting one finger, he knelt behind her, parted her cheeks. He doubted she'd ever been pleasured this way, and his suspicion was confirmed when he pushed into her tiny rosette— and she nearly exploded in the best possible sense.

"Oh, my God! Oh, God, yes!"

"That's right, baby," he crooned. "Incredible, isn't it? One day, this could be my cock. Would you like that, *bella*?"

"Yes . . . Julian, *please*."

"You're mine, Grace. I'm the only man who'll pleasure you. Do you understand?"

She stiffened, her hoarse response like a slap. "No. I'm not a piece of property."

"Grace—"

"Get off me."

He cursed himself, backing away just a little and urging her to lie on her back. "I'm sorry," he whispered, combing her hair from her face. "I pushed too hard, but it's only because I want you so much. Tell me what to do. What *you* want."

"Just be with me. No demands. Can you do that?"

"For you, anything. Give me another chance?" *Dios, please don't back away from me now. I can't breathe without you.*

At her nod, relief washed over him like a tide. He hadn't messed things up beyond repair. Crawling between her legs, he focused on Grace. On their pleasure, together.

Covering her body like a blanket, he reached between them and rubbed her clit in lazy circles. Kissed her with all the tenderness he possessed, sweeping his tongue into her moist heat. Tasting and probing.

"I need you," she pleaded, breaking away at last. "Inside me, please!"

With those words, nothing could've stopped him. He plucked one of the foil packets from the comforter, ripped it open, and rolled the condom on with practiced ease.

Scooping his hands under her bottom, he lifted her, and then guided the head between the lips of her sex and, in one smooth motion, buried himself balls deep. "Ahh, fuck, yeah."

They were seated together, his balls rubbing against her sex with delicious friction. He remained still for a moment, reveling in finally being inside her, where he belonged, letting her feel him, as well.

"Oh, *Dios mío*," he rasped, and began to move with long, slow strokes. "So good."

All the way out, then in to the hilt. A sensuous slide, claiming the woman under him. She writhed for him, mewling, lost to his taking her. She began to meet his thrusts with abandon, urging him to increase the tempo. He gladly gave his lady what she asked for, fucking her hard and deep, driving into her relentlessly.

"Julian, yes! Oh, God!"

"Come for me, baby. Come on my cock."

She shattered, her cries ringing in his ears, music to his soul. His balls drew up, the familiar quickening gathering at the base of his spine an instant before he shot. Holding her tight, he shouted, the force of his release rolling his eyeballs back in his head. On and on, spasming long after he'd emptied.

Drained at last, he pulled out of her carefully and kissed her forehead. "Be right back."

After disposing of the condom in the bathroom, he hurried to bed and cuddled in behind her, spooning them together. "I'm sorry for before," he said, regret spearing his gut. He stroked her silky hair, feeling like a jerk.

"It's okay. You just hit one of my sore spots."

"I didn't mean to. Are you all right?"

"I am. Better than, so quit worrying."

He heard the smile, the sated quality of her sleepy voice, and relaxed. "Okay."

"Stay?" She yawned.

"Until you tire of me. Sleep, baby."

Safe in her arms, he drifted off, happier and more content than he'd ever been. She hadn't promised him forever, but he'd take what she had to give, and shower her with all the love and affection she deserved. He'd see to her needs, in every way. And maybe one day, he'd own her heart.

God knew she already owned his.

11

Grace awoke to sunshine, a bone-deep sense of satisfaction, and two hundred pounds of warm male pressed half on top of her, whispering sweet Spanish nothings to her nipple.

Her nipple?

Curious, she cracked one eye open—and smiled lazily. Oh, yes. Her insatiable Latin lover was heaping praise upon her breast, tipping one of the shot glasses to dribble creamy brown liquid onto one perky nipple, and licking it off like a cat lapping cream.

"Mmm." She stretched languorously, forking her fingers through his black hair. "What on earth do you think you're doing?"

Grinning like a mischievous boy, he waggled his brows. "Making Buttery Nipples. Whoever invented these was a genius."

"I don't think—oh!—drinking your breakfast is a good idea. Julian!" She giggled, trying to wiggle away.

He pinned her firmly, worrying the peak with his teeth. "Not drinking," he murmured. "Enhancing your already divine flavor. Big difference."

"But—"

"Shh, *bella*. Let me play."

And play he did. *Oh, my.*

He drizzled the liquor down her torso, licking it as he went. With a particularly wicked gleam in his dark eyes, he filled her belly button with the sweet stuff, then sipped it clean. But when he pushed apart her thighs, hooked her calves over his shoulders, and held the glass over her sex, she couldn't stop her surprised squeak.

"You can't be serious!"

He was. The lukewarm liquid bathed her slit as he emptied the shot glass, pitched it aside. Then his wonderful, hot mouth sucked and laved off every drop. After he cleaned her folds, he latched on to her clit, his tongue sending shocks of ecstasy through her nerve endings. He clearly enjoyed what he was doing and she felt herself melting, opening to him as she'd done last night.

Giving herself completely to whatever he wanted, letting him take the lead. And loving it as she never had with any man.

"Yes! Oh, Julian, please!"

This time, he didn't make her beg further, though she would have if he'd demanded it. Vaguely she was aware of his groping the covers for the other condom. Ripping open the package and making himself ready.

And then he covered her, pushed his cock inside, and wrapped himself around her. Holding her, keeping her safe as he made love to her.

Making love. That's what it was. Sweet, passionate love, filling her again and again. If last night had been about bringing out her wild side, this was about his giving back to her tenfold. Showing her without words the depth of his emotion, his commitment.

No man had ever given all of himself to her before, with no promise from her of anything in return.

She watched his handsome face lost in joy, loving the play of his muscles under her fingertips, his gold cross dangling on her breastbone. His eyes caught hers and held as they moved together, the crescendo building, higher, stronger.

Julian's body went taut and his lips parted, his hips jerking in time to his orgasm. His release triggered her own and she joined him, clinging, riding the waves until they floated down together, sated.

"Thank you, *bella*." He kissed her temple and withdrew, rolling onto his back and cradling her against his chest.

For a while, they didn't speak, content to hold each other and contemplate the change in their relationship. Well, at least that's what she was thinking of. He might be daydreaming about his past conquests or the weather, for all she knew.

Raising her head a bit, she glanced up at him and found his expression serious, a slight frown on his face. "What's on your mind?"

"Nothing I care to get into and spoil our nice interlude," he said, stroking her hair.

"Something *is* bothering you. Oh, boy—I think I know what it is." Anxious, she propped herself on her elbow, resting her head in her hand. "We were having such a wonderful evening, I totally forgot to ask you about your visit to the police station. You did go and tell them about your accident and the bartender's death, didn't you?"

"Yeah. I saw Shane Ford. He's the homicide detective who worked Howard's case."

Her stomach sank. "I remember. That means . . ."

"It's official; we've got a serial killer. They have remains of two missing kids, but neither of them are Brett Charles. These were the first two who disappeared ten months ago, and they haven't been dead that long. Ford believes our man is holding them for weeks or months, getting his kicks torturing and doing God knows what else to them, then butchering them."

"Oh, sweet Lord. Charles and the others could still be alive?" While that might give the families hope, she couldn't fathom anything more horrifying than suffering for weeks on end at the hands of a psychopath, waiting to die.

"It's possible. Me, I'd want to go quick and clean."

"You're not *going* anywhere, quickly or otherwise," she said, poking his chest. When he'd been struck, what might've happened if he'd had internal injuries or hit his head a little harder . . . ? God, it was enough to make her sick. "What did he say about you and the bartender? Did he know?"

"Nope. Had no clue, and he was pretty pissed that the information fell between the cracks. I'm sure both so-called accidents will get another hard look. Ford's a thorough guy."

"I hope you're right. If anything happened to you . . ." No. Not going there. The notion was terrifying.

"Hey, I'll be all right," he said, leaning over to kiss her forehead. "Even if the hit-and-run was intentional, I'm sure he won't risk exposure again. The murders have probably hit the news this morning and he'll need to go to ground."

"Maybe he won't have the opportunity to snatch more victims, either. And I can't believe we're even having this conversation. This is unreal."

"I know," he said quietly. "But the police will figure this out and catch him."

As a lawyer, Grace knew this wasn't true the majority of the time. No sense in bringing it up, though.

Exploring, she skimmed a palm down his injured side. "Your bruises are healing nicely. Are you still in any pain?"

"Just a twinge here and there, nothing to worry about," he replied, giving her a reassuring hug.

"Your head?"

"Everything's fine, baby. I was a little sore when I went back to work on Wednesday, but I managed."

She snuggled closer. Damn, it made her warm and fuzzy when he called her by his pet names. Suddenly, he jerked upright, unceremoniously dumping her to the side. "Shit! What time is it?"

Scowling, she sat up and peered at the bedside clock radio. "Almost seven forty-five. Why?"

"Chingado!" Letting loose a stream of rapid-fire curses, he leaped from the bed. "I'm late! I was supposed to be on shift at seven!"

"Whoops." Eyeing his fine, naked backside as he disappeared into the bathroom, she stifled a giggle. "Sorry! If you'd reminded me, I would've set the alarm," she called out as the shower started.

"Evil woman, already leading me down the path to destruction," he yelled back.

"Well! Five minutes ago I was your baby."

Ducking out of the bathroom, he trotted over and planted a steamy kiss on her mouth. "You are. I wouldn't risk Sean's wrath for just anyone, and don't forget it, either." With that, he vanished again.

She did laugh then. Couldn't help it. The man was far too endearing for his own good—or hers.

Humming, she padded to the closet and donned her pink terry cloth robe, started a pot of coffee, and switched the television on to CNN. The coffee was only halfway finished when Julian strode into the room wearing his rumpled clothing from last night.

"If you can wait another two minutes, I can send a travel mug of coffee with you." The drive to Sugarland, she knew, would take at least thirty minutes with morning traffic, if not longer. She couldn't imagine dashing out without coffee.

"That's sweet of you, but I have to run," he said, taking her into his arms. He held her for a few seconds, nuzzling her cheek, her hair. "Wish I didn't have to go."

"Me, too. Sure you can't call in sick?"

He bit his lip, appearing tempted. "I'd better not. I think we should all be at work together, make a show of solidarity, since we had the intervention yesterday. Did you know about that?"

She nodded. "Kat told me the basics—not to gossip, it's just that she and Howard are so worried. She said Sean didn't cooperate."

"It went better than I thought it would, but he still refused to go for treatment. Things could be sticky around the station for a while." He kissed her cheek, eyes warm as they met hers. "Can I see you tomorrow? We can go for a drive, get some lunch. Whatever you want."

"I'd love that," she said, smoothing a hand over his chest. "Call me in the morning."

"Will do. I'll miss you, *bella*."

"Same here. Be careful out there."

"No worries."

Leaning into her, he gave her a brief, soft kiss, then was gone. After the door closed and his Porsche rumbled away, she stood in the middle of the living room as the latest disaster blared over CNN, and contemplated the long, lonely Saturday ahead of her.

How the heck should she fill the hours? Funny how this had never been a problem before. The condo—her entire world—seemed stark and empty. As though when he left, he'd taken all the light with him.

With a sigh, she headed for the shower, giving herself a stern pep talk. Tomorrow wasn't so far off. Besides, it wasn't like she needed a man to make her happy. She'd been flying solo forever, and she'd done fine, too. She wasn't going to pine for a man even if the sexy beast had spent the past twelve hours wining, dining, and making mind-blowing love to her.

Was. Not.

Blinking, she looked around the bathroom and realized she'd been standing in front of the mirror, bath towel in hand, letting the water run.

"Well, crap." Twenty-four hours until she could see Julian again. Might as well fess up.

Being alone really sucked.

Julian cursed all the way to work. When he wasn't replaying last night and this morning with Grace and grinning like a jackass. The woman had his balls in a hammerlock. She was worth every second of the shit he'd get from Captain Hard-ass over being late.

An hour and a half late, by the time he sprinted inside.

"Oh, man," Tommy crowed, glancing up from helping Zack polish the quint. "Did you bring us flowers, too?"

Zack laughed. "Woo-woo! Guess that explains a lot."

"Shitheads," he muttered, shrugging off his sport jacket. "Is the captain pissed?"

Tommy parked his butt against the fender. "I'm not sure he even knows you weren't here. He said good morning to me and Eve, went into his office with Six-Pack, and they've been holed up in there ever since."

"Yeah? He seem okay after the deal yesterday?"

"I wouldn't know. That's all he said, man. Ought to be interesting." Tommy waved a hand at Julian. "Get in there and change, and he might not have a clue. I'm not gonna say jack."

"Me, either." Zack shrugged and went back to polishing.

"I've had my hole ripped plenty by him. Wouldn't wish it on anybody, even you."

"Why, thanks, buddy. You're a regular Hallmark card."

"Don't mention it."

Leaving the two dickwads laughing at his expense, Julian crept inside, scouting for the big bad wolf. Eve, in the kitchen munching half a bagel, smiled when she spotted him.

"Duck when you walk by the office," she advised. "They're still in there."

He shot her a grateful look. "Thanks, Evie. Nice to know I can count on someone not to give me grief."

"Oh, I will. I'm just not awake yet."

He grinned and headed for the hallway leading to the rooms where they shared bunks. Unfortunately, he had to pass the office to get to the room he shared with Six-Pack. When he crouched and made his way past, he was relieved not only to get by undetected but to hear that their voices were calm. Whatever they were discussing, they weren't arguing.

He stripped and changed quickly, and had been hanging out in the kitchen with Eve for less than a minute when the duo finally emerged from the office.

"Close frigging call," he muttered, for Eve's ears only.

She snorted. "Was she worth it?"

"Oh, *yeah*."

"Was who worth what?" Howard asked, making a beeline for the coffeepot.

"The Porsche. She's worth every penny I paid," he said, filching the other half of Eve's bagel.

"Uh-huh," the lieutenant drawled, not buying a word.

Like he was going to tell a man who topped him by five inches and outweighed him by sixty pounds that he'd been banging his sister-in-law like it was last roll call to heaven.

Of course, he was serious about Grace, so—

Holy Christ, what if he and Six-Pack ended up related?

He sucked the bagel down his windpipe, choking and coughing. Eve pounded his back, short on sympathy.

"That's what you get for stealing my breakfast."

"My bad." He coughed again, accepting a glass of water from Six-Pack. "Thanks."

Sean leaned a hip against the counter, studying him with his piercing green gaze, but without the surly attitude Julian might've expected. "Running late this morning?"

Julian set the glass down and braced himself. He didn't have it in him to lie to this man. Not after all they'd been through. "Yes, sir. I just got here."

The captain considered this for a moment. "I think that's the most direct answer I've ever gotten out of you, Salvatore."

"Probably so," he agreed, waiting for the other shoe to drop. "Am I in trouble? Want me to scrub the toilets?"

"Won't be necessary. You're still a smart-ass, though." And then the most incredible thing happened—Sean smiled. A sincere one, offered like an olive branch.

After almost a year and a half of hell living with the captain around the station, the gesture was so unexpected Julian was hesitant. "You're not going to ream me?"

"Not unless you make it a habit." Smile turning sad, Sean clapped a hand on his shoulder. "I remember when I had a reason to be late. Enjoy every minute you can."

The captain strode out the door into the bay, and Julian stared after him, stunned. "Jesus."

"That's the closest I've heard him come to mentioning his family in over a year," Eve murmured, eyes trained on the exit. "Right out in the open, too. He's finally trying."

"He is," Howard said in concern. "But he's got a long way to go."

Julian swung his attention to the lieutenant, thinking it couldn't be easy being Sean's best friend. In fact, the stress must be really tough, especially walking the tightrope between the job and their relationship. But Six-Pack never complained, a testament to his strength and loyalty.

A call to a traffic accident curtailed any further discussion on the matter, and Julian wasn't sorry. His thoughts were occupied by a certain blond siren on her hands and knees, begging him to pound her hard.

Screaming when she came.

He knew he ought to focus on the nagging feeling he was missing something important regarding the Brett Charles kidnapping, but the feeling was like walking through a spiderweb. He wanted to brush it off his skin and think about happier subjects.

Like spending tomorrow with the woman he loved.

After some debate, Grace decided on casual. Khaki shorts and a red tank top were just the thing for a Sunday outing. Lunch, maybe a walk. No big deal.

A day alone, looking over some of her files, straightening the condo, and she felt almost normal again. Not so bereft or needy over Julian's absence. Order, control, and reason were blessedly restored. What a relief!

She enjoyed spending time with her hot fireman, looked forward to seeing him. But a little time and distance went a long way toward reminding her that she wasn't falling for him. He was a good friend who happened to be a fantastic lover. He fell into a nice, neat category in her life and surely he'd agree they were good together this way.

The knock on her door brought a surge of happiness and she had to check the impulse to rush to the door and fling it open. She was cool as a cucumber—but that didn't stop her pulse from racing at the sight of him on her threshold.

He wore a pair of cargo shorts hanging low on his waist, a snug blue T-shirt, tennis shoes, and a pair of dark wraparound sunglasses. A slice of flat, tanned belly between the edge of his shirt and the waistband of his shorts caught her eye. *Hot damn.* If they didn't get going, she'd drag him into her bedroom and let him have his way. Again.

Before he uttered a word, he drew her in for a blistering kiss. "Ready?"

"You bet."

She locked the door and they were on their way, to where she wasn't sure. "Got a destination in mind?"

"I do, that is, if you like fish."

"I love fish. Any kind, grilled, baked, or fried."

"Great! Why don't we head over to my neck of the woods and go to Riverview? It's a catfish restaurant overlooking the Cumberland, but they've got steaks and other stuff if you're hungry for something else."

"Oh, I like that place! I've been there once with my parents and Kat."

"It's nothing fancy, but the view is awesome."

"Thus the name."

He gave her a boyish grin. "Clever, huh?"

"Hey, it's all about marketing. People know exactly what they're going to get."

He held the car door open for her, gave her a pointed look. "If only all of life were the same."

"True."

Once they were under way, the smooth, upbeat strains of Carlos Santana filled the silence. Tapping her foot to the rhythm, Grace took the opportunity to study Julian's handsome profile, and wondered, not for the fist time, at the positive change in him over the past few months. If she were looking for forever—which she wasn't—was he the real deal?

Leopards and spots, he'd said. For his sake, she hoped he was simply learning to love the spots.

Twenty-five minutes later, he turned down the steep drive leading to the restaurant. Inside, the lunch crowd was thinning some and they were shown to a table. They both ordered iced tea and perused their menus, or she tried to, but couldn't stop eyeing how he'd perched his sunglasses on top of his head. Did he have to be so freaking cute that every waitress in the room appeared to be considering him for the daily special?

"I'm doing the lunch buffet," he said, snapping his menu closed. "Too many choices to decide."

"Sounds good." Laying her menu on top of his, she glanced out the window. "I've always loved the water, especially the Cumberland. It's always so peaceful and lazy."

"Usually it is. Looking at the calm surface now, it's hard to believe we almost lost Zack out there during a storm. Right there by the bridge, in fact," he said, pointing.

She grimaced. "How could I have forgotten?"

"It's easy to take for granted when you're not the one called to get people out of tight situations. To me, water rescues are the most dangerous, because of the brute force— tons of pressure per square inch. A rushing current during a flood can twist a hunk of iron or steel into a pretzel."

The waitress placed their glasses of tea on the table and told them to help themselves to the buffet. When she'd moved away, Grace said, "I heard you saved Zack's life."

He shook his head. "We all did our part. Six-Pack took

the real risk going in to get him." Standing, he held out a hand to lead her to the buffet.

Clearly, he was uncomfortable discussing how his teammate had nearly died, and his own heroics. She let it drop, and her opinion of him rose several notches.

In the line, she filled her plate with more food than a sailor could eat and eyeballed Julian's plate to see he had twice as much. The man must burn a load of energy to consume so much and not be as big as a tent!

Thinking of how he'd expended some last night, she flushed hot.

Once they were seated, she dug into a piece of catfish, crispy on the outside and flaky inside. Perfect. She'd have to walk around the block twice this evening to work off this meal, but it was worth every bite.

"Good?" He grinned, that darned dimple flashing.

"Excellent. If I keep eating with you, I'm going to grow a bubble butt."

"Not a chance. We'll work it off." The twinkle in his eye told her how, too.

"Really? Suppose you tell me how."

"I think I'll surprise you instead."

"I can live with that."

They finished their lunch, enjoying pleasant chitchat, trading anecdotes about their families. Grace was amused listening to stories about Julian's brother and sisters. She couldn't fathom living with five siblings, but Julian made the chaos sound fun, for the most part. It was obvious he loved them very much.

At last, he pushed his plate away. "Why don't we—"

"Jules! I thought that was you!"

Grace swiveled her head in the direction of the high-pitched feminine squeal and wished she hadn't. An absolutely gorgeous woman who could've been Carmen Electra's twin swooped in on their table—or more accurately on "Jules"— and wrapped him in an enthusiastic hug before he could even rise completely out of his seat.

"*Dulce*, it's good to—hmmf!"

While Julian, to his credit, did his best to disengage, his friend greeted him with a big, noisy kiss. On the mouth. Grace stared, feeling a bit like she'd been hit between the eyes with a hammer.

Dulce? He gives all of his women pet names?

Well, wasn't that fucking precious?

The girl ceased attempting to suck out Julian's tonsils and beamed at Grace. Who remained seated and gave the interloper a deadly smile usually reserved for her opponents in the courtroom. The one that said, *I spread people like you over my toast for breakfast every morning.*

The message wasn't received. "Hello! You must be Grace!"

"Well, yes, um—"

"Oh, Jules, no wonder you've been a stranger," she said, poking him in his uninjured side and taking the seat next to him.

The woman knew her name. And Jules had been a stranger. Those facts began to compute, and her fangs receded. But only halfway.

Julian sat down again and shot Grace an apologetic half smile, looking like he'd inhaled a bug. "Grace, this is my friend Carmelita Gutierrez; Carmelita, Grace McKenna." He glanced back at Grace, his laugh a bit desperate. "Carmelita has listened to me talk about you for hours. She's an awfully good sport."

"I'll bet."

Julian's friend leaned forward and spoke in a faked conspiratorial whisper. "We hardly ever talk anymore, and when we do, it's nothing but 'Grace this' and 'Grace that.' It's great to finally meet the woman who stole him away from me."

"I beg your pardon?" She narrowed her gaze at the woman, trying to decide if she was being sincere or catty.

"Well, Jules and I go way back, grew up together in San Antonio. After I moved here a few years ago, we got tight again. Shoot, we've been about as close as two people can be without tying the knot and popping kids. But we've never been serious like *that*. Sometimes you just need a friend to help you scratch the itch." She snagged a fry from Julian's plate and waved it at Grace. "You know how it is."

Speechless, Grace looked at Julian for guidance on how to field this conversation. But *Jules baby*, who had his face in his hands, looked about one second away from a coronary.

Alrighty. No help there. Grace forced what she hoped was a pleasantly blank expression. "And have you found a boyfriend to . . . scratch your itch?" *See me not leap across the table and throttle her.*

"There is someone I'm wild for, and he finally knows I'm alive," Carmelita said brightly. She laid a hand on Julian's arm. "Konrad asked me out!"

He blinked at her. "Who?"

"Where *are* you lately? Hell-oo. The guy I've been telling you about for weeks."

"Oh, yeah," he croaked. "Right. The techie geek."

She rolled her eyes. "He works with me at Fossier, for the tenth time. Don't you ever listen?"

"I'm a guy. My job is to pretend I'm listening."

"And to agree to everything the lady says."

"Pretty much."

As Grace listened to the dialogue bouncing between them, a couple of facts became crystal clear. One, these two shared a deep affection for each other, and the ache it caused in her chest didn't bear thinking about. Second, Carmelita didn't seem to have a mean, sneaky bone in her body. The woman was guileless and friendly, and that made it damned hard to dislike her.

Except for the part where she and Julian had been lovers. Frequently.

Yeah, girlfriend. That smacking noise is your cosmic bitch-slap of a reality check. Did you think his lovers were magically beamed to another planet the second he slept with you?

Did you honestly think you were his first fuck buddy?

Oh, God. That's what hurt most of all. They were childhood friends who shared a bond. The knockout babe next to him had enjoyed a loving, intimate relationship with him long before Grace had arrived on the scene.

She'll likely be around after he tires of waiting for me.

"Excuse me," Grace said, attempting to sound normal. "I need to use the ladies' room."

And then she fled. As quickly as she dared, before either of them noticed the tears stinging her eyes. What had possessed her to be so arrogant as to believe she could keep Julian's heart on a string? To think she'd just rock along, using him as her comfortable blanket with no regard for his feelings?

Carmelita might not love him in a romantic sense, but she was proof that this man didn't exist in a plastic bubble. Someone would love him one day the way he deserved.

But Grace didn't know whether she had it in her to be that someone.

In the restroom, she washed her hands and dabbed at her eyes with a tissue. Returning all splotchy wasn't an option.

She'd nearly succeeded in restoring a modicum of control when the restroom door swung open and Carmelita sauntered inside. She walked over and cocked a hip against the counter, all traces of the friendly airhead wiped from her face.

"Buck up, sister, because you and I need to talk."

12

Grace stiffened, every cell in her body prepared for battle. "I don't think so."

"Oh, but I do." The woman examined one red nail. "I don't have any designs on your boyfriend. Julian and I are close, but we're not in each other's hip pocket."

Grace opened her mouth to deny Julian was her boyfriend, but the words wouldn't form. "That's interesting to know, but I can't see why you'd feel the urge to tell me."

"Really? Then you're not nearly as smart as he says you are." She sighed. "Listen, I've never seen Julian gone over a woman before. He's been with one after another because nobody ever held his attention. Now he's head over heels and I've got to worry about him because nobody else will."

"I'm not planning to hurt him," she protested. A twinge of guilt pricked her conscience. "But we are still feeling out our relationship, and I'd appreciate being able to do that without his friends' well-meaning interference."

"Well, tough shit. Are you jerking him around?"

"Wow, you have a lot of nerve. . . ." The nasty retort hovering on her lips sputtered and died. Something about Carmelita's expression stopped it cold. A flicker of pain? This was more than the concern of a close friend. When it hit her, she felt numb. "You love him."

The other woman's gaze skittered away, and the fight left her posture. She didn't reply, but she didn't have to.

"Does he know?" Grace asked softly.

"No, and he won't." She gave a laugh tinged with sadness. "All these years, I'd have given anything if he would've looked at me, just once, the way he looks at you. I followed him halfway across the country, and he still never got a clue. Or maybe he didn't want to—who knows?"

Against her will, a wave of sympathy arose for the woman. "I've never been in your position, so I won't presume to claim to know how hard it must be. I *am* truly sorry."

"Isn't it ironic? He's got all the love he could ever want right here if he'd just open his eyes," she said, hand over her own heart. "Yet he's crazy about you, and I have to wonder if you feel the same about him."

"I am crazy about him! I adore him, Carmelita. Believe that," Grace said firmly.

"Yeah? Well, believe this. I grew up in one of the toughest barrios in San Antonio, and we take care of our own." Straightening, she fixed Grace with a grim smile. "I want to like you, and if you make him happy, maybe I will. But you break his heart, and I'll break you."

Carmelita turned and strode from the restroom, leaving Grace trembling. Not because of Carmelita's threat, but from the sharpness of her observations. If she'd noticed Grace holding back, so had Julian, at least deep down.

If she didn't get her head screwed on straight, she *would* hurt him. Badly. He deserved to be loved.

But do I deserve him?

How sad that she'd once kept Julian at arm's length because she believed he needed fixing, when all along it was she who was a mess. Pulling herself together, she hurried back to him, to try to salvage the rest of their day.

Julian picked at the rest of his fries, his appetite gone. He could strangle Carmelita and not suffer an ounce of remorse. Shit! What in the hell were they doing in there? Jesus, not cat-fighting. Please.

As if his thoughts conjured her, Carmelita emerged from the back of the restaurant and made her way toward him. She appeared tense, upset, but not irate. Well, he *was* pissed and she'd better get ready.

"Scratching our itch?" he hissed as she drew near. "What the hell was that about? Did you have to go and rub her nose—"

Leaning down, she kissed him on the mouth. "Gotta run. I'll call you."

"What? Get back here!"

But she was already moving off, dashing out the exit.

"Lovers' quarrel?"

Fuck! Reluctantly, he met Grace's pretty eyes as she sat down. Dammit, he couldn't read her. "She's not my lover, not since before you and I started seeing each other."

"Oh, for a whole week, then? Lovely."

"It's been almost a month." Christ, that sounded awful, no matter how a guy phrased it. "You *know* I haven't been celibate, Grace. What do you want me to say? That I shut myself in my condo and cried into my Patrón for months because you wouldn't give me the time of day?"

He'd die before telling her he'd moped his fair share.

"Not in the least. But I prefer not to trade bedtime stories with my boyfriend's former playmate. Call me strange," she said drily.

"I'm sorry, *bella*. I don't know what came over her—'boyfriend'?" His pulse gave a kick and his stomach did a funny flip.

Shrugging, she shot him a small smile. "Slip of the tongue. I haven't had one since high school, so what do I know?"

"Oh." He studied the table, at a complete loss. He couldn't guess what she expected of him, and frankly, he was exhausted from trying. A change of subject was in order. "Say, um, why don't we walk down to the dock at the bottom of the hill when we're finished eating and catch one of the boat rides up the river?"

"I'd love to."

It wasn't every day a man found himself in a sticky spot between two women—and not in a pleasurable context.

When they were done, he paid the bill and they walked down to the dock to await the next tour. Grace seemed okay at first, if a bit distant. She slipped her hand into his and some of the clouds diminished around his mood. Yet when he attempted to nuzzle her neck, steal a kiss, she turned her head and pulled away. Her withdrawal hurt something fierce.

Once the boat was under way, she sat close by his side. But emotionally, leagues lay between them. A deep, chilly chasm he didn't know how to bridge.

"Grace, I'm sorry."

"For what? For living your life before I came along?"

He had no answer for that one. Nothing that wouldn't dig him a deeper hole than ever.

He wondered if guys like Six-Pack would agree falling in love was damned hard work. If so, it was a miracle anyone ever did.

Near the point where the boat turned around to head back, however, it suddenly struck Julian that they were very close to the section of river where the two kids' bodies had been found.

Again, the spiderweb brushing his skin.

Later, he told himself. *Not now.*

After they disembarked from the boat, Julian drove them across the bridge to Stratton's for an ice cream, searching for another way to stretch the afternoon. He wished he could count on spending time with Grace this evening, either at her place or his, but the chance meeting with Carmelita had put a strain on things. Temporarily, he hoped. In any case, he sure didn't want to come across like he expected to get her naked, considering. He *did* want to, of course; he just didn't want to act like it.

Too soon, they were cruising to her place. When he pulled up in front of her building, his dread proved a reality. She shouldered her purse and laid a hand on his, giving him a sweet smile.

"Thank you for today. I really enjoyed spending it with you."

In other words, *Get lost.* Despite today's promising beginning, there would be no repeat of their last time together. He tried to smile back, but his face wouldn't cooperate. "I'm really sorry about lunch. Too much reality, huh?"

"A little, yeah. But I'm a big girl. The truth is, I also have court in the morning and I have files I need to study tonight if I hope to be ready. Rain check?"

Okay, make that *Get lost—for now.*

"How about dinner at my place tomorrow night? I'll cook." He'd never felt so exposed in his life, feelings waving like a banner.

She bit her lip, considering. "I'll call on my lunch break and let you know. Work for you?"

"Sure, baby." He brushed a flyaway strand of hair from

her cheek, then leaned over and gave her a thorough kiss, tongue sweeping into her heat, curling with hers. Just in case she thought he'd give up easily.

She broke away and opened the door, and he was pleased to see she was flushed, glancing at him as though having second thoughts about sending him off.

"Bye, Julian."

"Adiós, bella."

He watched until she disappeared inside, then pounded the steering wheel in frustration. "Goddammit!"

He had half a mind to call Carmelita and bawl her out. What in the hell had she been thinking? But he was so pissed he didn't even want to speak to her, which shook him. And saddened him, too, because something between them had changed with her stunt today.

She'd been his one constant for years, and now . . . he was standing on quicksand waiting to go under. Reaching for a dream he might never realize.

At home, he tossed his sunglasses, wallet, and keys on the bar, kicked off his shoes, and booted up his computer. Might as well make use of his empty evening.

Hoping to distract himself, he surfed the Internet for a while, reading online news and playing computer games. Eventually, however, his thoughts turned to Warren Vines and their confrontation. And to a story he wasn't convinced was true.

He spent a while searching the Net for any mention of the Vines family. Nothing, except a couple of blasé business articles on Warren as the head of W. H. Vines, his son Derek at his side like a good lapdog. About the company's move from Texas to Tennessee. Julian let his mind drift, and his thoughts snagged on something Grace had said the previous night.

Derek. Up against a sexual harassment charge. Because someone had found the nerve to stand up to him, as Julian hadn't done. What if Derek had molested other boys and in fact had never stopped in all these years?

What if . . .

"No." The idea was too fantastic. Too horrendous.

But he sat up straighter and decided to search anyway. Starting with something simple, he Googled *Murders in San Antonio 1994*. And promptly got over half a million hits. After checking the first couple of pages, he cursed. He'd never find anything this way. Some of the links were about specific cases that went to trial long ago. Some cases had never been solved. Some of the links were garbage.

Narrowing his search, he typed in *cold cases* after his original phrase. Right on the first page, a link close to the top was one he should've thought of, especially after speaking with Ford on Friday.

The San Antonio PD's Web site had a section dedicated to cold cases, so he clicked on the link. And what a creepy frigging section it was. Murder victims were listed in order of the year they were killed, beginning in the 1970s. There was a photo of the victim on the left and a paragraph on the right describing the circumstances surrounding his death.

Face after face. Both young and old, all lives cut short before their time. *Dios*, their stories made him sad. Before he knew it, he got caught up and spent more than a half hour reading the first few. Coming up for air, he realized he hadn't even scratched the surface. Wading through all these would take hours, possibly days.

What he was looking for might not even be there. This was why the searching was best left to the cops, who knew what they were doing.

What he needed was help from a cop he trusted. Phoning

Tonio crossed his mind, but he nixed that idea, fast. Tonio hated keeping secrets from Mama as much as Julian did, and he didn't want her getting wind of this.

Which left one person Julian knew of.

He half expected to get Shane Ford's voice mail, and was surprised when the man answered.

"Detective Ford. Can I help you?"

"Detective, this is Julian Salvatore. I need a favor."

The guy gave a short laugh. "You and everybody else. I'll want a good reason."

"Because it might relate to your murder investigation."

This got Ford's attention, and his tone sharpened. "How so?"

He paused, hoping he wasn't about to make a first-class fool out of himself. "I need you to use your pull to research any disappearances or murders of young adults that may have taken place in San Antonio, Texas, fifteen years ago. Maybe even further back."

A weighty pause. "What, might I ask, would that have to do with my case?"

"Call me paranoid, but not over the phone. I'll come by tomorrow and tell you."

"Listen, what are you doing right now?"

"Long weekend, and I'm beat. I'm going to crack open a beer and catch a baseball game."

"Tell you what—save me a brew and I'll come there," Ford suggested. "I'm not really on duty, just putting in some OT."

Despite his dread of spilling his story to the cop, Julian grinned. Ford was an okay guy. "You got it."

"Be there in ten."

Julian pressed the end button, waited a couple of seconds, and made another call.

Sometimes, a man just needed to hear his mother's voice.

"Hello?"

The sound of the cheerful voice on the other end made his throat burn. "Hi, Mama."

"*Hijo!* What have you been doing that you don't have time to answer when your mama phones? I've left two messages since Friday, and nothing! Are you all right?"

"I'm sorry, Mama." Seemed like all he'd been doing today was apologizing. He could picture his mama puffed up like a bantam rooster. "I'm fine. How's Tonio?"

"Humph. Why don't you call and ask him yourself?" But she relented and her voice softened with love and worry. "He works too hard. And the cut in his side isn't healing, *hijo*. He thinks his mama don't know, but I see how he favors it. He's tired, but he won't take any sick days."

Shit. "I'll call him. I promise."

"Good. Maybe he'll listen to his big brother."

He doubted it, but for Mama, anything. "And the girls? How are they?"

"Haven't you spoken with your sisters?"

"Not lately," he admitted, feeling guilty. "I've been busy."

"Well, Maria and Liza are pregnant again, and Sal and Robert are strutting around like peacocks. Constance is dating a nice young man who's a hotel manager on the River Walk. Tawny is still at home, fussing at me to take my medication." She heaved an exasperated breath. "I don't think that one ever plans to leave the nest."

Julian laughed. "You don't fool anyone. You'll cry for a month when she takes off."

"How are *you*, my baby? And don't tell me 'fine' again, because I know better. The tone of your voice never lies."

His amusement died. He didn't want to panic her, but there were times in a man's life when he still needed his mother's advice. Her support. "Honestly, I don't know. I . . . I've fallen in love."

"Oh! *Madre de Dios!* Truly? *Hijo*, this is wonderful!"

Wincing, he interrupted before she could launch a barrage of questions. "But she doesn't love me." God, his voice had cracked.

Several beats of silence passed as she weighed this. "Oh, *hijo*. How can you be certain? The woman who's finally captured your heart must be very special. And she must know what a wonderful man you are," she insisted.

"Grace enjoys my company, but I'm not sure she wants more. As in the whole picket fence–and-kids deal. She's a successful lawyer, beautiful and smart. But she's independent and she doesn't like her applecart upset. Why should she give up what she's got for a blue-collar guy like me?"

"Nonsense! If she's so smart, she'll grab hold before you get away and never let go! Besides, she doesn't have to give up anything and has everything to gain. Once she realizes that, she'll come around. Mark my words."

Julian swallowed hard. "Thanks, Mama. I needed to hear a friendly voice on my side tonight."

"I'll always be on your side," she said gently. "Are you sure nothing else is wrong? You still don't sound like yourself."

I don't feel like myself.

He longed to tell her. About witnessing Brett Charles and the man leaving the club. About the hit-and-run. The bodies.

His growing suspicions about who might be behind it all.

The whole horrible ordeal hovered on the tip of his tongue. If he spilled this, they'd be forced to rehash the painful past, which would hurt her. And then she'd be on the first plane out, put herself in the middle, and possibly into danger.

"No, Mama," he said in a low voice. He hated lying to her, and knew she suspected. "I'm just tired."

"All right. When you're ready to tell me what is wrong, I'll be here. *Te amo.*"

"Love you, too," he whispered.

Hanging up, he replaced the phone on the desk and went into the living room, considered tidying some, and decided, *Screw it.* He was having a beer with another dude, not a date. Grabbing a Bud from the fridge, he popped the top and made an experimental toast.

"Here's to single guys drinking, belching, and watching the damned game. With no women around to bitch about it."

Didn't make him feel any better, but it sounded appropriately rebellious.

The knock at the door snagged his attention and he went over and peered out the peephole before opening the door to Ford. "Shit, you look as wiped as I feel."

"You ain't lyin'." Ford swaggered in with a lean-hipped stride and ran a hand through his longish brown hair. "Nice digs."

"Thanks. Have a seat and let me get you a cold one. Bud okay? Or I've got Corona."

"Bud's fine, thanks." He flopped into Julian's recliner with a heavy sigh. "Goddamn, I could sit here and die. Happily."

"Tough week, I'll bet, with the murders hitting the news. Here you go, Detective."

"Shane."

"What?"

"You can call me Shane. We have mutual friends and I *am* drinking your beer, after all."

"Oh, right." An overture of friendship? Cool. He didn't get those often—from guys, anyway. "Well, bottoms up, Shane."

They took a few healthy swigs of their brews, and Julian wiped his mouth, eyeing the other man. "You ever been married?"

"Close a couple of times, but nope. No wife. You?"

Julian rolled his eyes. "I'm seeing somebody, or at least I hope I still am. And let me tell you, love sucks."

"I'll drink to that."

They did, and damned if they weren't ready for another round. He fetched them and handed one over.

"Guess I'd better go easy on these if I'm going to drive later. That would be a major bitch to add to my week, one of my own arresting my ass."

"Stay as long as you need to. The game will be on soon and you're welcome to hang out."

"I might take you up on the offer," he said with a nod. "First, though, I want to know about this extracurricular research project of yours. With the angle on the young people, I assume you're grasping at some sort of connection between any murders that might have occurred fifteen or more years ago and the ones here. The question is, why San Antonio and that time frame in particular?"

Shit, here we go. "It's just a hunch, based on something that happened to me when I was fifteen. Probably nothing, but I don't have the resources you do to look into it, except for using the Internet, and news articles won't give me the police angle from the inside."

Shane waited, the picture of patience and genuine interest. The cop wasn't simply humoring him, and that bolstered his confidence enough to spill. He related the entire story of his hazy, frightening encounter with Derek Vines, just as he'd told Grace. He capped it off by confessing his visit to Warren's office, and the conflicting tale Zoe told him.

When he was finished, Shane studied him for a few moments and whistled through his teeth. "That's a helluva story."

"There's something else—Derek is defending himself right now on a sexual harassment charge."

"Interesting, but circumstantial." Shane frowned. "Though it's pretty much common knowledge that sex offenders don't stop. They continue for years and escalate until they're caught. Not that this is true in Derek's case."

"You don't believe me?"

"Didn't say that. But since you didn't go to the police back then, there's no official record."

"Sonofabitch, why do I have to go through this every single—"

The detective held up a hand to forestall his tirade. "I'm not berating you, just stating a fact. You told your family, and the sad reality is, most young victims don't even go that far. You're to be commended for dealing with it as well as you have."

"So . . . you do believe I was molested?"

"I wasn't there, but it does sound pretty frigging creepy. In any case, I can see *you* believe it."

"And what if Derek was never caught? What if he *has* escalated?" Julian leaned forward. "Cody and I both saw Brett Charles with the older man and now he's dead. What if my hit-and-run wasn't an accident at all? Once these questions got stuck in my head, I knew I wouldn't be able to get rid of them until they're put to rest. Will you help me?"

"Since you've raised the question, it would be irresponsible of me not to, so yes. I'll make some calls, see what we can learn. It's a long shot, though," he cautioned.

Julian hadn't been aware of the elephant sitting on his chest until that moment. His breath left him in a rush. "I know, but I appreciate you checking."

"Now, how about that game?" Shane grinned, kicking his feet up.

Drinking beer, eating chips and Julian's homemade salsa, munching popcorn, and yelling at the television, he spent the most enjoyable three hours he could recall in quite a while—outside of being with Grace. Having someone over just to hang out was cool, and he wondered why he'd never had his team here before. He made a mental note to change that one day soon.

When the game ended, Shane stood and stretched. "Man, thanks for your hospitality. If you want, we could grab a beer at the Waterin' Hole sometime."

"Sounds good. How about when you have something for me?" He shook the detective's hand and saw him out.

"That'll work. I'll let you know what I find out, but it might take a few days."

"Okay. Take it easy."

"Back atcha."

After Shane left, he tossed the cans, put away the snacks, and watched a stupid reality show until his eyes crossed. He thought about calling Grace, but it was getting late and his brain was fogged from too many brewskis. Something told him that waking her up to slur in her ear wasn't the best way to win her.

Walking into the bedroom, he stripped down to his boxers and crawled between the sheets with a grateful sigh. In a minute he dropped headfirst into the sleep of the dead, deep and dreamless. Which was why, sometime later, he couldn't have said precisely what awakened him.

A prickle on the back of his neck. The sensation of eyes boring into him. A whisper of sound.

Lying on his back, very still, he cracked his lids open.

To see a dark figure standing over his bed, swinging something silver toward his chest.

13

With a yell, Julian rolled to his left, away from his attacker, as something hard glanced off his arm. He dived off the side of the bed but became tangled in the sheets, and the bastard was on him in an instant, the metal in his hand flashing in the moonlight.

Knife. Fucker's got a knife!

Twisting onto his back, he caught the arm inches from his chest, straining to hold off the attacker's weight. The tip of the blade quivered above his heart, the man grunting, cursing behind a ski mask, determined to achieve his deadly goal.

Since Julian was using both hands to hold the man's arm, he was unprotected when the guy grabbed his hair with his free hand and slammed the back of his head into the floor. Once, twice, three times, and Julian's vision exploded into stardust.

His grip loosened for a split second and the tip pierced his skin, and he knew he'd lose a contest of brute strength this way. Head spinning, he bucked, dislodging the guy, then brought up one knee and kicked as hard as he could, sending him reeling backward.

He leaped for the man, kicking the hand with the knife, sending it skittering away, and earning a satisfying howl from his nemesis. He brought the heel of his foot down as hard as he could on the attacker's wrist, enjoying the crunch of bone even more.

The man screamed, rolled to his knees.

"Like that, motherfucker?"

Adrenaline took over, fueling his rage, and he delivered a kick to the asshole's side that shot pain up his leg.

Having lost the advantage of surprise, and taking on someone capable of fighting back, the attacker scrambled up and fled. Furious, Julian tried to pursue him, but his foot was throbbing. So was his head, and his arm.

Silence returned, eerie in its suddenness. Gaze trained on his bedroom doorway, he backed toward the phone on his nightstand, grabbed it, switched on the lamp, and called 911.

And then the shakes set in.

He stammered out what happened to the dispatcher, who told him to remain on the line until the officers arrived. Yeah, like he'd hang up.

"Call Detective Shane Ford, too, and let him know," he said, teeth chattering. "He was here earlier, and this might have something to do with a case he's working on."

"We'll take care of it, sir. Just stay calm, okay?"

Keeping the phone tucked under his ear, he groped for the cargo shorts he'd ditched earlier and tugged them on. It was then he realized his right arm was covered in blood, and a thin line of crimson streaked down his chest. The room whirled and he sank to the floor, his back against the bed.

He must've taken a little trip into space, because the next thing he knew the room was full of cops, one lifting his head and speaking slowly. Or maybe it was his brain that was slow.

"Mr. Salvatore? We got paramedics on the way to take a look at you, okay?"

"S-sure."

"Can you tell us what happened?"

"I woke up and . . . there was this guy. With a knife. He . . ."

Tried to kill me. Mother of God, that man tried to kill me.

"Mr. Salvatore?" Still crouching, the officer spoke to someone else. "Guy's in shock. Where the fuck are the medics?"

"On the way. Be here in five."

"Think we got the knife over here," another one chimed in. "Don't anybody touch it."

"Julian? Jesus fucking Christ, are you all right?"

Julian blinked at the newcomer who squatted beside the first officer. "Shane?"

"Yeah, buddy. You just sit tight, okay? Anybody you want me to call?"

He nodded, and the movement was too much. "Grace McKenna. Number's in my cell phone," he rasped.

And the room, the blood, Shane, and the cacophony of noise all vanished into mist.

Grace peered at the digital clock as she reached for the phone, and came immediately awake. Two thirty. Middle-of-the-night calls never bore good news.

"Hello?"

"Grace McKenna?"

"Yes?" She bolted upright.

"This is Detective Shane Ford, Sugarland police. Your friend Julian Salvatore asked me to phone you. First of all, I want you to know he's going to be fine, all right?"

The blood drained from her face. "What's happened?"

"An assailant broke into his condo tonight with a knife. He—"

"Oh, my God! Where is he? Why didn't he call me himself if he's okay?" She jumped from bed and fumbled for the light.

"He fought the intruder off and the guy escaped, but he sustained some minor injuries in the process. Can you meet me in the ER at Sterling?"

"Yes! I'll be there as soon as I can."

"Drive carefully. Like I said, he's all right," the detective assured her.

"I will."

Grace hung up and threw on some clothes, chest seizing with anxiety. If he wasn't "fine" enough to make the call himself, then she wasn't reassured in the least.

She made the drive in a record fifteen minutes, too upset with herself to be unnerved by driving through the forested hills in the middle of the night. If she hadn't sent Julian away, he wouldn't have been home tonight for a knife-wielding lunatic to attack.

He'd been fighting for his life when he should've been safe in her arms.

Rushing into the ER, she ran to the counter, where a woman was reading a book. "Julian Salvatore," she blurted. "He was attacked and brought in here."

The woman glanced up and gave her a polite smile. "Through those doors, room three, but the police are with him, so you'll have to wait until—ma'am!"

Bullshit on waiting. A man exited the doors to the treatment rooms and she hurried inside, scanning for the correct cubicle. It wasn't hard to find. A uniformed cop and a brown-haired man in plain clothes were standing just inside the room, visible to anyone in the hall. The man in the blue jeans spotted her, and emerged to greet her.

"Miss McKenna?"

"Yes. Are you the one who phoned?" she asked, trying to peer around his broad shoulders.

"I am. I'm Shane Ford, and the two officers here are almost done. Why don't I fill you in and by then, you should be able to see him."

Forcing down her panic, she focused her attention on the detective, startled to find him quite handsome. His striking looks seemed so incongruous with the barren, ugly surroundings and their reason for being here; it made the scene even more surreal.

"What are his injuries?"

"He sustained two shallow cuts, here and here," he said, pointing to the center of his chest and making a slicing motion along his right bicep. "Neither required stitches, just cleaning and bandaging."

"Thank God," she breathed.

"Yeah, he got lucky. He sprained his foot, too, from kicking the shit out of the guy, but his head is bothering him the most. The assailant had him pinned at one point and slammed the back of his head into the floor a few times. He's got a knot and a bad headache, but nothing like before." His tone was gentle and reassuring.

She could see why Kat and Howard thought so highly of Ford. "Then they'll let him go soon, right?"

"I believe so, but they talked about monitoring him for a bit longer. He passed out before the medics arrived, and now he's in and out, looped on pain meds."

"Why would anyone do this to him? First the hit-and-run, and now a madman trying to—to *stab* him? What the hell is going on?"

Fury burned in her veins. As prosecutor, she could've put this monster away when the police caught him. Give her a gun and five minutes alone with him, and she'd save everyone the trouble.

"Julian has a theory about that and I'm helping him look

into something," he said grimly. "But I'll let him speak with you about it."

Terror gripped her. Someone had tried to murder her man, twice. And Julian might have an idea as to who and why? The urge to bust him out of here, now, and hide him somewhere was damned near overwhelming.

"If you have no objection, I'm taking him to my place, at least for tonight. I don't want him staying at his condo." The thought of his going back chilled her.

"Good idea. The glass on his sliding patio door is broken next to the lock, which is how the bastard got in. Until he has it repaired, he's not safe."

"He wasn't safe there to begin with," she muttered, digging in her purse for one of her business cards.

"True."

Taking out the card, she found a pen and wrote her home phone number and address on the back. "You can reach Julian here when he's not at work."

"Thanks." He tucked the card into his wallet. "Was he due on shift this morning?"

She paused, thinking. "No, he's on Tuesday." But, crap, she had to be in court by nine. She had a full schedule today and then they'd need to go pick up some of his stuff.

She couldn't think about that now. The need to be with him eclipsed all else. If she didn't get in there, she was going to make a scene. "I want to see him."

The detective gave her arm a sympathetic squeeze and stuck his head inside. "You guys done? I've got a worried lady friend here."

Both officers emerged and gave her a nod. "Ma'am," one said in greeting.

"How is he? Can I go in?"

"He's still in a bit of shock, but he's damned fortunate. Go ahead." The officer clapped the detective on the shoulder. "Catch ya later, Shane."

"I'm going, too. But first . . ." Ford removed his wallet again, and gave her one of his cards. "Should have given you this before. My cell phone number is at the bottom. Either of you can call me anytime, day or night."

"I appreciate it, and I know Julian does, too." Having a direct line to Ford eased her fears some.

"He's a good guy. Just tell him I said I'm working on the information and not to go and do anything stupid," he said cryptically. "I'll check on him tomorrow."

"Okay." Watching him stride down the narrow corridor, she shook her head. She'd get her answers later. At the moment, the only thing that mattered was lying in there alone. When his world was going to hell, he'd asked for *her*.

She stepped inside and her chest constricted. His head was turned to the side and he was staring into space. An IV ran into his right hand and a wide bandage swaddled his arm. Lifting his head, he spotted her, tried to smile, and failed.

"Grace," he said hoarsely. "I'm sorry, I shouldn't have told Shane to call you. I didn't mean to drag you down here to babysit."

"Are you kidding?" She pulled up a chair on his left side, leaned over, and gave him a careful hug and a lingering kiss before she sat down, curling her fingers around his. "I couldn't get here fast enough. I've never been so scared in my life."

"Makes two of us."

His dark eyes, she noted, were glassy. Either from pain medication or trauma, or both. "Tell me what happened."

His lashes fluttered closed briefly before he opened them again, his gaze not so cloudy. "You ever get the feeling you're being watched? Like there's a laser beam on you, connecting you to the other person?"

"I've had that happen, but never when someone truly intended me harm."

"I awoke from a sound sleep and it was like the air crackled with electricity. I sensed him before I saw his shadow over me with the knife."

She squeezed his hand. "God, that makes my skin crawl."

"Me, too, now. But at the time, survival instinct kicked in and I rolled off the bed before he had a chance to bury the blade in my chest. We fought and I managed to dislodge the knife from his hand, got in a couple of good licks. Think I broke his wrist when I stomped on it."

"I hope so! Did you get a good look at him?"

"He wore a ski mask, and he ran off before I could make a grab at it. But he was tall, maybe a little taller than me. Heavier, more solid and muscular."

"Not Derek, then," she mused aloud.

"You read my mind." Pausing, he linked their fingers together. "I've been lying here running over who'd have the most to gain by killing me."

"The man who left the bar with Brett Charles is the obvious candidate. Which I hope you told the police."

"I did. But I can't help thinking this has something to do with Derek."

She frowned. "Like he hired someone to kill you? Why would he do that? What happened was years ago. I mean, you did sort of throw down the gauntlet the other day, telling them what you remembered. But your family didn't take action against him back then and you'd have a hard time proving he molested you, given the circumstances. You're not a real threat to him."

"I might be wrong and wind up looking really stupid, but I believe there's something rotten going on with Derek. I've asked Shane to help me find out whether any disappearances or murders like the ones they're having here took place in San Antonio fifteen years ago."

Her jaw fell open as the implications hit her, hard. "My Lord, that would mean . . ."

"That I escaped something more horrible than I ever knew," he finished grimly. "And if so, for Derek to run across me here must've been quite a shock to his system."

"But then what about the man in the bar? It wasn't Derek."

"He could have a partner."

"Like who?"

"Warren, maybe. He's the one with the real power in the family, and the ruthlessness to back it up."

"Warren's a possibility. Remember what I told you about his practically trying to run my defense of Derek? I know for a fact he'd do whatever is required to protect his son, the family's name, and their fortune. He bullied my dad into assigning me to Derek's defense, with very little effort."

"He gets what he wants, and if what he wants is me on a slab—"

"Don't say it." A shudder wracked her body. "He's not getting to you, and besides, this is all speculation."

"*Bella*, it's not speculation that someone has tried to waste my ass twice. I don't see anyone else coming up with any other brilliant ideas why."

A pretty nurse breezed in with a smile, forestalling their conversation as she checked his vitals one last time. "All right," she chirped. "Let's take out this IV and then we'll get you sprung. I assume your lady friend is driving?"

Grace nodded. "Yes."

"Good. Take your pain meds for a couple of days, until the noggin and the foot are better. No operating heavy machinery while you're taking them," she recited. "You've got enough antibiotics in your system to last until you get your prescription filled tomorrow, and those should do the trick for your wounds. Keep them clean and call your doctor if they show signs of infection. Any questions?"

"How soon until I can go?"

"Just a few minutes while we get your paperwork. Be right back."

Fifteen interminable minutes crept by while they waited in silence, Grace chewing on Julian's awful theory. Did it make her a horrible person to pray he was completely off base, that he wasn't remotely connected to a series of grisly murders? Supposing he wasn't, however, they were left at square one with regard to answers.

Finally, he got his walking papers and he swung his legs off the bed. She winced at the sight of his foot, swollen, the toes bluish. She hoped he'd broken more than the bastard's wrist.

He held her hand and hobbled out on bare feet, shirtless, wearing nothing but his bloodied shorts. Glancing at her, he managed a lopsided smile. "Thanks for coming to pick me up, especially when you have to be at work soon."

"Get serious. I receive a call saying you've been attacked, and you honestly think I wouldn't rush to your side?"

"Well, no. I'm grateful for you, that's all," he said softly.

She wanted to say how grateful she was for him, too, how much he meant to her, but the admission stuck in her throat. "Let's get you back to my place and get some shut-eye. We'll take care of the other details like clothes and your medicine tomorrow, okay?"

He pulled up short. "What? No, *querida*, you're taking

me home. My patio door is broken and I can't leave my stuff in there to get stolen."

"Fine, then I'll stay with you."

His mouth tightened. "Absolutely not. He might come back, and I don't want you near there."

Bracing her hands on her hips, she glared at her stubborn lover. "Wonderful. When he pays you another visit, you can drool on him."

He blew out a breath. "Come on, baby. I'm too tired to fight with you."

"My point exactly. You're exhausted and ready to conk out. He might decide to return, and as tired as you are, you may not wake up. You're coming home with me, or I'm staying with you—take your pick."

"Dammit." He swiped a hand down his face, frustrated. "You win—just for tonight. I'll stay with you and get some sleep, but tomorrow I need to set my place to rights. It bothers me, leaving things unprotected."

"I understand, really." She stepped in to his body, wrapping her arms around him. She glanced at his bandages, hating them, what they represented. "Stuff can be replaced, though. You can't. Want to make a quick stop and get some clothes?" she asked, relenting some.

"Yeah," he said, burying his face in her hair. "I'd like that. I need to get rid of these shorts, and I sure don't want to hang out in them tomorrow."

"I can certainly understand. Let's go, then, so we can get your things and get out." She didn't want to stop there at all, but knew he'd feel better once they did.

Within a few minutes, they were at his place. She parked and was opening her driver's door when he stopped her.

"I'd prefer you didn't go in."

"Tough. I'm not staying out here by myself."

Too worn-out for another argument, he just shot her an exasperated look and got out. She followed close on his heels, not willing to be left behind. Independent or not, she wasn't stupid. In movies or books, the dumb heroine who stayed back always got slaughtered.

The knob on the front door turned and they stepped right into the brightly lit apartment. Julian was clearly annoyed. "Guess since the patio door is toast, the cops didn't see a need to lock the front."

"The patio must be how they got to you after you phoned 911," she observed. "This door hasn't been damaged."

"Thank goodness for small favors. Stay here for a second while I make sure we're alone."

Without waiting for a protest, he limped down the short hallway to his bedroom. She heard closet doors open and close, rustling noises. In a couple of minutes, he returned, glanced into the kitchen, and nodded.

"Everything's okay. Let me throw some things into my gym bag and we're outta here."

"You don't sound quite as reluctant to be away from here as you did earlier."

"Changed my mind. Come on." Taking her hand, he practically dragged her with him.

In his bedroom, he stripped off the stained shorts and yanked on a clean pair, along with a T-shirt he'd grabbed from a dresser drawer. A change of shorts, a shirt, and a couple of boxers went into the bag, as well as his navy blue fire department pants and polo shirt. He ducked into his bathroom and emerged with a stick of deodorant and his toothbrush, tossed them in, and zipped the bag closed.

"Ready."

Back on the road, she cast glances at him, keeping an eye on how he was holding up. She would have thought he'd crash on the way to her condo, but he seemed wired, staring out his window, bouncing his leg, drumming his fingers on the armrest.

"You okay?"

"Yeah," he said automatically. Then recanted. "No. I can't wrap my mind around the fact that three hours ago I was fighting for my life. If I hadn't woken up at the last second, I wouldn't be sitting here with you. I might be dead."

She laid a hand on his leg, and the bouncing stilled. "Well, you're not," she said fiercely, blinking back the sudden tears blurring the road. "You not only survived—you kicked his ass, and he'll be forced to think twice about risking exposure again."

"You're good for my ego." His quiet laugh dispelled some of the shadows. "Scratch that, you're good for me, period."

"Ditto."

"Such a romantic, too."

"Hey, I'm romantic! You're better for me than . . . carrot sticks."

"Jeez, I hope I taste better than orange cardboard." He chuckled. "Did I say you were good for my ego? Never mind."

"Kidding. You're really very bad for me, like a chocolate malt or onion rings."

"That's more like it."

She was glad to feel him relax, some of the tension easing from his thigh muscle. Getting him to rest might be more of a challenge.

She was right. Once she got him home and tucked into bed, he lay on his back staring at the ceiling, fidgeting with the sheets, picking at his bandages, and fairly vibrating with restless energy.

Cuddling into his side, she ran a palm over his flat stomach, intending to soothe him, sort of like one might a fussy baby. Shoot, she didn't know much about babies, but she knew when his stomach tightened and his breathing quickened his reaction was anything but peaceful.

His skin heated to her touch and she let her hand drift south, past his belly button, to the tent in his boxers. She rubbed the hard ridge, found the tip of him peeking through the slit, wet and silky.

Without a word, she sat up, flung back the sheet, and tugged the underwear down and off as he helpfully raised his hips. She crawled between his legs and he spread them wider to accommodate her, gasping when she suckled the head, licked the pearly drops.

"Let me make you feel good," she whispered.

"Yes, oh, yes, *please*."

She drew him in, sucking and laving the turgid flesh, gratified by his moans. He began to thrust, more and more vigorously as she manipulated his balls, increased the suction, driving him crazy.

At last she pulled off and shed her panties, leaving on the thin tank top, aware of his eyes, watching, glittering in the darkness. Primal. Sexual.

His silent hunger made her clit throb, made her ache to take him deep inside her and never let go. Straddling his lap, she guided the broad head to the part of her folds, and sank, slowly, seating him to the hilt.

"Oh, Julian." She splayed her hands on his stomach, adjusting to the sweet fullness of his cock impaling her.

"Ride me, *bella*."

Gladly. Rising and falling, she took him again and again, fanning the flames. Driving them higher, the glide of skin on skin so damned good it was unbearable. Her body quickened and then her orgasm burst in a blast of supercharged current as she cried out. She actually felt her sex spasming around his cock, milking him.

Which proved too much for him, and he joined her with a shout, hot jets of cream bathing her womb for endless seconds. They floated down together, breathing hard, grinning at each other in the darkness. Only then did she realize what she'd done.

Making love without a condom hadn't been smart. Not in the least. But they were consenting adults, and she was on birth control. She was healthy and she trusted Julian as she never had anyone else. But she had to say something.

"We didn't use protection," she said quietly.

Taking one of her hands, he kissed her fingers. "I have regular tests with the fire department, and I'm clean. Plus, I've never made love without protection before now."

"But you don't know about me. I'm clean, but what if I'm not on birth control?"

His voice quieted and his hand tightened around hers. "Are you?"

"Yes, but that's beside the point. We should've discussed this first, made sure we were on the same page. I can't believe I did that."

"My beautiful Grace," he murmured affectionately. "I'm sorry. It's just as much my fault as it is yours. But we're both healthy and we're not seeing anyone else, right?"

She nodded. "This is true."

"So we have nothing to worry about, as long as we're together." He rolled her onto her back, half-covering her with his body, snuggling her close. "Nap?"

"Go ahead, sleep."

It did her heart good to know she'd succeeded in relaxing him, making him happy. Nothing mattered to her more than lighting his world, making certain nothing bad ever touched him again.

Is this love?

"Grace?"

"Hmm?"

"Just want you to know . . . for as long as I live, you're the only woman I want to wake up next to."

His soft declaration shook her, turned her inside out, and left her trembling with its power. For the first time, she knew the meaning of unconditional love, given freely from a man to his woman.

Was she ready? Could she truly make him happy, shower him with the kind of love that lasted for decades, until they were old and wrinkled?

She puzzled the questions into the dawn, long after his breathing had evened out in blissful sleep.

Brett almost lost his mind when Kendra stopped singing.

Almost.

They'd come for her three times, dragging her off to the chamber of horrors, doing God knew what as he threw himself against the bars. Cursing them, screaming. Yelling at them to leave her alone and try a real man, because he'd give them a fight like they'd never seen.

He could, too. They'd brought him decent food and though he understood their self-serving reasons—to keep him relatively strong and solid for whatever evil games they had in mind—he ate. Every bite. He did push-ups, used the bars to lift himself repeatedly, building his upper body. He refused to quit, even if Kendra had.

He had to keep his faith, had to survive.

Survive was all he knew how to do.

And so, when they came for her the fourth time, and the horrible hum of the generator started, followed by shrill, animal shrieks as she died . . .

Brett sang.

Covering his ears, he sang loudly. Belted out every new age rock song he knew, because those were his favorites. They kept him bound to the real world, gave him hope.

He could endure. His family had to be frantic. People were looking for him. Dismembered bodies had been found, and the police were all over the Cumberland River like white on rice—he'd overheard one of them say so, all panicked and shit.

The bad guys were worried, and that made them human.

Humans, he could deal with. Hour after hour.

Until the cops found him, or it was his turn to scream. One thing for sure, though.

If and when that day came? He was taking one of those sick motherfuckers with him.

14

"You are staying here, and that's final!" Grace stamped one expensively shod foot, her glare threatening to fry Julian on the spot.

He couldn't help but laugh. "You did *not* just stamp your foot at me."

"Yes, I did! Stubborn, muleheaded idiot."

"What happened to my independent *bella* who was so determined to keep me at a distance?" Arching an eyebrow at her, he pulled his Sugarland FD polo over his head.

"That was before you almost became a Ginsu special! I'm worried about you, dammit!"

That was the problem. He didn't want her concern; he wanted her love. The day she said she loved him and couldn't live without him, he'd pack his shit and be on her doorstep before she knew what hit her. And not one day sooner.

Sitting on the edge of her bed, he calmly began to tie his shoes. "The manager said my sliding glass door is fixed."

"It can get broken again."

"I'll be ready."

"Everyone's luck runs out eventually," she countered, getting good and pissed by his lack of cooperation.

"I've got nine lives, and I'm only down four. I'm good."

"How can you be so fucking flip about this?"

"I'm not, believe me. The last thing I want is to paint a frigging target on my chest and wait for the final blow. Which is why I'm doing something about it, with Shane's help." Standing, he gathered her into his arms and pressed light kisses along her jaw, to the dainty shell of her ear. "Don't be mad at me, baby."

As determined as she was to withstand his gentle assault, her anger began to deflate. He was glad when she began to relax, and finally hugged him back.

"I'm not mad at *you*."

"I know."

"I love having you here."

Close. *But close, as they say, only counts in horseshoes and hand grenades.*

"I love being here."

I love you. Not yet, not like this, but soon. He'd tell her, and damn the consequences.

She rested her cheek against his chest and he reveled in her body pressed to his. He longed to pluck out the pins holding her hair in its prim, classy twist and let the tresses cascade down her back. He'd run his hands through the white blond silk, strip off her fussy power suit, and have his way.

"Do you think the detective will have something for you today?"

"Maybe. The San Antonio homicide guy is looking into the cold cases on his own time, so it might take a while."

He didn't want to disappoint her by telling her Shane had said the cop assisting him had been with the San Antonio PD only eight years. None of their homicide guys had been there more than twelve.

And when Julian had asked whether the older cops might remember any strange unsolved murders, Shane had reported that the homicide guy had cracked up laughing. He'd said San Antonio had more weird cold cases than warts on a hog's ass. From what he'd found on the Internet so far, he knew that was true.

"Maybe they'll hit on something soon," she said. "But I'm still afraid for you, staying alone. I wish you'd stay with someone, or check into a hotel."

"I'm not going to hide or put anyone else in danger." He kissed her temple. "This will be over before you know it, you'll see."

He'd sleep like crap, except for at the station, but she didn't need to know that, either.

"I wish we could go away somewhere and hide together. Like Bermuda."

"Me, too." Releasing her, he glanced at his watch and made a face. "But I have to run or Sean will eat my liver with a nice Chianti."

"Call me if you get a chance?"

"You bet."

He planted a blistering kiss on her pretty lips, just long enough to keep her wanting, then left before he wound up in trouble.

The drive didn't take long, the hour being early, and he made it to the station with ten minutes to spare. Of course, he hadn't given much thought to what story he'd tell the team about the bandage around his arm. Well, he figured Six-Pack knew about the attack because Grace had probably told Kat. But he doubted the big guy had said anything to the others. As luck would have it, everyone was hanging out in the bay shooting the breeze when he arrived. All eyes swung to him as he strolled in, trying not to limp on his sore foot, but it was Eve who piped up.

"What did you do to yourself?"

Glancing at his arm, he made a show of shrugging it off. "Oh, I just tripped and fell in the bathroom, scratched myself on the corner of the counter. No biggie." None of them knew his bathroom counters didn't have any sharp corners— and he couldn't have sliced the top of his bicep even if they did.

The lame explanation seemed to satisfy everyone except Six-Pack and Sean, who exchanged a look but kept quiet.

"Man, I thought Einstein here was the clumsiest guy I know," Tommy joked, jabbing a thumb at Zack. "After these last few weeks, I'm not so sure."

Knight chucked a dirty rag at Tommy's face. "At least I've got a hot woman to kiss my boo-boos, which is more than I can say for you."

Ignoring their antics, Julian walked inside, straight to the coffeepot, and poured a mug. Then he carried it into the common room, to the computer in the corner designated for general use. The machine was already on, and he launched the Internet browser, wondering how far he'd get before one of them came in and got into his business.

Apparently not far, because the thought conjured Sean and Six-Pack, who stood over him looking worried as hell. "I'm *fine*," he said before either of them started.

"Howard told me because he thought I needed to know, and I'm glad he did. Do you want to crash at the ranch until all of this blows over? Or I can stay on your couch. The asshole takes three steps inside your condo, I'll bash his skull in with a baseball bat." Sean crossed his arms over his chest, expression fierce.

"You'd do that for me?" He hadn't meant to sound incredulous, but hell.

"I still have a couple of redeeming qualities," Sean said

drily. "Loyalty to my men is one of them, even if I act like a dick most of the time."

Julian swiped a hand down his face, smiling in spite of himself. "Thanks, Cap, but I'm handling this."

"With that detective's help?"

"Yeah."

"All right, but the offer stands. You need anything at all, you'll let us know." An order, not a request.

"I will."

Sean, never one to waste time on warm fuzzies, went to attend to other matters, but Six-Pack remained behind. Julian knew what was coming before he opened his mouth.

"How are you, really? No bullshit."

No point in lying. Something about this man made others want to open up, always had. Even if it seemed Six-Pack was frustrated with him more often than not, Julian knew he cared. "Shaken," he admitted. "I'm just an average Joe, never intentionally hurt a soul in my life, and it's hard to take in."

"You have an idea why this person is after you?"

"I figured you knew. Grace didn't tell Kat, and so forth?"

"Nope. Grace didn't feel right about breaking your confidence. She only said you and Ford might have an angle, and that she's terrified for you."

Damn. "I hate that she's been exposed to this, Howard. I'd give anything if I could keep her out of this, but she won't budge. And there's something else. . . ." He met the man's brown eyes, wondering whether he was about to get clobbered, saving his attacker any further effort.

"You love her."

Julian winced. "How do you feel about that?"

One corner of his mouth tilted up. "I suppose I'll survive, but it's not me you have to sell. Grace goes her own way, and nobody's going to push her into something before she's ready. Even you."

"Think I don't know? She drives me crazy!"

"She's worth the wait."

"Yeah. Shit, what's a poor bastard to do?"

"Adhere to the primary rule of woman-taming—do whatever she wants. Happy wife, happy life."

"Sounds more like man-taming to me."

"The rewards are sweet, though." He paused. "So, you gonna tell me what these attacks on you are about?"

"No, because the more I say it aloud, the dumber it sounds. If I'm right, however, you'll be the first to know."

"Fair enough." Howard looked like he wanted to say more, but didn't. "I'll let you get back to the computer."

"Thanks for the ear."

"No problem. I'm here if you need me."

"I appreciate it. I'll be out in a bit to help with breakfast."

Once Six-Pack was gone, Julian continued his mission of poking into the past.

The answer might be one click away.

If so, he or the police would find it.

Something told him the answer had better come soon.

Grace picked up the phone from her desk and placed a call that should not have thrilled the ever-loving hell out of her. But she couldn't wait to wash her hands of Derek Vines and his filth by association.

With all her soul, now more than ever, she believed he was guilty of sexual harassment. Probably worse. Her one consolation was that Hayden Madison was going to get every single dime he'd asked for, and then some. She'd made sure of it . . . with a discreet phone call to his attorney.

She'd never used her position to stick it to a client before, and she hoped she never had occasion to do so again. She could get disbarred for this. In Derek's case, though, she felt justified.

"W. H. Vines, Derek Vines' office," his secretary intoned. "How may I help you?"

"This is Grace McKenna, Mr. Vines' attorney. I have a matter he's been waiting to conclude, and I know he'll want to take my call."

"Hold, please."

In seconds, the slimeball himself was on the line. "Grace! You have news?"

"I do. Mr. Madison has agreed to a settlement. Come down to my office in an hour and we'll go over it, and sign."

"Wonderful," he breathed, his relief palpable. "Was it what we offered?"

"No, I'm afraid not. We'll talk when you get here, okay? Bye." She hung up on him midprotest. Damn, this was going to be good.

While she waited, she let her thoughts drift to Julian and how his day might be going. He seemed to be recovering from the attack, and it sure hadn't affected his performance in the bedroom.

Heat suffused her cheeks and she giggled, glad her office door was closed. Wouldn't take long for her strange affliction to be correctly diagnosed, bringing Daddy on the run with a barrage of questions. There were some things daddies didn't need to know.

Such as what a masterful lover Julian was in bed, the only situation in which Grace enjoyed giving up control. He was fast turning her into a sex bunny, and she didn't give two hoots. In all her life, she'd never enjoyed herself more.

A knock on the door ended her reverie, and her secretary stuck her head in. "Grace, Warren and Derek Vines are here. I

put them in the conference room." Because nobody else could
see, Alice scrunched up her face and crossed her eyes, the
expression comical, giving her opinion of the two visitors.

Grace stifled a laugh. "Thanks, Alice."

Gathering the necessary papers, she stood and walked the
short distance to the conference room. Outside, she paused
and mentally fortified herself against the double onslaught.
She should've figured Warren would attend, as well, since
Derek couldn't take the proverbial shit without his being
there to wipe it—and he was footing the bill.

She walked in spine straight, head high, and closed the
door behind her. The men rose, offering their hands. Neither
man sported a brace or cast on his right wrist, nor any bruis-
ing, and she didn't know whether to be relieved or disappointed. Of course, Julian's attacker wouldn't be identified
so easily.

"Gentlemen," she said in greeting. *And I use that term
loosely.* "Let's have a seat and go over the settlement."

Derek leaned forward, elbows on the table, face anxious.
"You said on the phone he didn't agree to our original offer
of seventy thousand. How much does he want?"

Here we go. Schooling her expression to remain bland,
she said, "Two hundred fifty thousand dollars, or he takes
you to court."

A heartbeat passed, two, as they both stared at her, goggle-
eyed.

"Two hundred f-fifty thousand dollars? That's insane!"
Derek shouted. "That's one hundred thousand fucking dollars more than he asked for to begin with!"

My, you can add. "Yes, I'm afraid so."

Warren shot to his feet, pounding a fist on the table. "That's
outrageous! We will not be bilked dry by a candy-assed little
whelp spouting dirty lies about my son!"

Clasping her hands in front of her, she gazed at him calmly before turning her attention back to Derek. "Hayden Madison feels he has an ironclad case should he take you to court. If you choose to go that route, he's made it clear the sky's the limit on the dollar amount he'll seek."

"What? How?" Derek ran a hand through his hair, eyes wild. "It's my word against his! How can he think he's got a damned thing on me?"

Wow, look at the vein in his temple pounding. If Derek had an aneurysm, poor Madison would never see his money.

"It all comes down to skeletons, Derek." She let the statement drop between them like a bomb. Both men glanced at each other, looking like they were about to choke to death. Well, wasn't that interesting?

"What—" Derek's voice cracked. He paused and cleared his throat. "What the hell do you mean?"

"Skeletons. You know, those bony things that rattle around in the dark, waiting to be unearthed at the most inopportune moments?"

Warren lowered himself into his chair once more, narrowing his eyes at her. *Careful*, she cautioned herself. If they were indeed guilty of murder, she was treading a dangerous line.

"I'll be straightforward. Someone went to Mr. Madison claiming to have information on you. Damaging information, Derek. Mr. Madison and his attorney aren't inclined to disclose their source or what he gave them, but they are confident they can prevail in court."

"So why don't they?" Warren folded his arms over his chest, suddenly looking superior. "If they were so certain they'd win, we wouldn't be sitting here."

She'd anticipated this question. "You're forgetting the court costs and attorney's fees eating up a healthy portion of the award. Now, let's consider the potentially irreversible damage done to both Derek's reputation and that of your company, whether Madison wins or not. W. H. Vines will be dragged through the mud in the media. Questions will be raised. Is that what you want?"

Derek had gone as white as a sheet of paper. Warren was furious, but his anger was quiet now. A lethal entity reaching across the table, wrapping around her throat.

This was the moment of truth. Would they buy the story she and Madison's attorney had concocted? Apparently, Derek swallowed it whole. His face was a mask of pure fear, his emotions telegraphed for all to see. After they left, he'd drive himself insane trying to figure out who could've turned on him, ratted him out to Madison's lawyer.

Nothing left to do but deliver the final thrust.

"How we proceed is completely your decision. You have to ask yourself how much it's worth to make this all quietly go away. If you want to fight, I'll do my best for you in court. Your call."

"What a goddamned choice." Derek's bitter laugh sounded more like a sob. "I'll sign."

Checkmate.

Warren's expected second explosion didn't come. His silence was unnerving, but she gave every outward appearance of ignoring him. "For what it's worth, I think you've made the right decision."

A mound of paperwork and twenty minutes later, she straightened the documents and stuffed them into her file. They didn't offer their hands again and she didn't say it had been a pleasure. Even trade.

"I'll let Mr. Madison's attorney know when they can expect the money. Good day, gentlemen."

Derek practically fled, but Warren paused in the doorway,

glaring back at her, his eyes hard, glittering marbles. Though she met his gaze without flinching, her skin crawled and she had the sick sensation he saw right through her.

Turning on his heel, he stalked out and she exhaled a deep breath she hadn't known she was holding. Her heart pounded wildly in her chest and she felt dizzy. Maybe she needed lunch and, better yet, some fresh air. She had to get out of here for a while.

First, she made a brief call to Madison's attorney. "Bob, it's Grace McKenna. I have good news."

As expected, the man was ecstatic. Recalling Warren's parting stare, however, she gave Bob one piece of advice for his client—take an extended vacation, somewhere on the other side of the globe. As soon as possible.

Grabbing her purse, she headed for the elevator, calling to Alice on the way by to let her know she was going out to grab a bite. She had to erase the stain left behind by Derek and Warren. A nice, brisk walk down to Second Avenue might do the trick.

In the parking garage, she emerged from the elevator, and had taken only a few steps to cut across to the street when she heard voices raised in argument. Male voices.

About forty yards away, standing between two parked cars, Warren was waging an all-out verbal assault on his son.

Driven by instinct, Grace ducked behind a wide concrete support column, a nasty jolt of dread grabbing her at the thought of being seen. Why she didn't simply stride past them like a normal person who had every right to be there, she didn't know. But it was too late now and she was stuck here until they left.

". . . coming out of your trust fund, goddammit!" Warren railed.

"Shh," Derek hissed. "Someone might—"

"Don't dare shush me, you worthless little cocksucker," he said dangerously. "You don't know it's Salvatore. What if Gruber has turned? Have you considered that?"

"He wouldn't!"

Gruber? Who was he?

"Are you willing to risk it? You have a hell of a lot more to lose than a quarter million," he said with barely disguised loathing. "And something else—your inept lawyer has to be dealt with, and that fucking firefighter, as well."

"No! Not Grace! She doesn't know anything!"

Grace's eyes widened and her hand went over her mouth.

"You can pray she doesn't. Or you can get rid of her and all the other deadweight before you're buried along with it. Because when someone goes down for all of this, it won't be me."

One car door slammed and an engine started—Warren's, she assumed. The other followed suit. She waited until well after both had driven away before she emerged from her hiding spot. Then she retraced her steps to her office, dodged Alice's concern, shut the door, and sank into her chair.

"What have I done?"

Hand shaking, she picked up the phone.

"Hey, Jules! Telephone!"

Sandwich in hand, Julian strode into the common room, scowling at Tommy. "Damn, I'm right here. You don't have to yell."

"Oh. Sorry, but it's some chick. Sounds like she's crying." Skyler made a face. "Good luck with that, dude."

Crying? He swallowed his bite of turkey and Swiss, and reached for the phone. "Thanks, man." All sorts of terrible visions flashed through his mind. *Dios*, maybe something had happened to Mama, or one of his sisters. He was in no way prepared for the hysterical voice on the other end. "Hello?"

"Julian," Grace sobbed. "I need to see you."

His heart damned near stopped beating. "*Bella*, what's wrong?"

"I've done something terrible! I shook the apple tree and rotten apples came down, and now they're going to kill me and—"

"Baby, slow down," he said, trying to calm her when he was starting to panic. "You're not making any sense."

"Warren and Derek Vines!" she wailed. "They're going to take care of me and you along with all the other dead-weight! I heard them!"

Oh, my God. "Calm down, honey. Where are you?"

"In my office." In the background, she blew her nose, and stammered the firm's address and her floor.

"Okay, listen to me. I'm coming after you, baby, so you stay right there, you hear?"

"All right," she said in a small, scared voice.

That frightened him more than anything—his confident *bella*, reduced to tears. Terrified, needing him. "Sit tight, I'm on my way."

Hanging up, he pitched the phone, not caring where it landed, and rushed to the captain's office, dumping his sandwich along the way. "Sean, I have to go. It's an emergency."

The captain looked up from a stack of reports on his desk, frowning, but in concern rather than annoyance. "Does this have something to do with your attack?"

"It might. I just got a phone call and after I deal with this, it sounds like I might end up at the police station."

"Will you be back?"

"I don't know," he answered honestly. "I'll try."

Sean waved him off. "Don't worry, we've got you covered. It's a slow day anyhow."

Relief made his knees weak. "Thanks, I appreciate this. I'll make it up to everybody; I promise."

"I know you will." He nodded. "Get out of here."

Grateful, Julian hurried for his car and fishtailed out of the parking lot.

15

Julian set his GPS for Grace's work address, desperate to squelch the rising panic her phone call had brought. Shaking apple trees? What the fuck had she meant by that? He could only assume this had something to do with her representation of Derek, but he couldn't guess what had gone wrong.

Try as he might, he couldn't get her fear out of his brain. The miles between them didn't disappear fast enough to suit him.

He arrived at a towering glass behemoth of a building in downtown Nashville, sparing the briefest moment of awe that the entire structure belonged to her father. He was less impressed when he had to circle the damned thing twice to locate the entrance to the parking garage. There was something to be said for a modest location like his own workplace.

Luckily, he found a parking spot without much trouble, a lot of people being at lunch, he supposed, and took the elevator to Grace's floor. Stepping out, he glanced around the spacious lobby area, searching for a clue where to go next.

"May I help you?"

A militant-looking older lady with a cap of short steel gray hair sat behind a desk, eyeing him up and down with suspicion.

"I'm here to see Grace McKenna. She called—"

"Oh! The uniform! You must be Julian, her fireman," she said, waving a hand down a corridor behind her desk. "Where is my head? Alice, her secretary, told me to expect you. Down this way, dear, second door on your left. She's expecting you."

"Thank you." Despite his worry, he gave the secretary his best smile and made his way to Grace's office. He paused to deliver a warning knock, then went inside.

Grace spun around in her chair to face him. Her red-rimmed eyes widened and she launched herself into his outstretched arms, clinging like a burr.

"You're shaking, baby. Tell me what happened," he urged, rubbing circles on her back.

"Just hold me first," she whispered, burrowing against his chest.

"I can do that." He held her tight, kissed the top of her head. Rocked her in the protection of his embrace, giving her his support. His unconditional love, even if she didn't know it yet.

After a few minutes, she pulled back and met his eyes, somewhat more calm, but still afraid. "I thought I was so smart, sticking it to Derek, and I *did*. But I also stirred up a hornet's nest."

Taking her elbow, he guided her to one of the chairs facing her desk. He took the other and captured her hand, tightening his grip in reassurance. "How so?"

She hung her head, training her gaze on the floor. "God, Julian, I could get disbarred for this."

Her words gave him a chill. "You? I find it hard to believe you'd be capable of getting yourself into that sort of fix."

"Believe it. I did something highly unethical, albeit justified, and now it might come back to haunt me." She shook her head, as though not quite believing the whole thing herself. "After everything that's happened to you, there's not a doubt in my mind that Derek's a sleaze at the least, a murderer at worst. I arranged it so Derek was forced to pay significantly more than what his accuser was asking for in damages to begin with."

"How the heck did you accomplish that?"

"I—basically, the plaintiff's lawyer and I fabricated a witness. Someone who supposedly went to the plaintiff's lawyer and claimed to have damning information about Derek's past and his twisted proclivities, which his lawyer would reveal in court if Derek insisted on taking things that far. It was just a hunch on my part, but I thought there was nothing to lose. If he was truly innocent, he'd insist on going to court because he'd know no one could have any such information."

"And you were right."

"Yes. You should have seen him," she said, wringing her hands. "I thought Derek was going to have a stroke right here in the office. He was terrified of whatever this fictional witness might reveal, and he couldn't settle out of court fast enough."

"I'll bet." Julian's mind reeled at this. "You mentioned Warren. How did he take all of this?"

"As you might expect. He was furious, very vocal in the beginning, and then . . . he got quiet. Like the kind of calm Hannibal Lecter shows before he gives his creepy smile and guts somebody."

"Jesus. He didn't threaten you outright, did he?"

"No, he and Derek left. I called the plaintiff's lawyer, and then I broke for lunch and took the elevator down. Warren and Derek were in the parking garage, arguing. Or rather,

Warren was reaming his son, yelling about who the witness might be. You or—or someone named Gruber. Warren also said that Derek has a lot more to lose than the amount he lost in the settlement."

"My God, honey, what have you stirred up?"

"It gets worse. Warren told Derek something had to be done about his 'inept lawyer' and 'that fucking firefighter.' The last thing he said was if someone goes down for everything, it won't be him."

Julian's blood ran cold. There was no mistaking the threat to Grace, himself, and anyone else who crossed these maniacs. His mind whirled as he fought to remain calm. She was upset enough without his throwing his own fear into the mix. "Tell you what we're going to do. Can you clear your schedule for the rest of the afternoon?"

"I already did."

"Good. We're going to see Shane, and you're going to tell him what you just told me. Then we'll stop by my place and grab a few of my things before heading to yours."

"You . . . you'll stay with me?"

"Try to get me to leave." So it wasn't how he'd envisioned parking his toothbrush in her bathroom, and maybe it wasn't permanent. But her safety was more important than his pride.

"Thank you." Tears welled in her gorgeous eyes again.

"Hey," he said softly, brushing away a stray drop. "None of that. It's going to work out, baby. Come on."

He helped her up and waited while she shut down her computer, retrieved her purse, and locked her office. He led her past the curious stares of her secretary and a few co-workers, but other than a couple of muttered good-byes, most people paid them no mind.

"We'll come back tomorrow and fetch your car." She

didn't offer a single protest, and his fear increased. She was truly frightened and try as he might, he couldn't come up with a way she might have misinterpreted what she'd overheard.

At the police station, they had to wait a while to see Shane, who was out in the field but told the officer who called him not to let them leave.

More than an hour later, he came bustling from the back, an apology on his lips. "I'm sorry, you two. Things have gotten hairy around here. Come with me."

The detective led them to his small office and gestured them into seats across from his desk as he took his own. "Why don't you tell me what brought you by, and then I'll share why you've saved me a trip to see you."

Julian put his arm around Grace and gave her an encouraging smile. "Go ahead. He's here to help us."

Taking a deep breath, she began and left nothing out. When she finished, the detective had a stunned expression on his face—along with a hint of excitement.

"That was either very gutsy or an incredibly stupid stunt you pulled," he said. "Either way, you've given me vital information to add to my case."

"Which is why you wanted to see me?"

Shane picked up a ballpoint pen and chewed on the cap, nodding to Grace. "She's up to speed, right?"

"Yes."

"Nothing leaves this office."

"Understood." His pulse quickened. Shane had something; he just knew it.

The man flipped open a notepad, recapped the information he'd written—and the bottom fell out of Julian's world.

"San Antonio, Texas, 1994. Decomposed female victim found in a garbage bag in the Hill Country on the outskirts of the city, dismembered. Male victim discovered nearby, same MO, but he hadn't been dead as long. In 1995, another male, same MO, found in another shallow grave outside the city. The second male was never identified." He tossed the pad down, eyes lit. "Both less than five miles from the Vineses' land. You, my friend, are a fucking savior."

He sure didn't feel like one. In fact, he felt a little sick. "Can you arrest them? Those bastards need to be off the street."

"Not yet. This is all circumstantial, Julian. You lived there at that time, too, and I can't arrest you," he pointed out. "Living in cities where similar murders occurred more than a decade apart isn't a crime. What we *are* doing is cooperating with the San Antonio police, getting permission from the present owners of the old Vines estate to thoroughly search the grounds."

"And if you find bodies?"

He gave a tired laugh. "Wouldn't that be damned convenient? Just find them piled in the basement? No, it's a shot in the dark. Three victims were dumped away from the premises, so unless they broke their pattern, or really didn't have one, I wouldn't expect to find corpses awaiting discovery. But hope springs eternal. Perhaps they'll find forensic evidence."

"If they do, will you be able to get a search warrant for their place here?" he asked.

"Depends on whether the judge feels we have enough evidence. It's a crapshoot, but it's all we've got. Your stories will help, though."

"How long will the search take?"

"Once they get in there? A day or two. They'll go over every speck of the property with a fine-toothed comb. Should they find something, a few hours to get the warrant."

"We're looking at three or four more days, then." Julian longed to strangle Derek and his father with his bare hands. "That's not good enough. This kid, Brett Charles, might still be alive, and maybe others, too."

"I'm doing the best I can, Julian," he snapped.

"Sorry. I know you are. This is just so maddening. They're in this and now they're threatening Grace, as well." *Touch her and die, fuckers.*

"I don't think it's a good idea for either of you to be alone right now," he said, glancing between them.

"I'm staying with her again, until this is resolved."

"Good plan."

Julian stood, taking Grace's hand. "Let us know if something goes down."

"I will. And Julian . . . don't do anything stupid. I mean it," Shane ordered. "Stay far away from the Vineses—don't so much as blink in their direction—or I'm going to have your ass. Understand?"

"Perfectly." Didn't mean he'd listen. "They steer clear of me, we shouldn't have a problem."

"Uh-huh." The detective wasn't convinced.

"See ya."

Julian led them out and away from Shane's penetrating stare. It was like the guy was clairvoyant and saw the half-formed idea in his mind. The really *bad* idea. Which he would not act upon. Probably.

"You never did get lunch, did you?" he asked as they slid into his car.

"No, and I am a little hungry." Her stomach growled to prove the point.

"Same here. Why don't we grab a couple of burgers at Stratton's and go for a drive, unwind for a bit? Then we'll go get my stuff."

"Sounds nice." She gave him a sweet smile that warmed him all the way to his toes. And other areas, too. "The detective is right."

He glanced at her as he pulled out of the parking lot. "About what?"

"You really are a savior."

"Ha! My sisters will tell you I'm a pest. Oh, and let's not forget the guys on my team. Most days, I think they'd trade me for a cold beer."

"You sell yourself far too short," she said, refusing to play along.

"Nah, I'm about six one," he joked.

"Idiot." Laughing, she gently smacked his shoulder.

He loved seeing her violet eyes dancing and the tension drained from her posture, and he would do everything in his power to keep her distracted and happy.

Stratton's wasn't too busy by the time they pulled in and went inside. At the counter, he ordered cheeseburgers, fries, and soft drinks to go, and fifteen minutes later they were on the road again.

"Where are we going?" Peering into the bag, she snagged a fry.

"It's a surprise. There's something I want to show you." He tapped his hand on the steering wheel in nervous excitement, anxious to see her reaction. He drove out of Sugarland on I-49 for a few miles and finally spotted his destination.

A little thrill shot through him as he made a left-hand turn onto the weed-choked rutted path that served as a driveway. A large FOR SALE sign hung on the rotted barbwire fence, faded and starting to rust, and he stole a look at Grace before pulling through the open gate.

The rolling land was gorgeous, if shaggy with wild grass, dotted with towering trees, and graced by a secluded pond a ways farther down the path. He eased the Porsche along, over the bumps and ruts, thankful it hadn't been raining or he'd never be able to get back there.

"Wow, this is beautiful," she breathed, surveying the place with an appreciative eye. "No house?"

"Not yet. I know the land was used to graze cattle," he said, gesturing to a feed shed and holding pen about fifty yards off, now falling in.

"Well, this would be the perfect place to build one. The owner could do tons with this place."

"Yeah, it just needs a little TLC, and it'll be great." A slice of heaven, made even better shared with the right lady.

Don't get ahead of yourself, Romeo.

He parked beside the pond, popped the trunk, and got out to retrieve a quilt from the back. Leaving the trunk open, he carried it to a nice spot next to the bank of the pond and spread it out, while Grace stood beside the car holding the food and drinks, amusement tilting her lips.

"Do you always carry a quilt for spontaneous picnicking with your women?"

Straightening, he splayed a hand over his heart. "You wound me! I'll have you know that quilt is all-purpose, used for wrapping things I don't want to get scratched by sliding around in the trunk and . . . and . . . well, okay. Making out."

She rolled her eyes and began picking her way through the grass. "There's an image I needed."

"Jealous?" He puffed out his chest, pleased by the idea.

"I plead the Fifth."

"Lawyers—can't shoot 'em . . . ," he muttered in mock disgust. Remembering his manners, he hurried over, took the bag and drinks. "Stay there." He placed them on the blanket and strode back to her.

"What are you doing now?"

"Here, put your arm around me." Bending slightly, he hooked an arm around her back, one under her knees, and hauled her against his chest.

"Wait!" She squealed. "Put me down!"

"You want to ruin your fancy heels? Be quiet and let me show off."

She giggled, the merry sound, not to mention her body wriggling in his arms, her sweet scent teasing his nose, shooting straight to his cock.

"I've never played hooky to picnic in the country in the middle of the day, wearing my best suit and three-hundred-dollar shoes." She seemed pretty darned tickled about it, too.

"You deserved a break." He lowered her to the ground and plopped down beside her. "We both do."

"As long as it doesn't culminate in us getting hauled in for trespassing, I'm game," she said, kicking off her shoes. She pushed them to the edge of the blanket and dug into the bag, handing him his burger and fries.

"We won't. I've been here a half dozen times and nobody's ever said a word. I was *alone*," he added at her arch look. This, he noted, was met with smug pleasure. "Anyway, we're hidden from the road and the neighbors, so we can enjoy all we want."

"I wonder how much land this is." She unwrapped her burger and chewed in bliss.

He did the same and swallowed before answering. "Forty acres. The owner put it on the market over a year ago, but the economy has been so bad, it hasn't sold. He's steadily cut the price in the last few months and . . . I have to admit, I've had my eye on it for a while."

"Really? That's wonderful! Have you made an offer?"

Her genuine enthusiasm touched him, bolstered his confidence. Revealing a dream to the most important person in your life—especially when that person was the one you hoped to share your dream with—was daunting. "I think I'm going to," he said slowly. He realized he hadn't admitted it, even to himself, until that moment.

"Well, what's stopping you? This is a fabulous place."

"At first, the price. But now? Nothing, I guess. I've just never made this big a commitment before—the put-down-roots kind. But now I'm ready."

"Honey, I'm so pleased for you." She kissed his cheek. "I had you figured for more of a city man, but I can see I was wrong."

"Living in town is convenient, but the bustle gets old at the end of the day. I want a place that's my kingdom, where I can be myself. What about you? Are you a city girl?" Damn, was that too obvious? He took a sip of his cola and ate some fries, trying to act casual.

She shrugged. "I like living in Nashville. I suppose I've never really given much thought to a change of pace."

They finished their food and he struggled not to be deflated by her vague answer. But he couldn't say he hadn't been warned. Six-Pack had advised him not to push, and he wouldn't. Yet.

He liked to believe he was man enough to give her the space she needed, and to be happy with himself and the direction of his life first. A woman like Grace deserved a man every bit as confident and successful as herself.

God willing, he'd be that man.

"I feel like I'm supposed to be here, as though this is already home. I'm calling the Realtor this afternoon," he said, his mind completely made up.

"Good for you," she said softly.

And pulled him in for a kiss. A scorching-hot, tongue-tangling kiss that tasted like burgers and fries, and he didn't care. All coherence took a side trip when her hand drifted to his crotch and began to caress him to full arousal with the lightest of touches.

"I want you," she said, fiddling with his buckle. "Here. Now. And I want you to . . . take charge."

"Ah, shit, yeah." Two of his most treasured fantasies came together in his brain, and knowing they were both within reach at the same time blasted his self-control to dust. Quickly, he stuffed their trash into the empty bag, stood, and strode to the trunk, tossing it inside and placing their drinks there for safekeeping. Stripping off his shirt, he spread it on the ground at the front of his car and returned to where she sat on the blanket, watching curiously.

"Stand up," he said, his tone firm. She did, her face flushed with desire, waiting to see what came next. "Strip for me, down to the skin."

She shed her blue suit jacket and white blouse, then her bra, eyes never straying from his. Next went her pants and underwear, which she nudged aside with one foot. She stood totally exposed to him, tall, lean, and naked. His.

"Ah, Christ." He palmed his rock-hard erection through his clothing. "Take your hair down."

One by one, she removed the pins, pitching them onto the blanket with her clothes, until the whole shiny mass cascaded past her shoulders and down her back like a waterfall. She watched expectantly, gaze smoky, as lost as he to the sensual game they played.

He picked her up again and carried her the short distance to his shirt spread in front of the car and set her on it, unwilling to risk her stepping on something sharp. Last, he gathered up the quilt and her clothes, which he placed on the passenger's seat. Then he shook the blanket out and spread it over the hood.

Sidling close, he ran a palm down her back, skimmed her smooth buttocks. "Face the car." She did, trembling under his hand. "Good. The blanket is to protect your pretty skin. Do you know why?"

"I—I think so," she answered breathlessly.

"Oh, yes, you do. You see, I've enjoyed many sensual, satisfying adventures, but never this. The dangerous side of me has always wanted to take a woman right in the open, where anyone might see," he whispered into her ear. His pleasure grew when she shuddered, spread her legs, and leaned into his touches as his fingers explored the folds of her sex.

"God, Julian."

"Oh, you like that? You're going to love what comes next. My second fantasy is, I've dreamed of bending a beautiful, naughty woman over the hood of my fast car and fucking her hard and deep." He nibbled and kissed her neck, rubbed her clit. "Pounding into her, letting her know who belongs between her lush thighs. Lucky me, that woman is you, *querida*. I'm going to fuck you until you can't breathe, until nothing exists but me buried in your hot sheath. Now bend over and lay your upper half on the blanket. Brace your feet wider apart."

Madre de Dios! She was a feast waiting to be devoured, hair fanned over the blanket, taut butt poked out, inviting.

In two seconds, he'd toed off his shoes, shed his pants and boxers. Behind her, he smoothed his hands down her back, her pert ass, the outsides of her thighs. He crouched between her thighs, mindful that she deserved spoiling before he went at her like an animal.

Angling his head, he trailed his tongue over her slit, gratified by the tiny whimper from above. He let himself enjoy simply tasting for a bit, aware he was driving her into the proper head space, spiking her arousal, seducing her.

"Mmm, so pretty. Who does this belong to, baby?"

"Y-you."

"That's right." Parting her sex, he stroked into her channel with his tongue, sweeping as deeply as possible, causing her to moan. He continued his seduction in this way for a while before changing tactics. Fastening his mouth to her clit, he sucked the tender nub until she writhed over him, panting short cries, driven to the edge.

Before she went over, he stood, chuckling at her moan of despair. He positioned himself behind her, cock jutting proudly toward its goal, and grabbed her hips. He guided the head just into the entrance, teasing with the promise of what was to come, rubbing the tip in and out. Creating delicious friction.

"Please," she begged.

With a growl, he plunged in to the hilt. "Mine."

"Yes! Yours. I need . . ."

"Me, right here, always."

She ground backward against his groin. "Nobody but you."

His control frazzled and he began to shaft her, long slow slides that superheated the blood in his veins, sizzled in his cock. With every stroke, driving him mad, hips pistoning faster and faster until he was slamming his cock home, loving the noisy rhythm of their flesh slapping together. Her walls bathed him with fire, the flame spreading to every limb.

He quickened. His balls tightened. The fire consumed him.

And when she screamed his name, her channel convulsing around his rod, he exploded. Shot into her forever, giving her all of himself.

"I love you," he rasped. "*Dios mío*, I love you."

And so, he rendered himself naked and vulnerable in a way he never had before, had never been tempted to before this woman. This elusive, lovely, special woman. So right for him in every possible way.

It was official. He was ruined for any other.

As they came down together, he planted little kisses on her back, kneaded her shoulders. Whispered words in Spanish he'd never said to another soul, about sharing dreams, about tomorrow. About this place and how he hoped one day in the not too distant future she'd plan their home to suit her.

Forty years from now, he wanted them to sit on their back porch, holding hands, and remember this day with a fond smile. And how they'd re-created this moment by the pond many times since, the same as when love was new and the possibilities were laid out before them, the world theirs for the taking.

He softened and pulled out, desperate to squash the sudden, awful ache. Call him a sentimental fool.

He knew she had to have heard his declaration.

But not once on the drive back to town did she acknowledge his love—or give him the words in return.

16

I love you.

Three simple words had never thrilled—or scared—her more. She hadn't missed how he'd fallen silent as they dressed, his subsequent smiles and attempts at lighthearted conversation on the way back to town strained.

At an age when many women were fantasizing about finding the right man, falling in love, and settling into the status quo, Grace dreamed of taking on the world, one court case at a time. She had big plans involving the DA's office, and the picket fence fell into the nebulous "someday" category for her.

He loves me.

Sure, the sex was unparalleled. But not long ago, sex to him was an "itch" requiring a scratch. With Carmelita or whoever else was available. Was she supposed to believe he'd settled down? He had admitted he'd been quite the ladies' man.

Even if he'd changed, could she take the final step? Give over her heart, give up her independence, to a man who was a virtual tornado? Control and order didn't exist in his vocabulary.

Could the two of them ever work?

She recalled reading once that it's aerodynamically impossible for the bumblebee to be able to fly.

Tell that to the bumblebee.

Note to self—nothing's impossible if you believe. The jackpot question was, did she believe?

At his condo, she hovered in the living room while he packed his bag, and studied the photos of his family on the mantel. One group shot appeared to have been taken in recent years. A plump, attractive older woman, presumably his mother, surrounded by her children: Julian, his brother, and four sisters. Julian's parents made beautiful babies, because his sisters were pretty and his brother almost as stunning as Julian.

Julian would make beautiful babies, too.

Stunned at the errant thought, she turned away from the mantel. Fortunately, he walked into the room and interrupted her brooding, bag in hand and ready to go.

Once they were under way, she stole a glance at him. "I just want you to know how grateful I am for you coming to my rescue today. Overhearing that conversation between Warren and Derek was quite a shock."

"Not necessary," he said with an edge to his voice. "People who care for each other don't expect gratitude."

Okay. She was going to have to nip this awkwardness in the bud. "Well, people who care for each other express how they feel. I do care about you, Julian. And it means a lot to me that you dropped what you were doing to rush to my side."

He didn't respond. Damn, he probably thought she was a fickle bitch. She did care, dammit. She was even falling for him.

She just didn't want to.

At her place, he started to take his bag into her bedroom, but paused. "I don't want to presume. Am I sleeping in your room?"

Oh, that hurt. As much as she had it coming, his words lanced her chest. "Only if you want to." He didn't budge, making it clear that wasn't good enough. "I want you to."

He nodded, and put his bag in her room. When he emerged, he gestured toward the spare bedroom where she'd set up her office. "Mind if I use your computer?"

Man code for *I'd like to hide for a few hours.*

"No, go ahead."

A couple of hours later, she was watching the news when the music of his cell phone drifted from inside.

"*Dulce*," he greeted loudly, pleasure apparent. "How are you?"

On the sofa, she huffed to herself. *Dulce* meant sweet. She'd looked it up. A woman could torture herself for a very, very long time agonizing over how "sweet" his former lover was.

But he'd never done Carmelita over the hood of his Porsche.

So there.

His low, masculine tone drifted from the room for what seemed forever, and she resisted the impulse to hover in the hallway and eavesdrop. She paid not one iota of attention to the rest of the broadcast, couldn't have said if the entire state of California had finally slid into the Pacific, but she knew he ended the call at twenty-nine minutes.

The TV droned on, and she stayed put. Congratulated herself on not storming in there, wrapping her hands around his throat, and demanding to know what they'd discussed.

Does he miss her? Does he already regret spilling his guts and getting silence in return?

She heard him talking again moments later, perhaps leaving a message for the Realtor. After he went quiet, restlessness propelled her to wander into the office. Julian, who had at some point changed into shorts but no shirt, was surfing the Internet, reading an article, brow furrowed in concentration. His cell phone sat at his elbow.

"Hey," she said, ogling his muscular chest and washboard abs.

Turning, he blinked at her. "Oh, hey. Sorry if I abandoned you. I found a couple of old articles on the murders Shane told us about."

"Oh? Anything helpful, maybe something that strikes a chord?"

"Not really. It's just horrible, imagining what the victims suffered and thinking about their families. I wish I could do more."

She went to stand beside his chair and linked her arms around his neck. "You're doing all you can. Stop tormenting yourself."

"If I'd gone to the police all those years ago—"

"No. If you play that game, you'll drive yourself crazy. You didn't know then what you do now, so it's all moot."

"Maybe. But it hurts to think what I might have averted for other victims."

"*If* the Vines men are guilty. You have a theory at this point, nothing more."

"Don't forget the body count." He scowled up at her. "And the threats against you."

"Which might have been solely due to my part in the case Derek lost."

"Maybe."

"But you doubt it."

"Yeah. Too much coincidence."

Pulling up an extra chair, she sat and skimmed the article on the computer. "The second boy," she mused, "the one never identified. How can it be that nobody reports their child missing?" But she knew the answer.

"I think he was a runaway, or technically a street person, since they estimated his age as in his early twenties. All of the others have been local—victims of convenience. The killers don't have to look too hard."

"God, how creepy. Like a nest of spiders lying in wait."

"Exactly."

"Why not use street people exclusively?"

"They like them pretty and clean," he said ominously. "Easier to find what they want in clubs, where booze is flowing and inhibitions are loose."

"Jesus, you should've been a cop."

"Told you, Mama wouldn't hear of it." Glancing over, he gave her a tentative smile. An olive branch.

Seizing it, she smiled back. She hated the distance that had sprung up between them this afternoon, and wanted it gone. "Well, it's the police department's loss, fire department's gain."

He closed the article and poked around for a while longer, checking out other stories as she watched, content to simply sit with him. He didn't find any other articles, at least not the ones he was looking for. Just as he shut off the browser, the phone on her desk rang, giving her a start.

She picked it up, aware of his eyes on her. "Hello?"

"Grace?"

"Yes?"

"Hi, this is Shane Ford. Is Julian there?"

"Just a moment." She handed over the phone, whispering, "It's the detective."

He stuck the device to his ear. "Shane, what's up? Uh-huh. Ah, shit, no way," he groaned. "Where?"

Her skin prickled as she listened, on pins and needles, already dreading what news the cop had for them. After a couple more minutes, Julian pressed the end button and exhaled a deep sigh.

"They found another one. A male, but he doesn't fit Brett Charles' description—wrong hair color. They think he's a kid named Joey who disappeared while hiking four months ago, but they have to wait on a positive ID. Dismembered, like the others."

She swallowed the burning sensation in her throat. "Where was he found?"

"A mile from where the first two were discovered, along the Cumberland in a shallow grave. A lady out walking found the remains this afternoon when she threw a ball for her retriever and he didn't come back. She found the dog digging at something . . . and, well, you can guess the rest."

"Oh, God, how awful."

"You know what? We can't solve this sitting here, tonight. Why don't we cuddle on the couch with a glass of wine and forget about all of this for a while? How does that sound?"

"Heavenly," she said, standing. "I'll grab a nice bottle of Ledson if you do the honors."

"Deal."

She was acutely aware of his presence as he followed her into the kitchen, smelling faintly of cologne and sex, puckering her nipples. Trying to ignore his effect on her libido, she yanked a bottle of Chardonnay out of the fridge, grabbed the corkscrew from a drawer, and handed them over.

While he uncorked the bottle, she fished two wineglasses

from the cabinet and in no time, they were engrossed in a cable program on the end of the world in 2012. What that said about them, she didn't care to guess.

During a commercial, perhaps sensing her curiosity, he said, "Carmelita called me earlier."

"Oh?" Right, like she hadn't been dying to know every detail.

"Yep. She finally has definite dinner plans tomorrow night with Konrad, the guy she's been after."

But the one she really wants is you.

That tidbit would never cross her lips.

"Good for her. What else is going on?"

Since I could have grown a frigging garden in the time you spent on the phone.

"Not much. She gave me an update from home, said she talked with my oldest sister and Mama wants me to come for a visit, though Mama won't say so. Carmelita's family is bugging her, too, so she suggested we drive together, save expenses on gas for the trip."

"I'll bet she did." Whoa, that came out sort of nasty.

He craned his neck to study her face. "Why do you say it like that?"

"You two are close. I'm the interloper, 'Jules baby.' Do you think the idea of your taking a trip home with her thrills the shit out of me?"

A grin split his face. "You're jealous."

"You're damned right," she sputtered.

Cupping the back of her head, he gave her a tender kiss, lids heavy, dark eyes glittering. "I'm not going anywhere with her, and you're the only one I plan to take home to Mama, my *bella*. Never forget it."

That was dangerously close to the declaration of love he'd made by the pond, but for some strange reason, it didn't frighten her like before. Instead, the thought of being his one and only wrapped around her, steeped in the warmth of his body curled around hers.

This felt good. Right.

"Want to go to bed? I'm pooped," she said.

"Me, too." Taking her hand, he led her to the bedroom.

In short order, they were naked and snuggling—and his erection was springing to life against her thigh. Electric tension, fraught with desire, hummed between them. They needed, but it was softer, more languorous, not the animal intensity of before.

Covering her with his body, he settled between her thighs and entered her, linking their fingers together. He made love to her with gentle passion, coaxing them higher, higher, until they shattered and he poured himself into her. Held her close to his heart.

He didn't say he loved her, but he didn't have to.

She felt his love all the same.

Grace didn't have court for the rest of the week, so she made an executive decision—she called Alice and told her she wouldn't be in until Monday. The official story was she'd decided to work from home. She and Julian knew the truth.

For one thing, she couldn't bear to be near her office or the parking garage after what she'd overheard yesterday. Her fear was too raw, and Julian's solution—to hang out and be her protective shadow—wasn't feasible. Too many gossipmongers to bring Daddy running, getting into her biz. And Daddy certainly didn't need the stress of learning what was going on.

No, Julian was off duty and they were going to spend the day together, snooping. The recent deaths were weighing on him, and after some cajoling and outright arguing with his

detective friend, he'd wheedled out of the guy the two loca-
tions where the bodies had been found. The areas were no
longer roped off, but Ford didn't understand why he'd want
to walk around out there. Neither did she.

This evening, to get his mind off killers and victims, she'd
made plans for them to eat at a quiet Italian place she'd been
to before. And if she had to ravage his yummy body all
night long in order to keep him from fretting? Well, a girl
must suffer.

After a quick breakfast of cereal, followed by a steamy
shower together, they dressed in jeans and casual shirts. Grace
pulled her hair back into a ponytail, mainly to keep it out of
her face, but this incited her playful lover to pull and bat it
around constantly.

"Dang it, stop that," she groused as they walked to his
car.

"Why? I like messing with you." His boyish grin melted
her into a puddle.

"I'll mess with you," she muttered, annoyance gone.

"Promises, promises."

"You're insatiable."

"And you can't get enough of me," he boasted.

At least his ego was alive and healthy. Once they were on
their way, she took the opportunity to examine the cut on his
bicep. She was glad to see it closed and healing, along with
the smaller one on his chest hidden by his shirt. She hoped
they wouldn't make scars. Once this was over, she wanted
no reminders of how close she'd come to losing him.

Taking the county roads, he drove them to a spot a couple
of miles below Cheatham Dam. Where tire tracks were torn
in the earth, he pulled onto the shoulder. "The way Shane
described the area, this must be it. Several sets of tracks made
by their vehicles, all the way to the bank."

"Honey, I'm with Ford. I don't see what you hope to—"

But he was already out, a man on a mission. Drawn by some invisible force she couldn't comprehend. It was beyond macabre, scary as hell, being here. She wanted to throw him into the car and peel out, before they met the same end as the stupid couple in the slasher movies who always bought it because they were poking around in monster land like two dimwits.

Hurrying to his side, she took his hand, glancing around at the trees, searching for the slavering bogeyman. If something horrible befell them out here, nobody would ever know. Until it was too late.

"There," he said, pointing.

Indeed, the excavation site could not be missed. However, there was nothing much to see. The police had left no traces behind to tell the tale of what had taken place here, save for the scars on the earth. The grave was a simple hole, square-shaped and not very big, which was really gruesome; she didn't want to think about what the killer did to make a body fit into such a small space.

"Come on, Julian, there's nothing to see."

She looked over at him, hoping for agreement. Instead, he was staring at the hole, fists clenched, mouth drawn into a grim line. His eyes were strangely flat, his breathing harsh.

"Make the hole three by three," he said hoarsely.

"What? You're scaring me!" Stepping in front of him, she blocked his view of the grave and cupped his face. "What are you talking about?"

His gaze lifted to hers, filled with horror. "That day, in Derek's room, when I was coming around, I was trying to clear my vision, scanning the room for my clothes. I heard someone say, 'Make the hole three by three.' I was frantic to get away."

She felt like she'd been punched. "Are you sure? It's understandable with all of this going on, the stress, perhaps you *think* that's what you heard."

"No." He glanced past her at the ground. "I've been trying to remember all morning. Something about holes. I know what I heard, and it was real. Out of context, the phrase didn't make sense and I'd dismissed it, until now."

Desperate as she was to keep him from more pain, he wasn't conjuring this. And if one believed what he said, and she did, as a teenager he'd barely escaped a hideous death.

"You need to call Ford. While we're making tracks out of here," she emphasized with a shudder. "I'll drive. You call."

They slid into his car and he handed over his keys, then flipped open his cell phone. She gladly left the creepy place in her dust, and what's more, she had no intention of visiting the second site. One was more than enough.

Ford was away from his desk, so Julian reached him on his cell, relating what he'd remembered. "So, what do you say? Is it enough for a warrant, with the other stuff?"

They batted conversation back and forth, but she got the gist before he hung up. "No dice?"

"He said it's another good thread to tie the case together, but still not enough to search their place. Dammit!" He pounded the dashboard and fell silent for a moment. "He did say the San Antonio police got permission from the owners of the Vineses' old estate to conduct a search, and they'll start today. Everyone is being cooperative."

"That's good." She wanted to be reassuring. "We'll keep our fingers crossed for them to find something solid."

Ignoring his directive to head to the other site, she drove them to nearby Clarksville, swinging out to Dunbar Cave State Park northeast of town, just for the hell of it, and pulled into the visitors' parking lot.

"Have you ever been here?" she asked.

"No, but I've always meant to come by." He shrugged. "One of those points of interest I've never gotten around to, I guess."

"Want to see the cave? We can't hike through it because you have to make a reservation, but it's really cool to see up close."

"Sure, why not?"

Happy to have found a way to distract him for a bit longer, she got out and led the way, pointing out the visitors' center and the lake. "The mouth of the cave is farther than it seems, down that trail a ways. They say in the old days the locals used to hold dances and other events down there."

"Yeah? What else do they say?"

He grinned, and she knew he was humoring her. Fine by her, as long as he relaxed. "Hmm, let's see. It's closed from November to the middle of March because of all the bats in there sleeping. Or whatever bats do."

Throwing his arm around her, he laughed and kissed her head. "Hibernating, *querida.*"

"Whatever. Jeff Corwin, I'm not."

He seemed to find that really funny, but she didn't care if it was at her expense. This was fun. Who didn't like caves?

A few minutes later, they arrived at the huge mouth of the cave, and Julian whistled. "Wow, this is amazing. I can see the lure, why people are fascinated by them. You're looking at millions of years of history. Who knows what ancient people once lived down in there?"

"You have caves in San Antonio, right?"

"Oh, sure. Our most impressive one is Cascade Caverns, with the hundred-foot waterfall inside, but we have several other small ones. . . ."

Grace paused in her study of an interesting formation to

see why he'd trailed off. The man looked like someone had dropped an anvil on his head. His lips were parted, but they barely moved as he spoke.

"Oh, holy God. It cannot be that fucking simple. It *can't*."

"What can't?" Dread returned, full force, banishing the easy humor they'd managed to find.

As if in a trance, he walked slowly to the bars that blocked the entrance to the tunnel used for guided hikes, and wrapped his fingers around the metal. "These keep people out. They can also keep them in."

Cold seeped into her bones. "What do you mean?" But, God help them, she was afraid she knew.

"In San Antonio, the Vines estate has a cave entrance on the property," he said quietly. "All of the locals, especially us kids, were strictly forbidden from going down there. One year, they put up a gate a lot like this one, to avoid a lawsuit from somebody getting hurt, they said. Nobody questioned it, and why would they?" He turned to face her, expression haunted.

"Does their place here have a cave entrance?"

He nodded. "At the back of the property. I know only because we've had to take the boat out on a couple of water rescues in that area and the mouth overlooks the Cumberland. There are no bars across it, just some No Trespassing signs along the bank almost obscured by the brush."

"Bars would be too noticeable to the public."

"Maybe, but who would care?" Pulling his cell phone from his pocket, he hit speed dial. "I do have a hunch about one thing. Those San Antonio cops searching the grounds? They're looking in the wrong place."

Brett huddled in the gloom, rocking.

They'd come for him again soon. Do unspeakable things

to him, torture him with their instruments, try to get him to break.

He'd figured out their method. Once you broke, you were toast. The screamers were torn limb from limb. He knew because he'd heard. He'd been introduced to the rock chamber stained with rivers of inky blood, felt their ghosts hovering, filled with despair.

So he'd fought like a wild thing.

Surprise, assholes.

It had taken all three of them to subdue him, and even then they'd resorted to the needle. He was proud of that. Right now, fighting was all he had to keep him holding on.

He was alone, save for his faith. Stripped to nothing except what made him human, what separated him from those animals. He was bent, but he would not break.

He would escape from this hell under the earth. He only had to bide his time.

And wait.

17

"Have you gotten my damned messages? Call me." Julian snapped his phone shut and slumped on the sofa, cursing in frustration. "Where the hell can Ford be? Was he abducted by aliens?"

"Give the man a break, honey. His plate is full at the moment, and it's been only a few hours. I'm sure he'll get back to you the minute he has a chance."

Julian took a calming breath. "You're right. It's just that once I get my teeth into something, not knowing the outcome drives me up the wall. This is one reason why I wouldn't have made a good cop—everything moves too fricking *slow*."

Grace propped her feet on the coffee table and studied him in amusement. "You'd break a dozen rules on a daily basis. Not unlike now, I'm guessing."

"I only break one or two. On a good day." He had to get a grip or he was going to drive Grace loony tunes along with him. "All right, this is ridiculous. Let's check out the Italian restaurant you told me about."

"Sounds good. Anything's better than sitting here watching cable specials on the end of the world." She stood, stretching.

"And maybe by the time we're done eating, Shane will have given us the good news that our local sickos have been thrown in jail."

"I'll lift a toast to that," she said with enthusiasm.

Standing, he glanced down at his T-shirt and jeans. "Are we okay dressed casual?"

"We're fine. It's not fancy."

"Then after you, *bella*."

Julian took over the driving again, leaving his cell phone handy for Grace to answer if Shane called. God knew he was trying to put this entire sordid mess out of his head for the evening, but his gut churned. Staring at the bars over the entrance to Dunbar Cave had been a revelation of biblical proportions. The caves were the connecting thread between past and present, the invisible spiderweb that had been brushing his cheek for days.

Sure, the tie could be a coincidence.

But sometimes a person *knows*, deep down. When all the links fall into place and there's the unmistakable *click*, and every nerve ending sings. Then it becomes a waiting game to hear the good guys won, peace and security restored.

Except for the victims and their families.

Okay, Jules, you've done what you could. The cops will do the rest. With a mighty effort, he shoved aside the helpless frustration and concentrated on spending the evening with Grace.

"I made an offer on the land," he said, and pride swelled inside him.

Her reply was soft. "I'm proud of you. You're going after something you want, making it happen. That must feel awesome."

"Yes, it certainly does. What would make it even more

special is having somebody to share it with." He glanced at her, but couldn't make out her expression in the darkness.

"You have me."

"Do I?"

She fell silent and thankfully, they'd arrived. He pulled into a parking spot, shut off the engine, not making a move to get out. Neither did she.

"What am I to you, *bella*? Is it wishful thinking on my part to believe your feelings run deeper than just a friend?"

"That's not a bad thing to be," she countered, her tone a little trapped.

"No, it isn't." Scooting around to face her, he cupped her cheek. "But I want more. I don't need a promise of forever right now, but I do need hope. I've told you how I feel and I'll say it again—I love you, baby."

"Julian—"

"I love you," he repeated. "How do you feel about me? What is it you want? Tell me the truth, Grace."

"No, I . . ." Shaking her head, she made a strangled noise. "I don't know what I want."

"Even now?" He swore he felt his chest crack. Split open, torn asunder. Again, he'd pushed, unable to leave well enough alone. This time, perhaps too far.

"What happened to giving us room to progress naturally? What's the rush?"

If he wasn't so fucking sad, he would've laughed. He, unrepentant onetime ladies' man, had fallen for a commitment-phobe. Cosmic justice served cold.

"None, Grace. None at all. Let's eat, huh? I'm starved."

He wasn't, really. Not anymore. But he was determined to salvage as much of their evening as possible. No matter how badly he longed to hide out in his own place tonight and keep company with his Patrón, he wouldn't leave Grace alone. Even if he suggested that she stay with Kat and Six-Pack, she'd refuse. After overhearing Warren's threat, she'd not risk her pregnant sister's safety.

An untenable situation, being stuck in the same living space with a woman who didn't love him. He wished to God he'd never given her the ammunition to rip out his guts.

Their meal alternated between awkward silences and stilted conversation. A glass of wine didn't help, but three might, if he wasn't driving. But then he might say or do something even more incredibly stupid, reinforcing her low opinion of him as a keeper.

"Grace, I apologize for pushing," he said quietly.

"You feel used, and I guess I can see how. You don't trust my feelings for you, so what do we have?"

"No, you don't trust *yourself*." This seemed to startle her, and he gave her a sad smile. "You almost have it all. What's missing? I wonder."

"That's quite an analysis. What makes you so sure I'm missing anything in my life?"

"Because when I look at you, I see me . . . before I met the woman who made me believe, trust, and appreciate my gifts."

There was no mistaking the wetness in her pretty eyes. "How could I have done all of that? I've led you on a chase, bucked you at every turn. Hurt you," she whispered.

"Don't you see? Before I met you, I had no direction, always searching for the next best thing to make myself happy. Another woman, more booze, a fast car. And then I met you, so beautiful and unattainable." Reaching across the table, he clasped her hand. "You stopped me in my tracks, challenged me. And gradually I understood you were for real. You were the woman for me, no one else. I know how you feel; it's easier to cling to the safety of what you know than to jump without a parachute. But I'm glad I let go. For you."

His message was clear. *Will you let go for me?*

He didn't know how to put himself out there any more, to express himself any better. She looked down at their joined hands, then away, as he held his breath. Praying she'd say anything except they were nothing more than friends with benefits. If he was more to her, he'd wait forever if need be.

Staring at his plate, he was pretending fascination with twirling his spaghetti when her question took him off guard.

"When the danger is over, are you . . . will you stay? With me?"

He froze, his brain momentarily shorting out. Live with Grace? There was nothing he wanted more. But he remembered his original vow—when she declared her undying love, and not a second sooner. Maybe, to Grace, her invitation was tantamount to stating her feelings.

"Are you asking me to move in with you?" he asked carefully.

"Yes, I suppose I am." Biting her lip, she fidgeted with her napkin.

"Why, Grace?" *Please, tell me.*

"I love spending my days and nights with you. I value your companionship. Those are good reasons." She paused. "Will you?"

Disappointment bubbled, hot and unrelenting. He wanted the words so badly; he was dying inside. Stupid pride wouldn't let him leap at her offer. But she'd made a positive move, and he wasn't about to shut her down, either. "I'll think about it, *querida*. All right?"

She stared at him, surprise etched on her beautiful face. The second the words left his lips, he wanted to call them back, tell her he'd move in tonight. However, his gut told him he'd done the right thing.

"I really want to be with you, to spend all of our nights together. Please believe me," she said, voice betraying a bit of anxiousness.

"I do, and I want the same."

"Promise you'll let me know soon?"

"I promise, baby."

Smiling, he reached for her hand, curled his fingers around hers. Confusion and indecision warred on her face, but after a few seconds, she appeared to relax. He heaved a sigh of relief as she took a sip of her wine, visibly trying to regroup.

Yes, it seemed he'd made the right move for a change.

"Julian?" She nodded to a couple across the room. "Isn't that Carmelita?"

Well, it would be his luck tonight, wouldn't it? Turning his head, he peered across the dimly lit restaurant to the couple seated against the far wall at a cozy table for two. Sure enough, his friend was having dinner with a dark-haired man.

"That's her, and the date must be Konrad."

Carmelita looked great, as always, cinnamon hair tumbling over the shoulders of her black top. The man appeared enraptured by her bubbly conversation, smiling and nodding.

Julian's pulse stuttered unexpectedly. Something about the man's profile, how he tilted his head, set off alarm bells in his brain.

"Shouldn't we go say hello?" Even though Grace made the suggestion, she didn't sound too enthusiastic.

"No, I'll get the scoop later. Besides, they're leaving."

The couple stood and began to make their way toward the exit. She walked ahead of her date, and as she did, he put his right arm around her waist in a proprietary gesture. Julian caught a glimpse of something sticking from underneath the sleeve of his sport coat, and they were out the door before Julian realized what he'd seen.

"A brace. That man had on a wrist brace!"

"What? Oh . . ."

Grace registered his words as he pushed to his feet and bolted through the restaurant, dodging patrons and busy waiters. One waiter bobbled his tray full of dishes, but Julian didn't stop to find out if he'd caused an accident.

Grace called for him to slow down, but he ran faster, burst out the doors, and stood, scanning the parking lot frantically. Just then, the couple emerged from the shadows under a streetlamp, heading for a car parked alone in the gloom.

"Carmelita!" he yelled. "Wait!"

They were only a few steps from the car. He couldn't get to her in time.

"*Dulce*, wait! Stop!"

She heard him that time and turned, mouth dropping open to see him running full tilt toward them. The man with her spun, took one look at Julian, and cursed, reaching under his coat. Planting his feet, he extended his arm, something shiny in his hand.

"Back off!" the man bellowed, and the muzzle flashed.

At the pop, Julian hit the ground, gravel biting into his palms. No pain bloomed, no gunshot wound, and he scrambled to his knees to see Konrad—or whatever his name was— grab Carmelita by the hair and shove the muzzle against her temple.

"Get in and drive! Do it!"

"No!" He was on his feet and running again, racing to stop them. "Leave her alone!"

But the man was already shoving her into the Mercedes.

The one with the license plate that began with the same letters as the one he'd used to drive away with Brett Charles.

Dios, no, please!

He couldn't catch them, no matter how hard he ran. He saw the man's silhouette, the gun to Carmelita's head, as he forced her to drive away.

This time, however, he had the entire plate number.

"Oh, God." He stopped, panting, hands on his knees, trying to catch his breath. Footsteps approached, running, and he heard Grace calling his name. The gunshot! He turned, searching her from head to toe. "Are you hurt?"

"No, he missed us both," she said, out of breath. "Was that him? The guy who broke in and tried to kill you?"

"Unless you believe in impossible odds, yes. And that's the man I saw leaving the club with Brett Charles."

"What's he doing with Carmelita?"

Fear gripped him. "I think that's coincidence. Maybe." He took out his cell phone and dialed Shane again. When the man picked up and said hello, he nearly fell over. "Where the fuck have you been?"

"I was just about to call you. Got your messages about the cave idea and let me just say, we owe you one. That cave on the San Antonio property? The entrance had been covered up with rocks and dirt and it took our brethren there a while to find it. Man, it has holding cells built into it. They said the place was obviously used as a prison and torture chamber. The hellhole is fucking teeming with forensic evidence."

"Search warrant?"

"We're working on it. A few hours, at most."

"Not good enough. That bastard who broke into my apartment is the one I saw leaving the club with Brett Charles.

He was having dinner with a friend of mine tonight and I spotted the cast on his wrist, recognized him. He took a shot at me and Grace, then forced my friend to drive off at gunpoint."

"We've still got time to get the Vineses. This man, if he's connected to them, doesn't know we suspect them. All he knows is you recognized him. Does he have a name?"

"Konrad something, works at her accounting firm. Probably not his real name, but I have something just as good—the whole plate number on his Mercedes."

"Good job. Lay it on me."

He gave Shane the number and the name of Carmelita's accounting firm.

"We're on to him, all of them, so don't you worry," Shane reassured him. "They're going down, tonight. Sit tight, my friend. I mean that."

"Yeah." The lie stuck in his throat. "Call me." Hanging up, he looked into Grace's wide eyes.

"The cave idea panned out?"

He nodded, raking a hand through his hair. "They're about to get them all for kidnapping and murder. But the warrant will take too long for Carmelita, and anyone else who might still be alive, should 'Konrad' report in and they panic."

"What are we going to do now?" She fell in step beside him as he jogged for his car.

"*You're* going to go inside to call your sister and Six-Pack to come get you," he said. "*I'm* about to trespass on private property."

"Oh, no you're not! I'm going with you." Grace glared at him. No way was he doing this alone. "If there's the slightest chance of getting Carmelita and anyone else out of their clutches alive, we have to go now. There's no time to waste arguing."

"Dammit, Grace!"

"Safety in numbers, plus two people can accomplish more working together. In fact, extra backup is in order."

They jumped into his car and he fired it up, leaving the restaurant behind in a shower of gravel. "What extra backup?"

"Give me your cell phone."

He handed it over and she quickly placed a call. Her brother-in-law picked up on the second ring and she got right to the point. "Howard, it's Grace. We need your help."

"Anything," he said, instantly alert. "What's up?"

Ignoring the slight shake of Julian's head, she outlined what had happened tonight. "In short, the police can't move without the warrant, and by then it will be too late. We need reinforcements. Can you help?"

"I'm there, sugar. Directions?"

"Hang on." She handed the phone to Julian. "I don't know how to get there."

Julian took over, giving Howard the directions, with a dose of caution. "When you turn down their road, douse the lights and drive past the house. The road winds down through the trees and is eventually hidden from the house. You'll come to a fork. Hang to the left and drive along the river if it's not too wet to get your truck down there. Otherwise, you'll have to park and walk."

He paused, listening, then continued. "Yes, about a hundred yards down, we'll be waiting below the cave entrance. We'll have to climb up to it and it'll be pitch-black, so bring a good flashlight and shoes with tread. We'll all go together so we don't get lost. And Howard? Thanks, man."

He hung up and handed the phone back to her, but didn't speak. Studying his profile, she wished tonight had turned out differently. She'd hurt him so badly, she wanted to cry. Why couldn't she just say the words? Why wasn't she brave enough to take the leap as he'd done? Just let go of the rope?

What's wrong with me?

But this wasn't the time. Later, maybe, when all this was over.

Julian followed the route he'd told Howard to take, dousing his lights as they drove past the darkened house. Thankfully, the moon was bright, shining on the trees and the river to their left, so they weren't driving completely blind. However, the skeletal branches encroaching on either side of the car, reaching out like bony fingers, lent a special brand of creepiness to the mission.

As the car bumped over the rutted path along the river, Julian snorted. "If I'm going to be driving across fields and shit all the time, I might have to trade this thing in for a big-assed truck like Howard's."

"When you're the proud owner of that property, fixing fences and building your house, you're going to need one."

"You think so?"

"I know so."

His smile lit the darkness. "Thanks, baby."

To his credit, he didn't push, didn't ask whether she'd be there, overseeing the plans with him. Little did he know she very much could envision that future, at his side, creating their paradise together.

During her daydream, he'd stopped the car. Glancing around, she shivered, reluctant to leave the safety of the car. Coming here ahead of the cavalry had seemed like a good idea, but now she wished she'd urged him to back off and wait. Not that he would've listened.

They got out and shut their doors quietly, though there

wasn't a living soul around to hear. She hugged herself to ward off the sudden chill. "Can you feel it?"

"What, baby?"

"Evil."

He came around to her side of the car, pulled her close. "Yeah. I've been feeling that for about fifteen years."

"It's almost over," she said, resting her cheek against his chest.

"God willing."

They stood entwined until the whine of an engine, the crunch of the road under tires, approached. The outline of Howard's truck became visible and finally pulled to a stop behind Julian's car. To her surprise, two figures got out.

"Party started yet?" Howard's voice.

"We're waiting on the keg," Julian said. "Who's with you?"

"It's me. Sean. Couldn't let you guys get all the action."

Grace barely made out Julian clapping each of them on the back, thanking them.

"No problem," Howard said. "What's the plan?"

Turning, Julian popped his trunk. Fishing inside, he found what he sought and turned on the flashlight, keeping it pointed at the ground. "You guys bring one of these?"

"Check," Sean said, waving his.

"Okay. Grace and I will hike up there and check out the cave. Why don't you two go up to the house and make sure nobody's home, keep an eye out?"

"Since none of us are familiar with the layout, Sean and I will go up there with you first so we can see which way you've gone. Just in case we have to come looking for you."

"Good idea. Ready?"

Without waiting to hear whether they were, Julian led the

uphill climb. The grade was steep, the foot- and handholds tricky, but approximately ten minutes later they were standing at the mouth of the cave, shining their lights on the rather unimpressive crescent-shaped entrance.

"Doesn't look like much," Sean observed.

Julian started inside, ducking to keep from hitting his head. "Let's take a look."

Grace followed on his heels, the others behind her, and in a few steps, they all stood gaping at the sight before them.

"Oh, my Lord!" Grace's voice echoed off the huge cathedral ceiling. "Look at this place!"

"Dang, I feel like I should, like, genuflect or something," Howard said in awe.

"You're not Catholic, big guy."

"Still."

The soaring dome indeed had the feel of a church, though the floor was pitted and uneven. Two tunnels branched off the main chamber, and she dreaded venturing down either of them. This was nothing like the nice, safe guided tours given at the state parks. Anything could happen to them here and no one would ever be the wiser.

"Let's take the tunnel on the right to start with," Julian said. "We'll give the search about fifteen or twenty minutes and then head back to check in. I don't want to get lost and my theory is, if there's anything down here to find, they wouldn't want to have to walk far."

"All right. Keep your cell phone on vibrate," Howard put in. "Don't know what kind of reception we'll get, but every added precaution can't hurt."

"You guys be careful." Sean started back for the mouth, Howard behind him.

"Stay with me, baby," Julian said, heading for the tunnel.

"I'm on you like Velcro."

To prove it, she hooked a finger through one of his belt loops, trailing him through the narrow passage. The path was twisty, the footing tricky, and she had to concentrate not to knock him over.

Suddenly he stopped, and she plowed into his back. "Ow! A little warning, please?"

He waved the light on the ground in front of him. "Look at the dirt here."

Peering around him, she noted a wet, boggy area with dirt and mud in the path, likely caused by rainwater dripping through the rock. "So?"

"No tracks. If people passed through here all the time, we'd see muddy shoe prints going out the other side. The area is undisturbed."

"Brilliant, Mr. Holmes. Now what? Turn back or go a little farther?"

"A little farther, just to be sure."

The trip was brief. Moments later, the excursion ended in a small, empty chamber that some American Indian might have used as a bedroom.

Julian sighed. "Okay, we'll go back and call Six-Pack, let them know this one's a bust, then try the other one. What if I was wrong? I'm starting to feel like an idiot."

"Better than feeling guilty for hoping we don't find a thing so we can get out of here," she admitted. "This place is seriously giving me the creeps."

Latching on to his jeans again, she tried not to think about bats. They hadn't seen any so far, and she hoped they were out hunting their dinner. They made it to the main chamber without mishap, and Julian walked to the mouth of the cave for better reception and made the call.

"Hey, it's me. The right tunnel was a dead end, so we're going down the left one now. Any movement up there?"

Paused. "Okay, we'll see you soon." He flipped the phone shut and replaced it in his pocket. "All's quiet at the house."

"Great. Let's get moving so we can go home and open a really massive bottle of wine."

Taking her hand, he led her to the other tunnel, eventually letting go so she could follow single file again. She stuck close, noting the pitted hollows on either side of the path, perfect for some horror-movie monster to leap out of and rip them apart.

"Ugh, I hate these niches in the wall, or whatever they are—"

"Shh." He stopped, listening.

"What?"

"Listen."

At first she heard nothing. And then . . . a faint noise. Sort of high-pitched, echoing from the bowels of the earth. Every hair on her body stood on end as though she'd been electrocuted. "Is that . . . *singing*?"

"That's what it sounds like."

"Shit. Maybe we should go back, call the guys."

"This might be our only chance to see what's down here. Or who. Come on."

As they moved slowly down the dank corridor, the sing-song noise became clearer. As did the rancid stench that did not belong in a place of mere rock and earth.

Julian made a sound of disgust. "*Cristo*, I don't want to think what that smell might be."

And then, from somewhere just beyond them in the gloom, came a sound she'd never forget. A very human, raspy voice singing the low, haunting melody of "Comfortably Numb." Goose bumps broke out on her arms and she clutched at Julian's back.

"Oh my God, Julian!"

He picked up the pace as they rounded a bend. The flashlight beams glinted off metal. Bars. Cell doors.

Halting, he shone his light into the first one, and a soft exclamation escaped his lips.

"Ah, *Madre de Dios*."

Huddled in the corner of his prison, naked and filthy, a young man rocked, lost in his own world. Julian tapped on the bars to get his attention.

"Son, can you hear me?"

The singing and rocking stopped, and the young man lifted his head, face crumpling. "I won't scream. . . . You can't make me."

Oh, God, poor baby.

"We're not going to hurt you," Julian soothed. "We're going to get you out. What's your name, son?"

The kid squinted into the light and considered a moment, as though trying to recall.

"B-Brett," he said, voice breaking. "Brett Charles."

18

For the kid's benefit, Julian struggled to rein in his horror.
Because, shit, those slender shoulders were shaking and
Julian's terror would amplify the kid's.

"Brett! Cut it out and listen to me," he barked. The cries
became muffled as the kid made a visible effort to stop, and
the noise tore at his heart. "You want us to bust you out,
you've got to listen, okay?"

"O-okay."

"My name's Julian and I'm a firefighter with the Sugarland Fire Department," he told Brett, using the same friendly
tone he did with accident victims. Firefighters inspired trust
and a sense things would be all right. It would give Brett
something to focus on.

"A f-firefighter?"

"Yeah. How we found you is a long story you'll hear after you're back with your family, safe and sound. But first
you've got to tell me where I can find the keys, son."

"Keys? I—I don't know. Let me think."

"When they come down here, do they bring the keys with
them?" Dangerous ground. He didn't want to trigger a round
of hysteria by reminding him of his captors, but he needed
Brett's help.

"I—no! No, there's no jingling noise when they come,"

he said hoarsely, getting excited. "That comes later. After they've been to their room."

"So they get the keys from there?"

"Y-yes, I'm sure they do."

"Where is this room, Brett?"

"Keep going, to your right. Down there, not far. N-never takes them long to come back."

"All right. My lady friend and I are going to go look and we'll be right back."

"Please, no! Don't leave me here!"

"Brett, I'm Grace," she said from Julian's left side. "I'll stay right here and talk to you, okay?"

Brett sniffled. "All right."

He grasped her hand. "*Bella*, I'm not leaving you here in the dark."

"He's been in the dark this whole time," she said stubbornly. "A few minutes won't hurt. We'll be fine."

They didn't have time to debate. Sean and Six-Pack were going to wonder soon why they hadn't checked in. "Don't move an inch. I'll be right back."

Giving her a quick kiss, he moved up the corridor, glancing into the other cells. All were empty, and he tried not to imagine what had befallen the previous occupants. Most likely Brett knew, and coming to grips with his ordeal would take years of love and therapy.

Locating the door at the end of the tunnel took only a couple of minutes. Unlike the cells, this door was wooden, crudely fashioned. More importantly, it wasn't locked. He pushed the door open, swept the light around the chamber, and gasped. Fought down a wave of sickness.

He no longer had to imagine how the victims died.

The room was awash in dark stains that could only be blood. Several tables against the rock wall, the floor, coated in it. The tabletops bristled with all sorts of axes, saws, pliers, rods, hammers, and other items he didn't care to name. In one corner, a video camera provided silent testament to the truly evil acts committed here. Julian prayed the police found film.

In the middle of the torture chamber was a metal gurney covered in blood, scratches, and dents.

Bile rose in his throat and he averted his eyes, frantically searching for the keys. A hook on the wall? There were many things hung on the wall, none of them what he sought. He began scanning the tables, knowing better than to touch anything unless he had to. The cops would need this stuff as evidence.

Time was ticking away. He needed to get back to Grace and Brett. If he didn't find the keys soon, they'd have to leave Brett and phone the cops from outside. The thought of doing that to the kid was unacceptable.

He was about ready to try to find something else to force the door open, or maybe even blow the lock, when his light caught a glitter of twisted metal between two saws.

"Thank God." A small ring was nestled there, as though tossed carelessly by the last user. He grabbed it and hurried out.

In his beam he could see Grace sitting on the rocky floor next to the bars, holding the kid's hand as she talked to him in soothing tones. He was leaning against the bars as close to her as possible, seeking comfort.

"Hold on, Brett. We're getting you out," he said, joining them. "Baby, hold the flashlight for me."

After she freed his hands, he went through the keys, trying them one by one. His hands shook with adrenaline and a pure fear he'd never experienced before, not even the day he'd fled from Derek. But Brett seemed more calm and was actually standing, for which Julian was grateful.

The next-to-last key turned, and the lock scraped open. "Yes! Brett, can you walk?"

"I think so." He sounded distant, in shock, fading.

Julian pocketed the keys to give to the cops and opened the door. It gave with a loud squeal that made him cringe, and Brett hobbled out to meet them. "Here, let's give you some privacy, huh?"

He stripped off his shirt and quickly used the sleeves to tie it around Brett's waist, covering the essentials. The kid had enough to deal with, and he sure didn't need to face the oncoming barrage of cops and paramedics bare-assed naked.

"Th-thanks, man."

"No sweat. Put your arm around me and let's get the fuck out of here."

Brett did okay at first, but the closer they got to the mouth of the cave, the weaker he became. Julian was never so glad to see Sean and Six-Pack as the moment they emerged from the tunnel. His friends rushed toward them, surprised exclamations punctuating the darkness.

"Jesus Christ!"

"Is that him?" Sean asked.

"Guys, this is Brett Charles. Brett's been through hell and back, and he needs to get down to the truck while we call the cops." He spoke to his charge. "Brett, these are firefighter friends I work with. We're going to take good care of you."

"Yes . . . sir."

Brett's knees buckled. Julian kept him from hitting the ground and Howard scooped the kid effortlessly into his big arms, carrying him out of the cave.

"I called 911," Sean said. "We need to make tracks. We came back to tell you there're two men at the house, and one is holding your friend Carmelita at gunpoint. From where we were hiding, we heard them discuss coming down here to put her in a cell." Sean hurried after Six-Pack.

"Shit," Julian breathed. He made to follow them, but Grace grabbed his arm.

"Wait, what about the other cells?"

"They're empty."

"Are you sure? There are a lot of shadows and crannies. You could sweep a flashlight over something down there and not even see it."

She was right. What if he'd missed someone? "Catch up with them and I'll go back and check."

"No, we go together or not at all."

A low hum and whirring noise cut off their debate, and the cave was suddenly bathed in a pool of dim light. The lights were set into recesses and behind rock formations, out of the way and unnoticeable in the dark. Somehow, the place appeared more eerie with them on.

"I vote you go together, too," a voice said with a nervous laugh.

Shoving Grace behind him, Julian whirled to see Derek and Konrad blocking the way out. As Sean had reported, Konrad was holding a gun to Carmelita's head, fingers digging into her arm. Her eyes were wide with terror and confusion, and anger bloomed in his gut.

Assessing the odds, he noted Konrad appeared to be the only one armed. Derek had one hand in his pants pocket, fiddling with something. His dick, most likely. He kept glancing behind him as though expecting someone, probably Warren. Thank God Howard and Sean had gotten away with Brett. It occurred to Julian that the two men in front of them had no idea he'd been sprung.

The biggest challenge was stalling them until the police

arrived. At which point these men would surrender peacefully. Not.

Plan B, he had to get the gun away from Konrad, create a way for the women to get to safety. If only he could distract the bastard.

"You know, Julian, I'm very sorry it had to come to this," Derek said, sounding strangely sincere. "I'm sorry you had to recognize Carl here while he was with your friend. It's unfortunate, but sometimes things are out of our control."

Carl, not Konrad. He'd known the name was a fake.

Taking a deep breath, he pushed down his anger and decided to try to appeal to Derek's sensitive side. If he possessed one. "*You* can control this. I know you don't want to hurt anyone, Derek. I can see that."

Derek looked sad. "I've never wanted to hurt anyone, not even you, back then. But I owe her; can't you understand? She has a need only I can help her fulfill, and she's the only one who loves me. She takes care of me, sees that my angels make me happy."

He swallowed hard. "Make you happy, how?"

"I love them. They give themselves to me, and I'd never hurt them if it was my decision. But it isn't," he said, voice wavering.

Julian felt ill. "You rape them? You sick fuck."

"No! I love them! They're precious to me, but she knows best. They can't stay forever, and nobody else would understand. They'd lock us away and that's why I can't let you leave. I don't want this, but that's the way it must be. I'm sorry."

"You're all criminally insane," Julian said, clenching his fists. "Who is she? A figment of your imagination? *You* molested me that day, when I was drugged and out of my head. Right?"

"Wrong. I was the one who had the pleasure."

Zoe Vines stepped inside, and Julian's mind reeled. She was dressed in jeans, a blouse, and brown hiking boots rather than her designer clothes—more suitable for visiting her den. Behind him, Grace tightened her grip on his waist, but his attention was riveted on the beautiful monster in front of him.

This lovely, composed society lady was a madwoman. A mass murderer. A woman who had touched him as he lay helpless, long ago. A woman who'd molested God knew how many young people, butchered them horribly. She would've killed him, and he'd escaped a grisly fate.

He wanted to be sick.

Zoe sauntered closer, a catlike smile on her lips. "I'd had my eye on you all summer, so Derek brought you to me, like a good son. He drugged you, but I was the one who played with your delectable body, and you quite enjoyed yourself. Pity you don't remember." Her finger cupped his crotch, stroking.

"You twisted bitch," he snarled.

She went on as if he hadn't spoken.

"I'd intended to have Carl take you to our facility and keep you there with my other toys until I tired of you. Imagine my disappointment when you awoke while I was distracted by the doorbell."

Grace gasped, but he didn't have time to puzzle over her reaction.

"Why did you allow me to get away?" he asked, curious. "You knew where I lived, could have finished me anytime."

"Yes, I could have. But who would've believed a disoriented boy with little or no memory of what happened? Even your dear mother didn't believe you enough to risk the ugly story getting out. A veiled threat from Warren and she went away quietly."

He chose to ignore the barb about Mama. "He knows you kidnap and murder people?"

"Of course he does, but he doesn't get involved. Don't ask, don't tell," she giggled.

Of course Warren knew. They all needed to be locked up forever.

"There is one more reason I let you go. I suppose a sentimental part of me hoped we'd meet again one day, and the story would end the way it was meant to," she said.

That gave him chills. All these years, a murderer had never forgotten him. "I'll pass on the tearful reunion, thanks."

Reaching a hand out to Derek, Zoe waited as he placed a small object in her palm. He couldn't tell what it was before her hand closed around it.

"I generally prefer my flesh younger, but I confess I would have enjoyed a sampling of the delicious man you've become. Now you and your friends must die, and I have the dreadfully inconvenient task of relocating again."

At that moment, he spied Sean lurking at the mouth of the cave. He spared a second to wonder where Six-Pack was, but remembered Brett's fragile state. The young man couldn't be left alone, and someone had to wait for the cops. Sean moved on cat feet, sneaking up behind Carl, and nodded.

"You know what? Go fuck yourself, you crazy *puta*."

Sean lunged for Carl, hitting his gun arm into the air. The weapon discharged with a loud bang, sending a shower of rock down on them all. Several voices screamed.

Capitalizing on the distraction, Julian slammed his fist into Derek's face, dropping him like a stone. Spinning, he spotted Carmelita running to help Grace, who was sitting on the floor holding her head.

"Grace!" He took a step toward her, but saw Zoe fleeing out of the cave. "Dammit!"

He couldn't let her get away. He rushed out in pursuit as Sean dragged Carl along, having knocked the gun away and punched his lights out. Good for him. The man was spoiling for a fight half the time lately, and tonight he'd gotten one.

Julian stumbled down the slope after Zoe, and suddenly they were both brought up short by several cops bursting from the shadows, guns drawn.

"Freeze!"

He didn't move a muscle, and when Shane stepped into a beam from another cop's light, Julian's knees went weak. "Shane."

"Thank fuck." Addressing another cop, Ford pointed to Zoe. "Read Mrs. Vines her rights."

Very slowly, Zoe raised her right hand, a weird grin on her face. "Oh, I don't think so."

Shane turned to her. "Ma'am, drop what's in your hand. Now."

She inched the object higher, between her fingers, thumb hovering over a red button.

"Detonator," he whispered to Shane, blood draining from his face. "Zoe, don't—"

He ran back toward the entrance. "Grace, get out! Get out! Nooo—"

A thunderous blast shifted the earth under his feet, and blew him backward. Seared him with heat, pummeled him with shards as he fell.

Into nothingness.

Grace awoke to total blackness. Dust and dirt clogged her nose and mouth, and she coughed. "Ohh."

Coughing hurt. So did her right arm, badly. Sharp, sickening pain and she knew without touching it that the limb was broken. She touched it anyway and wished she hadn't.

The feel of the bone poking at her skin made her violently sick, and she retched.

Once the nausea abated some, she reached out with her left arm, trying to discern how much space was around her. She pushed to her knees and cradling her right arm against her stomach, she groped the floor. Searching for a loose rock. A way out. Something.

Carmelita!

She remembered. Julian's former lover had pushed her down when the explosion happened, shielding Grace with her own body. That the woman had done such a thing humbled her, and when they got out of there, she'd tell her so. Make her peace with Julian's friend.

"Carmelita?"

There was no answer and she called again, and again. Nothing. Crawling awkwardly, she kept fingering her surroundings, traveling in what she thought was an odd-shaped rectangle. Where could the other woman be? They'd been together, so she must've moved or been knocked aside.

She had to stop and rest periodically, sitting and panting through the searing pain. Perhaps she shouldn't be moving at all, in case she was inadvertently taking herself farther from rescue.

Julian was out there, and he'd be working to get to her. So would the police. She'd heard them outside, yelling "Freeze," so they must've captured Zoe, taken her along with Derek and Carl to jail.

What had caused the explosion? It surely wasn't natural, which meant it had been set. How?

Exhausted, dizzy, she resumed her search, calling for Carmelita. She was hurt, or unconscious. As soon as Grace found her, maybe she could help. . . .

Her hand touched something. Cloth. Under the cloth, a leg!

"Carmelita?" She shook the woman's leg, got no response. Feeling her way upward, expecting to find the woman's chest, she discovered a large boulder instead.

It took her a moment to process the terrible reality as she ran her shaking hand up the large rock, searching for the woman's neck to check her pulse. But there was nothing but boulder.

Carmelita was dead. Her entire upper half had been crushed.

"Oh no." She moaned, scooting away. "No."

Pulling her knees up to her chest, still cradling her broken arm, she laid her head down and cried. She'd never wanted something awful to happen to Carmelita. This was going to kill Julian.

"I love you," she whispered to him. But he wasn't there to hear her. She cried harder.

For all her fears of reaching for what she wanted, keeping him at a distance, it might end like this. With her alone in the dark forever, deprived of the happiness she might have found in his arms, his life, if she'd been bold enough to take it.

Oh, God, please find me. Please.

I love you, Julian. Find me.

He tried. Looked everywhere, crying her name.

Julian, I need you.

He needed her more. She was his life, his soul. Where was she?

Voices interrupted his search, pulling him toward them.

". . . think he's coming around. BP's good."

"Anything broken?"

"Don't think so. Just some nasty cuts and scrapes."

"Jules? Come on, man, rise and shine." Howard? He

thought so, but the voice was strangely muffled, like his ears were stuffed with cotton. A gentle hand rested on his shoulder.

"Grace," he croaked. Didn't they know he had to find her?

"I know, buddy. Take it easy."

"Where?"

"They're digging, trying to get to her," Sean said. "They'll find her."

"Digging?" Prying his eyes open, he winced. His brain was skewered by piercing floodlights. Gradually, his vision adjusted and he realized several paramedics were hovering over him, guys from Station Two, he thought, plus Sean and Six-Pack. He struggled to sit up and a couple of sets of hands steadied him.

"Whoa, not so fast," one medic cautioned. "We need to take you in, get you examined."

He pushed at their hands. "Let me up. Where's Grace?" They shot quick, uneasy looks at one another. But not quick enough. *The explosion.* "Where is she? She got out, right?"

Sympathy. Carved into their faces. Howard's hand resting on his shoulder, as though keeping him from flying apart.

Digging.

"Dios mío." He staggered to his feet, shook them off. "Grace? *Bella?*"

Dizziness assailed him, but he kept his feet, looking around in confusion. His love was somewhere in this chaos. She had to be. Cops and firefighters swarmed over the landscape, some talking into cell phones or walkie-talkies, some writing on notepads. Shane was nearby, making order out of hell, talking to some of his men and pointing toward the house.

But most of the men were tearing at the earth with shovels and other tools. Digging at the mouth of the cave that was no longer there. The entrance was sealed as though it had never existed.

"No."

Scrambling up the rise, he dropped to his knees and began clawing at the rock and soil with his bare hands. Distantly, he was aware of screaming her name, frantic for a response. To make a hole and get to her, hold her in his arms. Protect her as he'd failed to do before.

"Julian!" Strong hands pulled him backward, and he fought. "Get hold of yourself!"

"Let me go!"

Sean came around him and grabbed his bare shoulders, got in his face. "Do you want to be forced to leave? Because you're headed out of here unless you get a grip."

He stared at Sean, breathing hard, the words penetrating his panic. For all Six-Pack's kindness, his gentle support when a friend needed it, nobody could get in your face and cut the bullshit the way Sean could. "No. I have to help. She's in there alone—she needs me."

"Then calm your ass down and help. If you're a burden to these men working to get her and the other woman out, you'll put them in more danger. You hear me?"

"Y-yes, sir." Calm. He could do calm. For Grace.

And Carmelita. Oh, God, how could he have forgotten her?

"Good. Let's find you a shirt and something to dig with."

Glancing down at himself, he gazed dispassionately at the seeping cuts and bruises forming on his chest, stomach, and arms. He'd forgotten he'd given his shirt to Brett and wore nothing on top but his ever-present gold cross. The events of the past couple of hours seemed fragmented, like some weird acid trip, the whole thing hallucinated.

His friends returned bearing shovels for the three of them

and he set to work, trying to focus his energy on nothing but making a hole. Make the earth give way, get the women out. After a few minutes, however, the kid crossed his mind again and he glanced at Howard.

"Did they transport Brett to the hospital?"

"Yeah. Physically, he'll recover, but mentally? Damn. Some of the stuff he was babbling about while I was waiting with him made my hair stand on end." A smile curving his mouth took the sadness from the moment. "At least Shane got to make a happy call to the kids' parents. He said Brett's mom started screaming in joy and dropped the phone. The dad had to come on the line and figure out what the hell had happened. They're probably with their son by now . . . thanks to you."

"Me? No. Shane was already getting a warrant, so they would've found him anyway."

"That's right; you don't know." Howard gave him a look of satisfaction. "Shane said they were having trouble reaching the judge, and probably couldn't have gotten the go-ahead until tomorrow. By then, Brett might have been tortured again, or dead. You saved that kid's life, my friend. Because you solved the mystery, that boy has a future. Might as well face it."

His throat burned with a wave of conflicting emotions. As damned glad as he was for getting the kid out, what if the price was the life of the woman he loved? The life of a friend, as well? *No good deed goes unpunished. Fate gives with one hand and takes with the other.*

Pausing, he clutched his cross and said a quick prayer of thanks for lives spared. And one for those hanging in the balance.

Help us get them out.

They worked through the night, driven by coffee and sheer

will. Word had spread, and more cops and firefighters had showed up to help, though Kat and her parents hadn't.

Howard had firmly ordered Mr. McKenna to keep his wife and Kat at home to wait for word. They didn't need to be here if Grace was . . . gone.

An hour after dawn broke, a shout sounded on the far-right-hand side of where the mouth used to be.

"We're gettin' through!"

Men scrambled to assist in widening the opening. Julian tried to work his way into the middle of them, but there was no room. His friends made him move back and flanked him, lending their quiet support.

About a half hour later, two men from the new shift at Station Two ducked and crawled inside to try to locate the women. Eerie how the hillside was covered in people, everyone still as statues, nobody speaking. After an agonizing ten minutes, a fire hat poked out of the opening.

"One deceased," he said softly. "Gonna need some help in here getting her free. Still trying to locate the other lady."

A murmur rippled through the crowd, but Julian hardly noticed. One of them was gone. He'd lost either his woman or his childhood friend. He made a small sound in his throat, agony and despair. Blackness wanted to take him, but fear kept him upright as more firemen crawled into the space.

Fear and his friends at his back, Six-Pack's hand gripping his shoulder. "Julian, it's going to be all right. Hang in there, buddy."

It wouldn't. His heroics had cost a life. *Oh, Grace, please. No.*

A man backed out of the opening, carrying his end of the stretcher. A blanket covered the body, a small, pitiful lump, just a shell where a vibrant woman used to be.

He was frozen in place as the two men carried it past. A

third man approached him, sympathy on his craggy face. "I'm so sorry to put you through this, but I've got to give you a description."

That meant there wasn't much left to look at, and they preferred he not see. Not trusting his voice, he nodded.

"Female with brown hair, black pants . . ."

The roaring in his ears drowned out the rest. "Carmelita," he choked. "Gutierrez."

The man clasped his arm. "Again, I'm sorry. We're still looking for the other one, hoping for the best."

A strong forearm went around his chest, holding him from behind, preventing him from sagging to the ground. Grief threatened to drown him, take him down to where nothing mattered. His breathing hitched as tears spilled down his face. He thought they might as well be blood.

Endless minutes scraped by and finally, two more men emerged bearing another stretcher. Julian saw dirty blond hair trailing over the side, a splint on her right arm, and an IV.

Alive.

"Oh, my God! Grace!" Breaking away from his friends, he stumbled to her, staring down at her pale, bruised face. Too still. "Baby, can you hear me?"

"We need to transport her, Julian. Meet us there, all right?"

"I want to ride with her," he insisted, keeping pace with them.

"Nope, you'll meet us. Your lady is hanging in there and you need to get checked out yourself."

"But—"

They slid her into the back of the ambulance, and the one who'd been speaking hopped in. The other one shut the doors and they were off. Taking her to safety.

Battered, but alive.

Sean and Six-Pack appeared in front of him, expressions determined.

"Well, let's go after her," Sean said. "You've done all you can here. Now Grace needs you more."

Through his tangled emotions of grief over Carmelita and overwhelming relief that Grace would be all right, he had to wonder. Did she want him anymore?

Their dinner the night before haunted him. She wasn't ready to commit. And perhaps she'd been right. He'd done nothing but push her where she didn't want to go.

He'd nearly gotten her killed.

He couldn't force Grace to love him, and he could see the truth very clearly now.

Julian Salvatore had finally grown up. Now he had to do the right thing. Even if it destroyed him.

19

Grace pried open her lids, blinking away the layer of grit coating her eyeballs. Mostly. She tried to grab a coherent thread of thought and hold on, but her head felt as though an evil scientist had sucked out her brains and replaced the space with fluid.

She felt dull, her body heavy and floaty at the same time. How was that possible? Oh, her brain was floating outside her body, that's how. She was also lying flat on her back. Her bleary gaze traveled south and she tried again to process the situation.

IV in her left hand. Cast and sling on her right arm. She was a boneless chicken with broken wings. No, one broken wing. Except if you're boneless, they can't be broken. Whatever.

Okay, add good drugs to the list. Dripping happy juice through the IV thingie.

Maybe she could order one of these for the condo.

"Grace? Hey, *querida*, welcome back."

She turned her head toward the sound of the beloved voice. Happiness swelled that had nothing to do with drugs—well, maybe just a little—and she gave him what must be a goofy smile. "Julian, you look . . ." She frowned, belatedly realizing he looked awful.

Not his appearance, but something else. He smelled good and his hair was clean, so he must've showered. His little gold cross rested outside his T-shirt where it belonged. No, what bothered her was his smile. It didn't match the sadness in his dark eyes, which were smudged with circles underneath. His face looked ravaged, as though he'd aged a decade.

"How do you feel?" he asked, stroking her leg on top of the blanket.

"My chicken wing is broken." Damn, drugs made the weirdest things come out of a person's mouth.

"Yes, it is, but in about six weeks it'll be well. Are you in any pain? If so, I'll buzz the nurse."

"Hmm." She thought. "Not really. Just floating."

"All right. Grace, do you remember what happened?"

"An accident." No, that wasn't right.

"Not exactly." He paused, looked away for a moment. "We found Brett and got him out of the cave. But then we got caught and—"

"The explosion," she breathed. Everything came back in a rush, spinning her mushy brain. "Carmelita."

"She's . . ." His voice broke. "She's dead."

"I know. I'm sorry." She wanted to reach for him, but couldn't, trussed up like she was.

"It's not your fault. It's mine. All of what happened to you and her is my fault." He sounded so desolate, her heart broke.

"No. That makes no sense." Not much did, in fact. She struggled to keep up with his thinking.

"If it weren't for me, neither of you would've been put in danger."

"That's crazy!" she blurted. "Not your fault. Things happen for a reason—wings get broken—and you fix them!"

"Some things can't be repaired, Grace," he rasped, making a visible effort to retain control of his emotions. "I want you to listen to me. I'll always love you, but I want you to know that I finally understand something. Real love is letting go when you know you're not what the other person needs."

"What?" She blinked at him. "What are you saying?"

"I want what's best for you, and I know it isn't me. I hung on, pushed too hard, and I refused to see things from your point of view. I thought if I held on tightly enough, I could make you feel what I did." He cleared his throat, continuing with an effort.

"All I ever wanted was for you to be happy, *bella*, and I realize now it can't be with me." Leaning over, he brushed a kiss against her lips, and stood.

"But—"

"Good-bye, Grace."

"Wait! I have something to . . ." *To tell you.*

But he was already out the door. Gone.

Julian borrowed Kat's spare key to Grace's condo, with a promise to give it to Howard when he returned to work next week, and fetched his belongings. Five minutes, in and out, before he could change his mind.

Next, he went to see Brett at his parents' house outside Nashville. Shane said they'd phoned and left several messages at the police department, desperate to thank Julian in person, and didn't know where to reach him. Julian had agreed, after some coaxing. They needed closure, Shane told him.

He'd expected the meeting to be awkward, and he dreaded the boy's reaction to seeing him again. He was afraid Brett would associate him with the trauma he'd been through, perhaps be withdrawn or angry. He needn't have worried.

Brett was coping, one day at a time. He was a stronger young man than anyone, even his own family, had realized. He spoke some about how he'd survived a month in the dark, by keeping his mind focused on survival. He was saddened by the fate of the others, but noted they'd mentally given up. They weren't murdered until they broke, and that, to Brett, was the key.

Brett's parents were awesome people, serving soda and warm cookies and reminding Julian of his own mama. Food fixed everything from the common cold to broken hearts. They hugged the stuffing out of him and thanked him profusely for putting together the threads that led to their son's rescue. After Brett went upstairs to nap, they spoke in hushed tones about the other victims. The San Antonio PD had located several graves at the Vineses' old place, and several more at their current one.

The truth was, the authorities might never know how many victims there were. But at least they could rest easy knowing the entire bunch, including Warren, had been charged with multiple counts of kidnapping and murder. The court trial would be a nightmare, but Julian would face it when it came, knowing those monsters would never again see the light of day.

That was poetic justice.

After saying good-bye to Mr. and Mrs. Charles, he went for a long drive. He couldn't face anyone else right now, even his friends, as supportive and well-meaning as they were. He wanted only to be alone, to fortify his courage for Carmelita's funeral in three days. How he'd face her family, he didn't know. They'd flown her body home to San Antonio, and he'd made his plane reservation for tomorrow.

He'd called Mama, and her sweet voice telling him to come home had been the last straw.

He drove, the hot bubble in his chest, the rage, hurt, and sorrow, needing to be lanced before his heart exploded and killed him outright. But maybe that would be kinder.

Before he was aware of exactly where he was headed, he'd turned down the rutted path onto the land. The property he'd made the offer for, it seemed, a lifetime ago. The car bumped along and he thought, *I really do need a truck.*

He'd add that to the list.

Right after burying his best friend.

And losing the woman he loved.

Putting the car in park, he got out and walked over to the pond. And inevitably, he recalled making love with Grace right here, in this spot. The place he'd hoped to make theirs forever.

The bubble in his chest burst and he sank to the ground. He stared, unseeing, over the water, trying to breathe through the pain, to hold it off a bit longer.

He lost. Burying his face in his hands, he let the tide of grief wash over him, carry him away. He didn't know how long he sat there sobbing, but eventually he was spent. Drained. Cleansed in a sense, like maybe now he could handle the rest of what he must go through this week.

And after that, maybe he could get on with his life.

He looked around the property with new eyes, and a small kernel of hope took root. This would be his.

Whatever the future brought, for him, it began right here.

Grace stared at her nosy, interfering, wonderful sister, and smiled at their hatched plan. "It's perfect! Why didn't I think of an all-out ambush? He doesn't stand a chance."

"Well, drastic measures are now called for. You've left him how many messages since he returned from San Antonio?"

"Five."

"Five! Stubborn ass. I think it's buried in the genetic code."

"Surely Howard's not this muleheaded."

Kat snorted. "Frequently. Are you sure you want a man?"

"Ha! You don't fool me. Even when you're pissed at him, you glow."

"I know, dammit. The way he lights me up even when I want to stay mad is programmed into *my* genetic code." She grabbed her purse. "Ready to storm the Bastille?"

"When you are." They left, Kat helping Grace into her Bimmer and setting a covered chocolate cake at her feet. Then she hopped in the driver's side and they were on their way. Grace glanced at her sister. "I appreciate your taking the week off work to chauffeur me around like this. Broken chicken wing and all," she said, lifting up her arm in the sling.

"I still can't believe you were babbling to Jules about chicken wings when he came to see you," Kat teased.

Grace found she could smile, even laugh, because she knew something Julian didn't.

This little separation wasn't going to stick.

Kat pulled into the station and parked in a visitor's slot. The big bay doors were open today to let in the warm June breeze, and a few guys were visible, hanging out near the quint. The two women approaching, especially one bearing a cake pan, drew lots of attention.

"I have chocolate cake!" Kat announced to whistles of appreciation from the team.

Grace sought Julian and found him leaning negligently against the door of the ambulance on the other side of the bay, feet crossed, hands in his pockets. Their gazes clashed and she winced at how empty his eyes were, how blank.

As though she were a stranger he'd never bent over the hood of his Porsche in the sunlight. "Hi," she said, giving him a tentative smile.

Vaguely, she was aware of the rest of the team following Kat inside as though she were the Pied Piper, intent on a fudgy treat. But Julian didn't move. Just relaxed there like a lean, lazy cat, with not a care in the world.

He nodded, but didn't budge. "Hey. How are you?"

Time to bring out the big guns. "Well, if you'd bothered to return any of my five messages, I'd have told you."

There. A flicker of emotion. Quickly hidden, but not fast enough. "I've been busy."

"Yep, being a coward."

He pushed off the ambulance and straightened, a muscle in his jaw clenching. "I did what's best for you. Call me whatever you want."

"Coward."

"Grace—"

She stalked him, moving into his space, and laid her good hand on his chest. "Damn, a fireman in uniform turns me on."

"What are you doing?" His eyes widened.

"If you need to ask, you're further gone than I thought."

With that, she grabbed the back of his neck, pulled him in, and kissed him. His hesitation lasted a split second; then he melted into her, crushed her against him. He swept his tongue into her mouth and he tasted so fine, smelled spicy and all male. All hers.

He broke the kiss and stared into her eyes, expression agonized. "Why are you doing this to me?"

"Because you didn't ask what I wanted." She paused, hoping to convey every ounce of emotion she felt for him. "You left me in my hospital bed, alone and hurting for you. You took it upon yourself to be judge and jury over us, to blame yourself for what happened. You assumed you knew what I wanted and needed. But you *never asked me*."

"I asked you before," he said hoarsely. "You didn't know."

"Ask me again."

"What do you want from me, *bella*?"

She tilted her face to his, whispering into his lips. "I want no man but you. I need to spend the rest of my life with you. Julian Salvatore . . . I love you. With all my heart."

Making a strangled noise, he wrapped his arms around her, held her close. His heart thrummed madly in her ear and she snuggled into his warmth. Several seconds passed before he replied.

"Say it again."

"I love you. *Only you.*"

"Oh, Grace. *Dios*, I've missed you."

"I missed you, too. Let's not do this again, okay? Whatever we face, we face it together. Deal?"

"Deal." Cupping her cheeks, he tilted her lips to his. "I love you, too."

A smattering of applause broke out, along with whistles and catcalls. Blushing, Grace turned her head to see that every single one of his friends, along with Kat, had drifted into the bay, some still munching on chocolate cake.

"Thank God," Eve said, rolling her eyes. "He's been a real asshole."

"No fucking shit."

Laughing, Tommy leaned against the quint, blond hair falling over his pale blue eyes. "More power to you, man. I'm not *ever* falling in love."

Smiling, his eyes only for Grace, Julian said, "Famous last words, my friend."

Julian counted himself the luckiest bastard on the planet. His lady was riding by his side on a gorgeous day, laughing, holding his hand . . . and wearing his engagement ring.

The Eagles were crooning about "the long run" on the radio; they had a picnic packed and the whole day ahead of them. *Life is good.*

And he no longer felt guilty about enjoying the second, and even third, chance he'd been handed. Carmelita would've wanted that for him, just as he would have for her. He intended to live every moment to the fullest.

Making a left turn, he swung his new Ford truck down the familiar bumpy path onto their property. They'd signed the mountain of papers less than an hour ago and driven straight out here for the official "we're in huge debt" party.

He'd never been happier.

Pulling up next to the pond, he parked and hopped out, then skirted the truck to take the blanket and picnic basket from Grace. He spread the quilt on the ground and set the basket in one corner. "Wine?"

"I'd love some."

He pulled a bottle from the basket and uncorked it, then handed it to Grace while he fished out two glasses. "Do the honors?"

"You bet." Her right arm healed, cast history, she poured two healthy portions of Chardonnay and placed the bottle aside, on the ground. "A toast?"

"To us. And to all of the future picnics we'll have right here by our pond."

"I'll drink to that!"

They clinked glasses and sipped their wine for a few moments, enjoying each other's company and savoring the fact that this was their place. Their slice of heaven they'd build, together.

"Julian?"

"Do you remember my telling you that Kat and I used to visit our aunt in San Antonio during the summer?"

"Sure, why?"

"The Vineses were neighbors with our aunt, if you'll recall."

Puzzled, he waited for her to continue.

"I know we haven't talked about what happened to you that day, all those years ago, but . . ."

"No, we haven't." Neither of them had wanted to focus on anything except the future, and loving each other. "What's on your mind?"

"Remember when you told me about it? You said the doorbell rang, and you ran away."

"*Querida*, I can't imagine what—"

"Hear me out." Scooting closer, she touched his arm. "When you told me, something niggled at the back of my mind. Then, when Mrs. Vines was holding us in the cave, she said the same thing—she answered the door while you escaped. That's when it clicked into place."

She took a deep breath. "Honey, I was the one who rang the doorbell."

Julian stared at her, pulse drumming in his head. "What?"

"My aunt sent me over to borrow a cup of milk and two eggs. Mrs. Vines answered the door, and she was scary-pissed, at first. But when I explained what I needed, she composed herself and went to get it for me. While I waited on the porch, I saw a boy run across the lawn and down the street."

"Grace, my God," he breathed.

"I thought it was weird, but then Mrs. Vines came back with the stuff. I left, and never thought one more thing of it."

"Until the night we found Brett."

"Exactly. I've wanted to tell you, but I wanted to wait for the right time." She smiled. "But today, with us celebrating our new beginnings . . . it just seemed to bring everything full circle, you know?"

"You're amazing, that's what I know." Scooting close, he nuzzled her ear. "You've saved my life twice, and I'm the luckiest man on earth."

Right now, his thoughts weren't on floor plans or home decor. His mind wasn't on fixing fence posts or paving the drive. Or even on the delicious food in their basket.

His wicked mind was on the delectable woman in his company. His woman. Carefully, he placed his wineglass on the ground outside the blanket, digging it into the ground a little so it wouldn't fall over. He did the same to hers, laughing at her indignant protest.

"Hey! I wasn't done with that!"

"We'll get back to it," he said, capturing her mouth with his.

If he lived to be one hundred, he'd never get enough of tasting her, of marking her as his. He'd waited long enough, and he never planned on wasting one minute again where Grace was concerned.

Lowering her onto her back, he nibbled at her neck, the flesh exposed by the part in her blouse. Impatient, he undid the tiny buttons, pulled the shirt from the waistband of her pants, and helped her off with it. As he encouraged her to sit up briefly, the bra went next, and he laid her down again, drinking her in.

"*Dios*, you're beautiful. I want you naked and spread for me, right here in the sun. I want to make love to you, baby."

"Oh, Julian, yes."

She buried her fingers in his hair as he suckled her breasts, one after the other, feasting on her, loving how her sweet little nipples pointed skyward. Her skin was so creamy and perfect, he couldn't help but sample every inch. He slid her pants and underwear down her legs, tossed them aside.

Standing, he got rid of his own clothing and gazed down

on his gorgeous woman, his blood fired, his cock standing at attention. "Spread your legs for me."

She did, every inch the sex siren, showing off her pretty pink slit, tempting him. She tempted him even more when she pinched her nipples, ran her hands down her stomach. With one hand, she fingered her clit, whirling the nub in lazy circles as she canted her hips, mimicking a nice, slow fuck.

"Ah, God, you drive me insane."

Crouching between her legs, he cupped her ass cheeks in his hands and lifted her to his mouth. His tongue flicked her moist slit, sliding along the wet skin from back to front, laving until she writhed under the attention, begging for his cock.

"Julian! Do me, please, now!"

Kneeling, he lifted her butt, pulled her forward, and impaled her fully on his cock.

"Oh, God! Yes!"

She was so uninhibited, perfect for him. All his.

He fucked her with strong, sure strokes, taking his cues from how her body sang for him. She was completely open, his to have however he wished, and so he pounded her hard, drove into her until she yelled his name and tensed, her channel convulsing around him.

The tingling sparks began at the base of his spine, the tightening of his balls, and then he erupted. Shot his cum deep inside her, on and on, his exultant yell probably startling every speck of wildlife in the area.

As he finished shuddering his release, she grinned up at him. "Wow. If that's what I can expect for the next forty or fifty years, sign me up."

Pulling out, he rolled onto his back, settling her head on his chest. He particularly loved how her white blond hair fanned over his naked body. "You already signed up," he informed her, pointing at the modest solitaire on her ring finger.

"Hmm. So I did. And you know, I think it's the best decision I ever made, my sexy fireman."

Okay, so he puffed up a bit at that. What red-blooded man wouldn't? "I hope you always feel that way, *bella*."

"Under one condition."

"Anything."

"Well, don't get me wrong—this way was fantastic and all, but . . ." She rose up and peered at him, biting her lip.

"What?"

"The truck is great, but don't ever sell your Porsche. I'm kind of fond of the hood."

Bursting out laughing, he hugged her close. How had a man like him ever snared the most beautiful woman in the world, who loved him to distraction?

"I love you, baby."

"Not as much as I love you."

Yes, indeed, life was good. And in the end, how well a person was loved, and loved in return, was really the only thing that mattered.

Just to be sure she knew, he showed her. One more time.

Turn the page for a special preview
of the next book in the
Firefighters of Station Five series,

LINE OF FIRE

Coming from Signet Eclipse in May 2010

"Go wide! Go wide!"

"Come on, Skyler! Pass the ball!"

Tommy Skyler peddled backward, fingers gripping leather, muscles tense. A good quarterback never rushed.

A *star* quarterback locked on his receiver, fired, and planted the pigskin dead in his chest. Every single time.

For a couple of seconds, Tommy was back at Bryant-Denny Stadium. A crowd of over ninety thousand. Half of them on their feet, screaming his name.

Better than being a rock star. Almost better than sex.

He'd go down in fucking history.

Zeroing in on his target, he pumped his arm and let the football fly. It left his fingertips, spiraling in a perfect arc toward his receiver.

He had a split second to see Eve Marshall catch the pass with a muffled *umph* before his lieutenant at Fire Station Five, Howard "Six-Pack" Paxton, broke Julian Salvatore's block. Barreled into Tommy like a two-ton freight train and put him on his back, the wind temporarily knocked out of his lungs.

Tommy heaved a breath, then barked a laugh as Six-Pack rolled off him. "Jesus. You missed your calling, man. You should've played in the pros."

"Nah. I was completely disillusioned when I found out the players couldn't date the cheerleaders. Ruined it for me." The lieutenant pushed to his feet, brushed the grass off his regulation navy blue pants, and offered Tommy a hand.

Tommy took it, letting the big man yank him up. "I hear you. One of the dumbest rules on the planet, if you ask me."

"Maybe that's changed by now?"

"Got no clue."

He suppressed the twinge in his chest. Once upon a time, he knew practically everything there was to know about the world of pro football. A world that had been his for the taking. And he'd been out of the loop for only two years.

Fuck, it felt like a lifetime. Might as well be.

"Great pass," Eve said breathlessly, jogging over. She tossed the football back to Tommy, who caught it, grinning.

"Nice catch."

Eyeing their pretty teammate, the only female firefighter at Station Five, he was distracted from answering right away. The woman had some serious mojo goin' on, if a man didn't mind 'em a little tough—both mentally and physically.

And Tommy *so* did not mind. From the top of her dark head to her lean, muscular body, to her long legs, the woman was strong as hell. The curve of her angular jaw hinted at more than a thin streak of stubbornness—more like a will of iron. He should know. He'd flirted with her, half seriously, over the past couple of years, only to be firmly shut down.

Oh, she didn't mind his teasing, even seemed to get a kick out of it, but never failed to get across that their byplay would not evolve into something else. Ever.

Should his ribbing cross the line, she'd tear off his balls and feed them to him for lunch.

Not that Eve was his type anyway, since he'd met—

"Skyler? Yoo-hoo!"

He blinked at her. "What?"

Eve propped her fists on her slim hips. "I said, maybe *you* should've gone pro. Focus, kid."

"I'm not a kid, Eve," he said, suppressing a sigh of annoyance. *Now, where have I heard that song and dance before?* "And yeah, I thought about it. Didn't work out."

She frowned at his clipped tone, the absence of his usual comeback filled with innuendo. Something she wasn't used to from him, he figured. "Why not?"

He barked a short laugh, surprised at the bitter sound. "I decided being rich and famous didn't appeal."

Tommy barely caught her scowl as he spun and strode for the bay. Behind him, he heard Julian caution quietly, "Leave it alone, Evie."

"What? What'd I say?"

Three loud tones over the station's intercom system ended her protest, and Tommy broke into a jog as the computerized female voice began to relay their call. Saved by the bell.

Or not. Crap. Had he heard correctly?

Zack Knight, their FAO—fire apparatus operator—stuck his head out of the bay and yelled. "Come on, slackers! Haul your asses!"

Tommy rushed into the bay and skidded to a halt next to the big quint, shoved his feet into his boots, and yanked up his heavy fire-retardant pants. The others followed suit as Tanner joined them.

Tommy glanced at Zack. "Did she say—"

"Scaffold collapsed downtown," Sean interrupted, jerking on his own gear. "Two construction workers dead, one clinging to what's left of the scaffold. Forty-four stories up."

"Shit," Tommy breathed. Quickly, he donned his coat and reached for his hat. "Aerial ladder on the quint's not gonna reach."

"One of you will have to rappel down to him, get him into a safety harness." Ready, the captain yanked open the passenger's door of the quint, braced a boot on the running board, and hauled himself up. "Let's go!"

Tommy climbed into the backseat of the cab, followed by Julian. Zack slid behind the wheel and Sean took the place of the commanding officer in the passenger's seat. Since the two commanding officers never rode in the same vehicle, the lieutenant took the ambulance, Eve joining him.

Tommy glanced at Julian, musing that just a couple of months ago their resident bad-boy jerk had been practically shackled to the lieutenant's side. Out of sheer necessity, not brotherly love, for damned sure. But exorcising one's demons, not to mention finding true love, had a tendency to change a man for the better.

I don't need to change, but I wouldn't turn down the lovin'.

As if. Settling back in his seat, he frowned, attempting to force his mind away from a certain cute-as-a-button nurse with shoulder-length curly brown hair and liquid brown eyes. Freckles across her pert nose. Smart as a whip.

And harboring an apparent aversion to getting too close to him, no matter how hard he tried.

"I can hear your brain grinding, amigo. What gives?"

Tommy studied Julian, surprised, not for the first time, by the genuine concern on his friend's face. "Dude, am I that obvious?"

"To me." Julian shot a pointed glance to their companions in the front.

Tommy gave him a small smile, grateful the man had his back yet again. Jules wasn't the type to flap his lips in front of the others, especially about two very painful subjects—

the elusive Shea Ford for one. And for the other, exactly how Tommy's dreams of the NFL had died.

On the topic of Shea, at least, he could let his friend off the hook. Besides, Zack and the captain weren't paying attention anyway.

"Same girl problem, different day," he replied simply. Julian nodded in understanding, giving him a grin.

"Still giving you grief about being too young? I *told* you the first thing you need to do is give your vocabulary a dude-ectomy! A woman doesn't mind her guy having the *stamina* of an eighteen-year-old, but she doesn't want him to *sound* like one."

Tommy laughed in spite of himself. "Girl advice, coming from the man who used to change women more often than his boxers. That's scary, Jules."

The other man arched a black brow, his teeth white against his bronzed face. "Caught me a fine one, didn't I?"

"Touché. How is Grace, by the way?"

"Uh-uh, no changing the subject. So what seems to be the problem with you and your lady? I mean, you said you've been out together, right?"

"Yeah, for a quick burger, and once we went to a movie." Tommy shrugged, not letting on how much her rejection of him as a man truly hurt. "We had a good time. But I might as well have been her brother, considering the distance she kept between us. When I dropped her off after the movie, she shook my freakin' hand, man."

Julian grimaced. "Ouch. Even a brother would get a hug."

"No shit. She just won't let me close."

"I hate to say this, but . . . maybe there's just no spark."

"No, that's one thing I'm sure of," Tommy said firmly. "Seriously, you could power Sugarland for a week with the electricity we got goin' on when we're together. It's not that she doesn't feel it, but like—like she doesn't *want* to feel it, you know? Just because I'm a couple of years younger than her? That's so wrong."

"Well, there's another possibility." Julian waved a hand at his friend. "Maybe the problem isn't you at all, but something going on with *her*. Ever think of that?"

Tommy blinked at him, the light dawning. "I'm such an idiot. Why didn't I think of it first?"

"Because you're a *guy*. And in typical guy fashion, you've thought of nothing but your wants and needs right from the start. What about what *she* wants and needs? I grew up with four older sisters. Believe me, I know what I'm talking about."

Tommy felt his cheeks grow hot. Dammit. "Aw, crap. I've really screwed up everything."

"Not necessarily. Give her time; be there for her. Listen to what she has to say. It's not a race, so don't push her away by moving at warp speed."

"I never thought of it that way before," he muttered. "Thanks, du—Julian."

The other man snickered at his self-correction. "There's hope for you yet, kid."

"Not a kid." He sighed, mulling over Julian's advice. Had he been so self-absorbed he'd missed some serious signals from Shea? Ignored her needs? If so, that was about to change. Maybe there *was* hope for them after all.

They fell silent and he focused on the problems they faced as they neared their destination. When the building came into view, the collapsed scaffold crumpled against the unfinished side like a pile of pickup sticks, Tommy gave a low whistle.

"We've got a worker stuck up there? Fuckin' A, this is gonna suck."

The others muttered in agreement, and the tension in the cab became palpable. Zack pulled the quint past the construction fence, well away from danger should the rest of the structure come down. The second he stopped, they jumped from their vehicle, gazes automatically fixed on the wreckage before them. The captain began barking orders.

"Howard, I want you, Salvatore, and Skyler on the roof. Take the ropes and harnesses, and decide who gets to play Spider-Man."

"I'll do it," Tommy volunteered.

Julian looked relieved and Howard said, "You're in."

"Marshall, you'll work the ground with me," Sean continued, ignoring Eve's scowl. "There's no telling what damage, if any, has been done to the framework of the building or whether it'll shift, so let's move it!"

Eve stepped forward, voice hard. "I'm just as capable of—"

"Not now, goddammit," the captain snapped. Then he turned his back on her and keyed his radio, calling the battalion chief to find out his ETA.

Tommy didn't blame Eve for being pissed. Wasn't the first time Sean had passed her over for the more strenuous or exciting task. But nobody had time to debate the matter. Tommy helped the lieutenant and Julian with the gear, then followed on their heels. On the way, his gaze fell on two man-sized lumps covered by a black tarp, at least a half-dozen workers standing by, looking on mournfully.

Jesus Christ. How awful to start a workday as normally as any other and have it end in tragedy. He averted his eyes and took in the distance from the roof to the scaffold, concentrating on the job ahead.

This wasn't going to be easy. Even from here, the piteous cries of the worker drifted to them, raising the hair on the back of his neck. The only thing worse than hearing the man's panic would be if it abruptly ended, in a bad way.

They rode the construction lift to the roof and set about securing the rope and pulley system to nearby support beams. Tommy quickly shed his heavy fire coat, which did nothing to relieve the stifling July heat, but at least his movements wouldn't be so restricted. The pants and boots he left on in the interest of time.

He yanked on a pair of gloves, then let Julian help him with one harness; the other, connected to his own, he'd put on the worker as an extra safety measure before they were both lowered to the ground. Ready to go, he sat on the ledge of the roof, bracing himself until the rope was drawn taut.

Julian tried an encouraging smile, but it came out more of a grimace. "Be careful, man. Better you than me."

"I'm so touched, thanks."

"All right," Howard said. "When you're ready."

Tommy nodded. "Go."

As he eased himself over the side, the line remained tight, giving him a sense of relative security. He wasn't afraid of heights—just the fall and the sudden stop at the end. As long as the equipment did the job, he was good.

He held on to the rope, using his feet to "walk" down the side of the building. Technically he wasn't really rappelling, since he was being lowered by his teammates, but he figured that was semantics. His ass was dangling more than forty stories above the ground, so what the hell difference did it make what it was called?

Foot by foot, he crept downward. Two stories. Three. Sweat rolled down his spine, and into his eyes. Glancing below, he finally caught sight of the worker clinging to a metal pole a few feet from the side of the building. His hard hat was missing, revealing a balding head. Beefy shoulders, gut riding over his belt. Big sonofabitch, probably outweighed him by fifty pounds or more.

Fantastic.

"Hurry!" the man bellowed, panic cracking his voice. "I can't hang on much longer!"

"Don't move!" Which, of course, the man did, becoming more agitated the closer Tommy got.

"I—I can't help it! I'm slipping!"

"I'm almost there," he called, hoping he sounded reassuring. "Just a few more seconds, okay? What's your name?"

"R-Russell."

"I'm Tommy. Hold tight, Russell. I'm comin' your way."

"Oh, God, I'm gonna fall!"

Dread settled in the pit of his stomach. This situation had clusterfuck written all over it. "No, you're not. Look at me, all right? Focus on *me*."

At last, Tommy became level with Russell, quickly assessing his only option. Carefully, he pushed away from the wall with one foot and used the other to test the sturdiness of a crosspole. Gradually, he put all his weight on it, relieved when it held. He needed only one minute more. Maybe luck was on their side.

Bracing one hand on another pole to steady himself, he began to inch toward Russell, talking calmly, crossing the few feet separating them. "Easy does it. I've got a harness here with your name on it, connected to mine. Soon as I get you strapped in, we'll—"

The structure shifted, shuddering under Tommy's boots. For Russell, that was all she wrote.

The bigger man yelled, eyes rolling, terrified, as he scrambled toward Tommy.

"No! Stay right—"

Tommy barely had a split second to react. Russell launched

himself across the remaining distance, forcing Tommy to catch him in an awkward bear hug.

Just as the rest of the scaffold collapsed.

Tommy's boots slipped and he swung free, toward the side of the building, with 250 pounds of deadweight in his arms. Metal groaned, rained down on them. One rod struck Tommy's fire hat, sending it flying.

Along for the ride, struggling to retain his hold on his heavy burden, he braced himself for the impact with the side of the building.

Tommy hit the bricks on his right side, pain exploding in his head and shoulder. The world spun crazily, but he held on to Russell. Who clung to him for dear life, screaming like a little girl.

Shut up, jackass! This predicament is partially your fault.

That's what he wanted to yell at Russell, who was too far gone to care. *Just focus on getting him to the ground.*

From above them, Howard yelled, "Hang on! We're sending you down!"

They were moving, Tommy realized through the buzzing between his ears. Lower and lower. Peering over Russell's shoulder, he saw another engine company had arrived, bringing more firefighters from another station as backup. Yellow coats and pants everywhere, rushing toward him.

The ground came up to meet him, and Tommy stood on rubbery knees, releasing his hold on the worker. Several pairs of hands grabbed Russell and led him away. More hands worked at Tommy's harness, getting him free.

". . . okay?"

Tommy blinked, trying to find the speaker. "What?"

A hand gripped his shoulder. "I asked, are you okay?"

Eve's worried face swam in front of him, and he waved her off. "I'm fine. Ready to run laps."

His grin felt wrong, like his muscles wouldn't work. He shook off another pair of hands and took a couple of steps so they could see he was perfectly all right.

Tommy's knees buckled.

The last thing he saw was the captain lunging to catch him.

A crackle on the desktop radio unit interrupted, and as Dora snatched it, Shea braced herself. The paramedics always radioed ahead when they had a bad situation and were bringing in a trauma case.

"Sterling ER, charge nurse Carlisle speaking." Dora scrabbled for her pad and pen.

Shea waited, dread building, while Dora took down the pertinent information on their incoming patients.

"All right. We'll be ready." Replacing the handset, Dora cleared her throat. "That was one of our fire captains. We've got four men coming in from a scaffold collapse on a construction site. Three are workers with relatively minor injuries—cuts and bruises, a sprained ankle, and a cracked rib. The fourth man is a firefighter. Got his head busted open rescuing one of the workers, but he's stable."

Her stomach gave an unpleasant lurch and she peered at Dora's spidery handwriting. At this point no names were taken, so she scanned, trying to locate the age of the firefighter. But the woman scooped up the pad, already in action. "Is he—"

"We need four rooms ready. Round up the others while I drag Brown's ass from the doctors' lounge. Get movin', girl!"

Dora's most amusing quality was her rough, no-bullshit personality. It was also her most formidable. Shea hurried to prepare for their arrivals, squelching the unease skittering along her nerves. There were plenty of firemen in Sugarland, and the one coming in was stable.

The man was most likely nobody she knew.

Three other nurses helped her make sure the rooms were prepared, the necessary forms and charts on hand. Dr. Brown arrived with the young resident Dr. Freeman, and none too soon.

The first wave began, two men wheeled in on stretchers, one after the other. Anxious, Shea studied each of the firefighters with them, and finally let out a relieved breath. These guys weren't from Station Five.

Thank God.

Dora and one of the other nurses assisted Brown and Freeman with the two construction workers, taking their vitals and checking their complaints. On the counter near Dora sat the notepad with the victims' information. Might as well look, put her fears to rest.

Shea took a step toward it, but her attention was diverted by a big construction worker shuffling through the doors, one arm slung over the shoulders of a companion, his fleshy face scrunched in pain.

"Let's go into room nine," she said in a calm, soothing tone, gesturing to the next cubicle. "What's your name?"

"R-Russell Levy. Christ, I think that guy broke one of my ribs." He panted as his friend led him to the bed, where he sat with a groan.

"I need you to unbutton your shirt so we can have a look." He struggled with the buttons and his friend pushed his hands aside, finishing for him.

"All right, lie back for me. This side?" She helped him as he nodded, and noted the bruise forming around his torso. He winced as she gently probed the area in question. "Is this where it hurts?"

"Damn!"

She took that as a yes. The rib was likely cracked, but she wasn't allowed to say so. "How did this happen?"

"Firefighter grabbed me when the rest of the scaffold fell, and squeezed me like a fuckin' boa constrictor. Kept me from plunging over forty stories." His eyes widened as he recalled the terrifying experience. "Sweet Jesus, I coulda died! How is the kid, anyways?"

Shea froze. "You mean the firefighter?"

"Yeah. He got the livin' shit knocked out of him when we hit the side of the building."

"I don't know. He hasn't been brought in yet." Taking Levy's wrist to get his pulse, she asked casually, "Do you know his name?"

"He told me, but I was so freakin' scared I don't remember what it was. Strong sonofabitch, though."

Schooling her expression to remain neutral, she eyed the man's substantial girth. No way could Tommy have held on to this giant. She forced herself to concentrate on caring for the patient, jotting down his vitals, which were fine. Next, she handed his friend a sheaf of forms.

"The doctor will be in soon to take a look, and I'm sure he'll want a couple of X-rays. You might have to help Mr. Levy fill these out—" A commotion outside broke into her instructions. "Excuse me for a moment."

Shea stepped into the hallway just in time to see a gurney burst through the double doors, being pushed fast by two firefighters, one holding up an IV bag, and trailed by three more. These men she recognized because she'd met them all before. Among those bringing up the rear was Zack Knight, her best friend's fiancé. Under different circumstances, she'd smile and say hello.

But her gaze was fixed on the blond-haired man on the

gurney, his eyes closed. Eyes she knew were as pale blue as the summer sky. The gauze pad and the hair on the right side of his head were soaked with blood, with more smeared down the side of his face.

Her knees turned to water and she leaned against the desk for support, the breath sucked from her lungs. Captain Sean Tanner's voice competed with the roaring in her ears.

"Open head wound," he barked to Dr. Brown, who'd emerged from one of the rooms. "He's unconscious, but his vitals are stable. He took a blow to the right side of his body, but he sustained no broken bones and there's no evidence of internal bleeding."

Shea closed her eyes, and her hands began to shake. *Oh, God. Tommy.*

"Shea! Need you in here."

Dr. Brown's firm order got her moving. Part of her fought the wild urge to run out the door, jump in her car, and high-tail it home to hide. She didn't want to see Tommy like this. Tommy was strong, sunny, gregarious. Sexy.

The pale man on the bed appeared heartbreakingly young. Vulnerable. Despite the well-defined muscles roping his bare chest and torso, to see him now, nobody would believe he'd used nothing but his upper-body strength to keep a man almost twice his size from plummeting to his death.

Which was precisely what Tommy had done. At great risk to himself.

Working like a well-oiled machine, two of the firefighters, Dr. Brown, Shea, and a tech surrounded Tommy and prepared to move him from the gurney to the hospital stretcher.

"On three," Dr. Brown said. The move went smoothly, and the doctor glanced at the anxious group of firefighters. "The captain can stay in case I have questions; everyone else, out. Give us some room, please."

Sometimes Brown stretched the rules when it came to injured men in uniform. Nobody protested.

Zack gave her a slight smile and nod before filing out with the rest. Moving to Tommy's side, Shea worked with quick efficiency, hooking him up to a blood pressure cuff, pulse oximeter, EKG monitor. Dr. Brown pried open one of his lids, then the other, shining a penlight into his eyes.

"How long has he been out?"

The captain straightened, rubbing his stomach as though to soothe an ache. "Not long, maybe fifteen minutes. We got him here pretty fast."

Brown nodded. "Pupils are a bit dilated but reactive to light. I imagine he'll come around soon," he announced. He pocketed the light and bent over his patient, prying the gauze from the side of his head. Peering intently, probing, he made a humming noise in his throat. "Can't stitch that. The wound is too shallow and abraded, skinned more than punctured."

"He'll have a mild concussion," she said. *Please let that be all.*

Brown grunted in agreement. "Most likely. I'll feel better once he's cleared by neurology, awake, and talking. Get these wounds cleaned and dressed while I order a CAT scan."

"Will do."

After donning latex gloves, Shea parted the hair above Tommy's temple and began to clean the area with antiseptic. He moaned and stirred some, starting to come around, which made her dizzy with relief. The noise also brought the captain immediately to his side.

"Skyler? Can you hear me?" Sean leaned over, rugged features lined with concern.

Tommy turned his head toward the man's voice and groaned something unintelligible.

"Don't move," Shea said, carefully turning his head toward her again. He sucked in a sharp breath in response to her ministrations, but held still.

"He's already coming awake. That's good."

"Yes, it is." She set the bloodied cloth on a tray and grabbed a fresh one. "Okay, it's clean. Since the bleeding has stopped, I'm not going to try to tape a bandage over it— it wouldn't stick without shaving his scalp."

"Like my hair where it is, thanks," Tommy mumbled.

Shea's heart leaped and she looked into his face. Slowly, his lashes fluttered open and she found herself staring into unfocused crystal blue eyes. She'd never seen anything more beautiful.

"You're lucky your brains are still inside your skull, kid," Sean said, relief stamped on his face.

"Brains. Yeah, brains are good," Tommy muttered.

The captain's lips curved into a smile. "Time for a little test. What's your full name, son?"

He hesitated for a couple of seconds. "Thomas Wayne Skyler."

Shea began to clean the scratches on his right arm, hiding her surprise. Why hadn't she known that before? Hearing his full name made him more . . . real, somehow.

Sean continued. "How old are you?"

"Twenty-three."

"Who am I?"

Those pale eyes, a tad clearer now, danced with mischief. "My asshole of a captain. Sir."

Sean laughed, the sound rusty, unused. "Since it appears you're going to survive, I'll let you get away with that. Just this once."

"Thanks, Cap."

He hasn't really noticed me yet. How will he react when

he sees me? Will he be glad? Angry? Distant? God, anything but the last.

Shea quelled her trepidation and took the plunge. "What about me? Do you know my name?"

He turned his head and blinked up at her for a few seconds. Then his face broke into a wide, happy smile. A smile that stole the oxygen from the room. Made her light-headed. "Shea. How'd you get here?"

"I work here, hotshot. Remember?" Finished cleaning his arm, she tossed the cloth and peeled off her gloves, then discarded those, as well.

His happiness dimmed some. "Oh. Right."

Had he thought she'd come especially to see him?

She crossed her arms over her chest. "Quite a heroic feat you performed. Do you recall what happened?"

He snorted. "Told him not to move, but he panicked. Jumped on me. Almost turned me into a human wrecking ball."

"You did good, kid," Sean praised.

His cheeks colored, but he gave a slight nod. "Thanks."

The captain rose to go. "They're going to do a CAT scan as a precaution, but I believe you'll be out of here in a few hours. When they spring you, go home. Get some rest, and we'll see you in forty-eight."

As she watched him leave, Shea heard Tommy say, "How have you been, Shea?"

She found him watching her, gaze intense. Hot. Not a trace of his ordeal in evidence, save for the obvious scrapes on his face and the ugly bruise forming on his right arm and shoulder.

In fact, with his blond hair tousled and framing his angular face, bronzed male nipples tightening from the chilly temperature in the room . . . he looked good enough to eat with chocolate syrup and a cherry.

Down that path awaited disaster.

"Just fine," she said, hating how her voice squeaked. "You?"

His reply was a soft caress. "Lonely."

One word. One glorious word conveying a wealth of meaning, and her blood sang.

What does that mean? He's waiting for me? Breathe.

Suddenly, he sat up on the bed, swaying a little. "Whoa."

She grabbed his arm to steady him. "What are you doing? Lie back down before you fall over."

"No. I can't ask you this while flat on my back." He removed her hand from his arm and curled his fingers around hers.

Oh, no. "Ask me what?"

"Will you go with me to Zack and Cori's wedding this Saturday? Be my date?"

Her throat shrank to the size of a pinhole. Why was it so hard to tell him? "I can't. I—I already have a date."

His smile wilted. And the genuine hurt in his blue eyes was something she hoped never to see again.

Slowly, he let go of her hand and she felt the loss of his warmth like a physical blow. "I see."

"I'm sorry, Tommy. Really. But . . . save me a dance, okay?"

What a stupid thing to say. She had to get away from the pain etched on his face.

"I—I'm going to get another nurse to stay with you."

Shea turned and fled the exam room without looking back.

Fleeing the pain in her heart wasn't quite so simple.

ABOUT THE AUTHOR

Jo Davis spent sixteen years in the public school trenches before she left teaching to pursue her dream of becoming a full-time writer. An active member of Romance Writers of America, she's been a finalist for the Colorado Romance Writers Award of Excellence, has captured the HOLT Medallion Award of Merit, and has one book optioned for a major motion picture. She lives in Texas with her husband and two children. Visit her Web site at www.jodavis.net.

ALSO AVAILABLE
FROM
JO DAVIS

Trial By Fire
The Firefighters of Station Five

Lieutenant Howard "Six- Pack" Paxton loves three things: being a firefighter, riding his Harley, and his bachelorhood. That is, until the curvaceous Kat McKenna falls into his arms at the scene of a fire—and melts the six-foot-six tower of bronze muscle...

But just as passion ignites between them—and they explore new heights of ecstasy—a ruthless arsonist with a deadly secret and a thirst for vengeance becomes their worst nightmare.

**"Sizzling romantic suspense...
so hot it singes the pages!"**
—*New York Times* Bestselling Author
JoAnn Ross

**Available wherever books are sold or at
penguin.com**

Penguin Group (USA) Online

What will you be reading tomorrow?

Tom Clancy, Patricia Cornwell, W.E.B. Griffin,
Nora Roberts, William Gibson, Robin Cook,
Brian Jacques, Catherine Coulter, Stephen King,
Dean Koontz, Ken Follett, Clive Cussler,
Eric Jerome Dickey, John Sandford,
Terry McMillan, Sue Monk Kidd, Amy Tan,
J. R. Ward, Laurell K. Hamilton,
Charlaine Harris, Christine Feehan...

You'll find them all at
penguin.com

*Read excerpts and newsletters,
find tour schedules and reading group guides,
and enter contests.*

Subscribe to Penguin Group (USA) newsletters
and get an exclusive inside look
at exciting new titles and the authors you love
long before everyone else does.

PENGUIN GROUP (USA)
us.penguingroup.com